Quoth
the
Crow

**Look for other new *The Crow* novels
forthcoming this year:**

The Crow: The Lazarus Heart
by Poppy Z. Brite

The Crow: Clash by Night
by Chet Williamson

Published by HarperPrism

THE CROW ™

Quoth the Crow

DAVID BISCHOFF

Based on characters by
JAMES O'BARR

HarperPrism

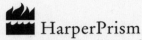

HarperPrism

A Division of HarperCollins*Publishers*
10 East 53rd Street, New York, N.Y. 10022-5299

Copyright © 1998 by Edward R. Pressman Film Corporation
All rights reserved. No part of this book may be used or reproduced in any manner whatsoever without written permission of the publisher, except in the case of brief quotations embodied in critical articles and reviews. For information address HarperCollins*Publishers,*
10 East 53rd Street, New York, N.Y. 10022.

ISBN: 0-06-105825-4

HarperCollins®, ![]®, and HarperPrism®
are trademarks of HarperCollins*Publishers* Inc.

The Crow™ is a trademark of Edward R. Pressman Film Corporation

HarperPrism books may be purchased for educational, business, or sales promotional use. For information, please write: Special Markets Department, HarperCollins*Publishers,*
10 East 53rd Street, New York, N.Y. 10022-5299.

Cover illustration © 1998 by Cliff Nielson

Designed by Lisa Pifher

First printing: January 1998

Printed in the United States of America

Library of Congress Cataloging-in-Publication Data
is available from the publisher.

Visit HarperPrism on the World Wide Web at
http://www.harperprism.com

98 99 00 01 ❖ 10 9 8 7 6 5 4 3 2 1

To Dean Koontz
Past, present, and future master

A flap of the wing to:
Jimmy Vines, Martha Bayless, Robin Shurtz,
John Douglas, and Jeff Conner

Quoth the Crow

prologue

I was sick—sick unto death with that long agony; and when they at length unbound me, and I was permitted to sit, I felt that my senses were leaving me. The sentence—the dread sentence of death—was the last of distinct accentuation which reached my ears ...

... The thought came gently and stealthily, and it seemed long before it attained full appreciation; but just as my spirit came at length properly to feel and entertain it, the figures of the judges vanished, as if magically, from before me; the tall candles sank into nothingness; their flames went out utterly; the blackness of darkness supervened; all sensations appeared swallowed up in a mad rushing descent as of the soul into Hades. Then silence, and stillness, and night were the universe.

—Edgar A. Poe, *The Pit and the Pendulum*

THE HOUSE SCREAMED.

It was one of those bloodcurdling cinematic screams, the kind horror movie scream queens were famous for. It seemed to rattle the windows of the little rowhouse building, shake the walls. The bass aspect throbbed the foundation, the high ululation reaching up to the flat roof, shaking the gravel and tarpaper.

It sounded, Count Mishka thought, rather like Jamie Lee Curtis.

In fact, it was Jamie Lee Curtis, doubled and manipulated like a Tarzan yell. A digital stitching of classic distress from both *Terror Train* and *Prom Night*.

The youth, all dressed in black (black shirt, black boots, black jeans, black T-shirt, black earring, black nose-ring, black eye liner, black razor-cut, black scarf, black jacket—all not merely black but stylishly *Gothic* black with bits of shine and gloss on hems and edges, a little touch of glitter around Alfred E. Neuman/Prince Charles ears) giggled.

He pushed his new door alarm again.

Another female scream, this time a little bit shorter and cut off quick, as though some killer had just slashed off her head.

Brinke Stevens and Linnea Quigley? Yes, surely. Nice and sexy, even in terror. Especially in terror.

Yum.

Dusk, bleak and autumnal, settled over the snug Baltimore neighborhood. A dog barked in an alley. A woman in a hooded coat bent toward a destination. The smell of fresh tarmac hovered from a construction site a few doors down.

A gull, a little off base from its harbor environs, swooped over the line of tiny Fells Point rowhouses.

Carrying his loot under his left arm, Count Mishka, known to his parents and the government as Richard Mark Henneman, slotted the key to his house with his right hand.

The keys jingled as the door opened. The last of the pre-recorded door alarm screams the Count had engineered wafted away in the shadows like dark smoke.

A cold chill seemed to blow through the house.

Richard shivered, with something more than the cold.

What the hell? he thought. *Is this house haunted?*

Cool, he thought.

The gang would approve.

For a year now Richard Henneman had allied himself with a self-described "elite" group of local Goths—that post-punk, funereally festooned subculture whose fierce rejection of mainstream commercialism was often obscured by equally rigid, narcissistic obsessions, scorched-earth cliquishness, and an unhealthy addiction to black nail polish. The Gothiques, however, had of late, become a much more closely bound unit. A unit bound not just in blood . . . but in money. Lots now. A great deal more in the future. Yes, the Gothiques were quickly becoming Goth, Inc.

And all because of a teensy little *murder*.

How delicious!

The Count's hallway was splattered with blood.

Movie poster gore.

Bloody fanged Draculas from Bela to Gary menaced. Luckless women with deep cleavage held up their arms, screaming. Alongside these posters were framed collages Richard had made of pictures Xeroxed from his favorite fan-boy genre mags, *Fangoria*, *Shivers*, *Midnight Marquee*, *European Trash Cinema*, and their lesser-known brethren. Exotic movie makeup and mayhem. Decapitated heads. Eviscerated bodies. Slobbering monsters trailing guts, rarely their own.

Art, pure and simple.

Frozen moments of pure pop cinema at its zenith.

Chuckling to himself, the Count turned on the living-room light, kicked the door closed behind him, and headed straight for his holy of holies, his entertainment center. He bowed slightly to the fat Buddha above the television set. "Much incense to be burned tonight, oh Enlightened One!"

He dumped his treasures on the couch, dug out the new Iggy Pop CD; well, not so new really, as it was the *Raw Power* remixes, a twenty-year after-the-fact revision of the classic album that had been "ruined" (according to hardcore fans) by David Bowie's attempt at making it sound commercial, back when Mr. Pop was still called Iggy Stooge. The Count put the disc in the CD player and hit random play (the most important development in modern conveniences since the remote control). Immediately, Iggy and the Stooges started blaring proto-punk through his new Bose satellite speaker system.

"Rock my world, Iggy!" said the Count. He pogoed through the narrow dining room, through the narrow kitchen, where he opened the Sears Hotpoint refrigerator, pulled out a fat can of Fosters, and ripped off the poptop, letting the foam spurt up, Aussie-style. Back in the old days, he had to drink National Boh. Now the Count drank *good* stuff. "Go, Iggster, go!" He laughed, letting beer run down his mouth and shirt.

The Stooges electronically obeyed.

The bass throbbed and screeching guitars rang. The drums ripped and hammered. "I am the world's forgotten boy!" Iggy shrieked.

Iggy rocked the walls, postered with Goth rock, darkwave icons. The Sisters of Mercy, The Cure, The Mission, The Damned, and Bauhaus; newer acts like Switchblade Symphony, Laibach, Chem Lab, Attrition, Lycia, Dorian Gray, Die Laughing, London After Midnight; and even molding oldies like David Bowie (hey, Trent digs him), Kiss, and Alice Cooper (Marilyn Manson should be paying them royalties for stealing their acts) to show the catholicity of his taste.

Iggy rocked the bookcase, holding film and TV books and a few horror novels. Iggy rocked the racks bulging with plastic-covered comics. Iggy rocked the CD racks and the record stacks. Iggy rocked the multimedia racks stocked with hundreds of videos near the thirty-one-inch Sony TV and various video players, dripping with yet more videos, laserdiscs, and DVDs.

Iggy rocked *all*.

The Count's collection of pop culture and effluvia flowed out from the living room, filling the dining room. Rolling up the staircase were more piles of videos and CDs, on up to the top rooms of the house, which were also filled with bookcases, comics, posters, action figures, Japanese robots, and other arcana.

Many of these things had been stolen.

Richard was an excellent shoplifter. He'd found, as a prepubescent youth, that his hunger for comics and such far exceeded his allowance. Deft of finger, fleet of foot, and big of coat, he found his forté was in theft. What he didn't want to keep, he sold or traded, thus starting up a most wonderful collection. At the age of fourteen, he'd broken into a comic shop at night, cut off the lock on the collector's case and stolen a treasure trove of old Marvel and DC comics, even some EC titles from the fifties. By the time he was eighteen, he had so many comics and books, tapes, CDs, and records that he operated a store out of his college campus apartment, making a major killing on Image Comics (love those variant covers!) during the market's speculator boom.

Alas, he'd been thrown out of college as a sophomore for numerous offenses. Unchastened, his larcenous activities continued, refining his skills while building his stock and trading capacities—but his constant hunger for more and more loot kept his vision low, a victim of his own compulsive appetites.

Then he'd met the Gothiques, or rather, Le Salon des Gothiques, the funky basement hangout presided over by one Baxter Brittle.

His talents were quickly discerned by salon director Brittle, a boozehound artist and erstwhile editor of Tome Press, blessed with a recent inheritance (namely the Cork'd Sailor bar, home of said basement), whose own collections were often augmented by the Count's activities. Previously just a spotty nerd with a light touch, Richard Henneman's social activities increased. He achieved the identity of "Count Mishka." He even got semi-regular helmet polishing from a few of the Goth chicks attracted by Brittle's garish personality (and free booze).

However, it had only been in the last year, with his induction into the inner circle of Baxter Brittle's trust, that his monetary situation truly improved. He bought a small townhouse in Fells Point and moved the contents of his apartment and storage spaces here. True, soon he was going to have to rent another storage locker, but such was the volume of the flow of materials through his possession (some, like tonight's stuff, actually *bought*) that he was able to keep selling things and making a profit in addition to the moneys achieved from his work at Tome Press.

Iggy rocked the book vault.

The elaborate cabinet, a genuine antique of solid oak, had been a gift from Tome Press. ("For extraordinary services rendered," said Brittle.) All the locks had been refitted with modern hardware, and the interior made air-tight and moisture free, perfect for housing rare books, just like the special cases used by William Blessing for his famous Poe collection.

Iggy Pop railed on about penetration and shake appeal while the Count laughed. Shaking his head to himself, he chuckled as he inserted the magnetic key into the antique facing of the lock. He opened the cabinet and looked at his most prized of treasures. His "double-bag" items.

Behold! he thought. First editions. *Signed* first editions, a collector's best investment, guaranteed to appreciate in value. From Stephen King to Anne Rice to Clive Barker to Dean Koontz to Ramsey Campbell to Robert Bloch to Shirley Jackson to Richard Matheson, they were all here. And a nice tight copy—or better yet, an unread, signature-only copy—had more built-in security value than any 401k plan or IRA account. There was a first edition of Bram Stoker's *Dracula*, signed. Ambrose Bierce. Some nice Lovecraft. Dozens of wonderful collectable valuables, ah, yes.

Glorious stuff indeed.

However, the totally primo material he had only just recently obtained . . . The most valuable, the oldest . . . the most magical . . .

And for free!

There they were: a solid set of first editions by Edgar Allan Poe. These from an era when first printings ran in the mere hundreds, and often were just privately issued. Fruit of that terrible night of four months ago that had turned, somehow, into such a bonanza.

Even now, as he did every night, his fingers drifted over the leather spines of the old, custom-made clam-shell slipcases (valuable relics themselves) that held the fragile volumes from the corrupting influences of light and air and unnecessary handling. He felt a palpable thrill, an exquisite energy humming within these repositories of magic.

Ah, yes, who could have predicted that through a death and a burglary, such luck would fall upon his collector's head!

Tome Press was doing very well indeed, expanding by leaps and bounds. Richard Mark Henneman, being one of the Inner Circle, was now Vice President in Charge of Special Projects. Which meant, in addition to his usual cool duties of overseeing a small press turning into a large press, looking into other avenues of expansion. Being a music maven and motion picture nut, it was natural that the Count's interests should be stirred by the desire to "produce." And to judge by the idiots already doing so, how hard could it be? concluded the Count. Just today he had spoken with some film students about Tome Press making its first horror movie. And he was sure he could get one of those one-man studio "bands" like Trust Obey to do the music, then make a soundtrack deal with Projekt, Tess, or Cleopatra. The possibilities were endless.

Man, what a blast!

Touching the volumes of Poe was like getting jolts of power.

Raw power! Hey!

Goth, Inc. was headed for the stars!

"And we're along for the ride, huh, Iggy?" the Count said, closing the cabinet.

Iggy bellowed and groaned and retched in reply.

"Give me danger, little stranger," they sang together.

He took another chug of Fosters, then wiggled into the living room. He took a carefree backward half-gainer (after placing his hefty beer can on the coffee table, already groaning with Cool Stuff) onto the couch.

He grabbed one of his controls.

Aim. Press of button. Off with Iggy's head!

He hit another button and *Interview with the Vampire* zapped onto the thirty-one-inch TV screen. The Count mimed along with Brad Pitt's dialogue, then took another swig of Australian brew.

Yes, after a long day in the salt mines, it was time for a little lie-down. Then, up in time to hit Fletcher's, where Death On Two Legs, a new band he was interested in, was playing. He'd check out the babes, do a little Ex . . . have a good time shmoozing . . .

And then, maybe find a willing female (his personal goal: an honest-to-God honey from the Goth Babe of the Week website) and come back to the bachelor pad to watch trailers for sixties horror films and partake in some hot sex.

Man, talk about a perfect prospective evening!

Even as the ominous music swelled from the vampire video, the Count found exhaustion closing in on him, cushioned by the beer. Sleep was cool, but all in all, he'd rather do it during the day. Night, he'd always felt, was full of so many other possibilities.

As he slept, he dreamed he was flying on the back of a giant black bird. The creature dived and spun above foggy lands of mysterious castles, streaked with rainbows. Lightning and heavy metal music thundered in dark caverns.

Far out, he thought. *Amazing.*

Dreams were good. Even bad ones.

Maybe especially bad ones.

"After all," he mumbled hazily, rising up from his nap, "I wouldn't be in business without them."

Vaguely he reached out for his can of Fosters to jump start

his neurons. His hand clenched on emptiness where the can had been.

"What the—" he said, blearily rising up.

"Looking for this?" said a voice.

A dark form stepped forward and pressed the can into his hand.

"I went and got you a fresh one, Count. Warm beer doesn't really make it when you're just waking up from a nap."

Someone else is in the house . . .

Who?

The Count looked up from his place on the couch.

A figure seemed to swim in front of him.

The light from the dining room made a nimbus around his body, but around his head there seemed a halo of pure darkness.

Somewhere (from the second floor?) came the sounds of wings, flapping.

Click.

Gears warmed from their freeze.

"Hey, man. I haven't got much worth stealing. A little money in my pocket—my TV set and—"

He turned and gestured toward the towering entertainment center.

Where there had been a brand-new Sony XBR thirty-one incher, there was now only an empty space.

"Whoa! You already *got* it."

He started to get up.

The figure leaned over.

Stuck a Heckler and Koch HK-4 in his nose.

The Count flung himself back on the couch.

He recognized the gun.

It was his.

"Oh, shit. Looks like you've got the run of the place. Guess you're going to take what you like, huh?"

"I know exactly what I want, Mr. Henneman. That is your name, isn't it, Count? Richard Mark Henneman."

The man's voice was harsh and scratchy, and somehow off . . . like a special-effects voice, pitch-shifted, controlled anger through clenched teeth.

"Yes. Yes, that's me." The bore of the gun was cold and heavy as it pushed into his nose. And it hurt like hell.

"Look, sorry to be in your way. Just take the stuff, okay? I don't care. Just don't shoot me."

"No?"

"No! That . . . would be really stupid!"

"Would it?"

"Look, are you trying to screw with my head or something? I told you to take what you like. I'll even show you, okay? Just get the gun out of my nose!"

The gun pulled back.

The figure stepped away.

It appeared to be a dark man dressed in a dark coat, but as he moved back, some of the darkness about the face seemed to fade away. It was an older man, with taut and aged skin. Dark glasses. Was he being burglarized by some retiree?

Cool!

"Look, Grandpa. I promise I'll cooperate. You can even have the gun. That cost me a pretty penny, I'll tell you . . ."

And I wish I kept it on me at all times . . . Your head would be all over the living room . . .

He couldn't really shoot, but the thought was delightful and helped keep down the fear. Mick Prince had helped him buy the gun, and was going to show him how to use it. Mick was showing the Count lots of neat new things.

The Count wished that Mick were here now.

He'd know what to do.

"You have no idea who I am!" the man yelled. "No idea!"

Without warning, the man flung his gun arm across the table, sweeping it free of the books and tapes and videos and the drug paraphernalia box.

Stuff went flying across the room.

Two glasses crashed against the opposite wall.

This sucker was *strong* for an old duffer!

The Count cringed backward. He started pushing at the couch with his feet to push himself off and to somewhere safe.

With surprising quickness, the Dark Man reached out and took a fistful of his shirt with the gun-free hand. He then hauled the Count over to the coffee table and slammed him down on top of it.

The Count was so dazed by this that he barely noticed the

Dark Man's next motions. He tried to get up, but soon realized he'd been restrained. There were several belts tying him down. He could only move his head, his hands, and his feet—and those not terribly far.

"Shit! How can I show you the stuff!" he complained, not liking this turn of events, cold reality beginning to penetrate.

"I know exactly what I want and where it is," said the Dark Man. "Now, though, I need a few things I can only get from your brain."

"Huh? Information? What? Jeez . . ."

Everything seemed dark and fuzzy about the stranger. Around the room, the ceremonial candles had been lit, though above, on the ceiling, darkness held sway. The Count sensed a form, a presence up there, somehow hulking huge and ominous.

For a moment the Dark Man remained silent, perhaps to allow more time for the fuse of dread to ignite in his captive's heart.

Then he knelt down by his side.

"I have powers now . . . strange powers . . . I perceive things as I had not before . . . in life," he said, in a solemn whisper. "In life, Mr. Henneman. I perceive, Mr. Henneman . . . Count Mishka . . . that beyond the sins and minor atrocities you've already stitched into the cosmos, there are greater evils which are your destiny. Imagine, Count . . . Imagine, say, if Joseph Goebbels of the Third Reich had been earlier recognized as the villain he would become. Oh, the better world it would have been had he been excised from existence. Snip snip, go the scissors of fate, always, Count. But too often, too late for the world. I am seriously considering helping those scissors along tonight." The Dark Man pulled out a large pair of pruning shears, their newly honed blades bright in the flickering candlelight.

"Jesus! What are you going to do with *those?*" the Count gasped. "Look, I told you—"

"You have no idea who I am, do you?" said the Dark Man. "Let me inform you." He started to come closer. "I am Doctor Phibes, Mr. Henneman. I am the vilified Shakespearean actor of Vincent Price's *Theatre of Blood*. I am Peter Cushing in *Tales From the Crypt*. I am Claude Rains in *Phantom of the Opera*. I could go on, Count. Am I speaking your variety of cinematic dialect now?"

"What are . . . I don't . . . You're making no sense!" squeaked the Count.

Snip, snip went the shears.

The Dark Man knelt beside him, removing his dark glasses. Candlelight reflected on gray, scaly skin. The Count got a faint scent of ripe roadkill. He looked into the eyes, and saw something he remembered. Something just a few months back.

Then he recognized the eyes.

He opened his mouth to speak, or at the very least to scream, but nothing came out.

Oh God, oh God, oh God . . .

"I see the spark of recognition in your eyes, Richard," said the Dark Man. He slowly put his glasses back on and then stood. "It does my soul good. I think, perhaps some good can come out of my death. And that is why I'm here. Not just vengeance, you see. Not just redemption. But for the good for future generations!"

Still paralyzed with horror and disbelief, the Count watched as the Dark Man withdrew something from his pocket. It was the remote control device for his television . . . What was he doing with—?

Click, click.

The hulking form that the Count had sensed before, up in the darkness near the ceiling, suddenly lit up.

It was his massive Sony XBR, somehow suspended by its cable and electrical wires from the lighting fixture in the ceiling. In gorgeous Technicolor, Peter Cushing's Van Helsing was holding a stake, his hair flopping about wildly, as he battled Christopher Lee's Dracula.

The huge TV set dangled six feet above Richard Henneman's head.

The Dark Man began to intone.

"'I now observed—with what horror it is needless to say—that its nether extremity was formed of a crescent of glittering steel, about a foot in length from horn to horn; the horns upward, and the under edge evidently as keen as that of a razor. Like a razor also, it seemed massive and heavy, tapering from the edge into a solid and broad structure above. It was appended to a weighty rod of brass, and the whole *hissed* as it swung through the air.'

"Quiz time, Mr. Henneman. What is the source of that quote?"

"I . . . don't . . . know . . ." the Count managed to squeeze out.

"Perhaps I should approach the subject through the media that you are familiar with."

Suddenly on the screen flashed scenes from a movie that the Count had seen. Vincent Price in a cowl. Stone steps, a dungeon . . . A bosomy woman . . .

Then, the guy from *Millennium* (cool show!) in a cowl too. A dungeon. A bosomy woman, naked . . .

"Pit . . ." he said. "*Pit and the Pendulum.*"

"That's right, Count," said the Dark Man. He reached up with the shears and pushed hard on the TV set. It started swinging back and forth, back and forth.

Strobing light.

"There was Roger Corman's classic interpretation . . . and the more recent Stuart Gordon version," said the Dark Man. "And I don't need to tell you about Dario Argento's graphic quotation of the tale some years back."

Back and forth.

Back and forth.

Strobing light across the dry and dwindling skin of the Dark Man, flashing on his glasses.

"What is this?" cried the Count. "Baxter! Is this some trick? Baxter? Is this your sick and twisted sense of humor?"

Back and forth went the television, spurred on by the shears of the Dark Man.

Back and forth.

Strobing light.

Scenes from movies sprayed from its gigantic cathode ray, garish scenes from *Night of the Living Dead*, old Universal horror movies, fifties monster movies, eighties slasher movies, Stephen King movies, Clive Barker movies, forgotten movies he'd bought from Sinister Cinema and Video Search of Miami, read about in *Video Watchdog* . . .

Back and forth, they went.

Strobing light.

"Oh, what a rainbow of delight, Count! Pain and blood and horror in ninety-minute packages! Such decadent fun, don't you think? But not as much fun as joining in on my melodramatic death scene. Not as much fun as jumping on the bandwagon of my estate, barreling toward commercial hell."

"Stop it!" cried the Count. "Just cut it out!"

"Maybe. Maybe I'll let you go, if you tell me where your other royal friends are. The . . . uhm . . . Marquis I believe his name is, hmm?"

"He'll be at the Cross Club," said the Count. "Yeah. He usually hangs out there, this time of week."

"Thank you."

However, the Dark Man who claimed to be William Blessing, risen from the grave, did not release the Count from his bonds.

"Hmm. I see you also collect those paragons of culture . . . comic books." The Dark Man limped over to a bookcase and grabbed a handful.

Back and forth . . .

Swish . . . swish . . .

. . . went the Sony over his head.

"Oh, and what do I see? *The Sandman* by Neil Gaiman." He limped back and tossed the pile onto the Count's chest. "These issues feature that cute little bit of jail-bait, Death. I'll make a deal with you, Count. You explain to me what these comic books are supposed to *mean* exactly, and I'll let you go!"

"What?"

"To me it's obvious, but then I'm a professor of English. Perhaps if I got it straight from a dedicated fan I could learn some nuance I might have missed, hmm?"

The Count looked aghast. How could he answer a pop quiz with Death when there was a 100-pound television swinging above him like a wrecking ball?

"Sandman's, uhmm . . . like, this prince of dreams . . . and he . . . uh . . . goes back and forth in cool mythologies . . . and . . . like . . . uhm . . . is . . . uhm . . . cool and . . . uhm, profound . . . and uhm . . ."

"No. I didn't think you could tell me," said the Dark Man, with a slight trace of sadness. "What's the purpose of collecting something if you can't be bothered to understand it? Is it cool because others like it, or because *you* do? You see my point, no? Well, you will soon enough."

Then the Dark Man reached up and cut the power cord and cables with the heavy shears. *Snip.*

The Sony XBR thirty-one-inch stereo television came down from its pendulous trajectory with unnatural speed, as if hurled from a great height.

The Dark Man watched.

He felt no joy, no satisfaction.

But neither did he feel sorrow.

The TV's edge smashed into the bound man's face like an anvil on an apple, crushing first it (a splash of blood and brains all about), and then the end of the coffee table. With a crack and splintering and the sound of a splatting melon, the television set pushed the table down, hurling the rest of the body up, whipping it, cracking it.

Glass shattered and flew, some into the Dark Man's legs.

Though it cut his flesh, he barely registered the pain.

Electric sparks shot out from the set, and for a moment from the cut wires. Smoke wreathed the wreckage and gore.

Then with a sputtering, the electrical charge faded.

The feet of the Count spasmed, then went still.

The Dark Man stood silently for a moment.

From a pocket inside his coat, he pulled a single black feather.

The feather of a crow.

He tucked it into one of the Count's hands.

"Fly into the dark now, my foe," said the Dark Man. "Fly to where neither you nor I know."

Then he turned and departed for his next assignation . . .

. . . remembering.

. . . the first bullet stabs into his chest. Its impact is astonishing, tearing forcefully through skin, ribs, right lung, veins, arteries, then

exploding out of his shirt and cashmere sweater. It feels as though a grinning demon has stabbed a red-hot poker through him, searing and scalding . . .

The demon, though, wears the contorted mask of a wild-eyed lunatic, a huge gun held out before him.

The Dark Man walked the streets of night, the streets of Baltimore, for his next rendezvous. These men had killed him, destroyed all that he'd held dear. Now it was their turn to die.

The Dark Man walked the streets of Fells Point.

. . . remembering . . .

. . . Amy! Oh, my dear God! Amy! Don't hurt Amy!

. . . burglars! Madmen! Killers!

Help! Oh, dear Jesus! Help!

All through searing manic pain as he flies against the bookshelf. Precious ancient volumes are knocked from the shelf. The smell of vellum and old paper, the odor of wax mixed with fresh blood.

The image of his assailant burns into his mind, every ragged stretch of facial sinew, every pore and bend of nose. The hard, thin lips. The thick, curling eyebrows. The granite eyes. The greasy black hair, tied behind into a ponytail with a ring of bone . . .

And, peripherally, the image of the other attacker, holding his wife. A muscular ape of a man with a buzz cut, thick brow ridge, no chin, an oozing look of lust in his piggish eyes.

He scrabbles against the shelves of his library, against the slime of himself, trying to push himself back, thinking "Save Amy, save the collection . . ."

Then the gunman sneers . . .

. . . and he knows in his soul it cannot be.

The Dark Man walked through the streets of Baltimore, his home.

Baltimore, Maryland.

He had been born here in the city, and he seemed to grow up with a sense of its history and promise. Now, he could smell the waters of the Inner Harbor to the south. Baltimore, on the Patapsco River two thirds of the way up the Chesapeake Bay. Largest city in Maryland and one of the largest natural harbors of the world. A city of American growth, American architecture, American heritage. Now, as he walked, he could almost taste, amongst the stink and the humidity, steamed blue crabs in the air, cold cheap lager, rich bay spice.

Baltimore.

A good place to die.

But no place to rest . . .

Yet.

The Dark Man walked through the dark folds of Little Italy . . .

. . . remembering . . .

The weapon explodes a second time and to his pain-heightened senses it seems to squeeze out its bullet in slow-motion amidst the halo of fire. He can feel his denial, feel himself crying "No" again, feel himself reach for some kind of inner power to push back the metal charging for him.

When it connects, the force of it smacks him back against the base of the shelving where he'd been pushed by the first. It rips and gouges and tears through his already bloody shirt into his abdomen, a buzz saw of power ripping flesh and life with abandon and spitting out raw hunks of him onto the floor. He can feel it drilling through him, cutting through his solar plexus and his internal organs with mad indifference, chewing up what is left of his life and spitting it out.

His assailant is saying something but he cannot hear it. He realizes that his assailant has been saying things all along, accusing things, but he cannot register them . . . cannot retain them.

His only thoughts are of Amy, his wife, his beloved . . .

And how powerless he feels, how consumed with pain.

Blood blood blood . . .

He falls to the floor, blood overwhelming him, blood covering his awareness.

The deep black blood of unconsciousness amidst a final thought: Amy.

The Dark Man walked the downtown streets of Baltimore.

Past the new clean walls of Harborplace, past the Aquarium and past the bright hotels, past the moon glowing in the windows of the office buildings.

But he is not dead.

. . . not yet.

He clambers from the darkness, back to save Amy, to save his collection, to save . . . save . . .

He opens his eyes and groans . . .

And he looks into the eyes of the greatest horror of all . . .

The Dark Man walked toward the Cross Club.

He heard the beat of wings and he looked up and saw a dark form, flapping through the city canyons, above the cars and late-night activity.

He followed.

And as he followed the crow, the Dark Man remembered his dream.

His dream of Edgar Allan Poe.

one

I pray to God that she may lie
Forever with unopened eye . . .
Far in the forest, dim and old,
For her may some tall vault unfold
Some tomb, which oft hath flung its black
And vampyre-winged panels back,
Fluttring triumphant o'er the palls,
Of her old family funerals.

— "Irene"
Edgar A. Poe, *To the Humane Heart*

December 8, 1811

THERE WAS SOME KIND OF BIRD IN THE WINTER FOREST.

"William," Edgar had said. "William! A bird!"

A big *bird.*

A black *bird.*

Black as the dark cellar beneath the theater where he and William would hide and play while mother rehearsed. Black as the night when all the candles were out in their boarding house and clouds moved across the stars and the moon like giant wings. Black as the suit the somber Doctor had worn when he'd come to visit Mama yesterday.

"Where?" His brother William stood up from where he'd been sitting on the porch.

"There! In the tree . . ."

But where Edgar pointed now there were only branches. Skeletal branches, clacking memories of trees once filled with green and fruit and life, now barren with December's cold.

"I don't see any bird, Edgar," said William, who'd proceeded to continue playing soldiers, not including Edgar in his game.

Now Edgar stood by a window. In the room was a nurse with one-year-old Rosalie. Standing by a bed were a number of family friends, theater people mostly. William now clung expressionless to a woman who had stayed with Mama all night.

Edgar sat by the window, fidgeting and staring out at the trees. That big bird fascinated him. With its vibrant *"Caw! Caw!"* and its knowing eye, its sharp beak and its powerful claws, it seemed so strange and yet so forthright. Like a mystery that answered a puzzle. He tried to keep looking for the bird because what the grownups in the room were saying troubled him, even though he didn't understand much of it, and not just because it came in strained whispers.

"She can't last much longer."

"What will become of the poor children?"

"I can't help them! I've enough of my own!"

"They'll have to be separated. Such a shame. And they seem to love each other so much!"

"The poor woman. Such talent! Such a sweet singing voice. She shall sing for Jesus himself, I think."

"She is going to a better place."

Mama, going someplace? Edgar had thought. But how could that be? She was in her nightclothes, tucked very nicely in bed. No, the adults must be very wrong, for even though he was only three years old, he well knew that if you were going someplace you got dressed up . . . and at the very least you got out of bed. But Mama had been in bed for days and days . . .

True, it wasn't like Mama at all. Mama was mostly always out of bed. Mama was an actress. A famous actress, William had declared. *"She has trod the boards from Richmond to Boston!"* his five-year-old brother had declared once, striking a melodramatic pose. *"Sirrah, she has won even the cold hearts in New York City and Philadelphia with her dulcet tones. She is simply the best actress and singer ever."*

Edgar certainly knew his mother was the most beautiful creature in the world. But his mama was the one who would hold him and put on his coat and tie his shoes and tell him it would be all right when he fell down and scraped his knee. The woman who painted her face and put on frilly outfits and danced and sang in Time Tells a Tale or cried and swooned in the melodrama Tekeli, or, the Siege of Montgatz almost seemed someone different—and yet very wonderful nonetheless.

A flash of wing . . .

A blur of black . . .

There . . . just on the horizon of this dismal Sunday morning. Was that the strange bird?

"I wonder if her husband knows she is ill."

"That scalawag. David Poe! No one has heard from him. Left the family last year, the drunkard."

"A terrible father."

Edgar barely remembered his father. Somewhere deep inside him were memories. Somewhere deep were feelings. However, at this moment, the possibility of a glimpse of that dark avian emissary seemed the most vital matter, not the hushed chatterings of these people hovering around Mama's bed.

Where was it?

"Edgar? Edgar, come here dear. Your dear mama wishes to speak to all her children." Edgar recognized the voice. It belonged to Fanny Allan, who had taken much interest in his family. He liked Fanny, very much. She was a sweet lady. Her husband, John, however—he was stern and disapproving and frightening. Edgar wasn't sure he liked John Allan.

"I'm trying to find the bird!" Edgar said. "I know it's out there!"

"The bird can wait, sweet child," Fanny insisted. "Your mama needs to speak to you immediately."

Edgar sighed. He got down off the chair near the windowsill and he walked toward the bed. William was already there, looking sad and confused and holding Mama's hand. Another woman held Rosalie, Edgar's infant sister, who stared at her mama with big, dark eyes and uttered no sound at all.

Edgar walked to the side of the bed and leaned against it.

"Edgar?" said a soft, wispy voice. "Edgar, is that you?"

"Yes, Mama."

He didn't like the way she sounded. Mama's voice was very feminine, but it was also a very strong soprano. This voice was but a *ghost of mama's, and it rasped from her mouth as though pulled through pain.*

Groaning, William Blessing woke up.

He was sweating and gasping. His sheets were wet with sweat.

"Oh dear," said the sleepy voice of his wife, Amy, turning over and placing a comforting hand on his shoulder. "That awful Poe dream again?"

"Yes," said William Blessing. "The dream. The dream about the crow . . ."

"Maybe," she said softly. "Maybe you should write a nice romance novel next."

two

Gaily bedight,
A gallant knight,
In sunshine and in shadow,
Had journeyed long,
Singing a song,
In search of Eldorado.

—Edgar A. Poe, "Eldorado"

MICK PRINCE KICKED OPEN THE DOOR.

Fumes from booze and dope poured out into the hallway, followed by the smell of rancid food and vomit. Drawn tattered window shades leaked morning across listless bodies still drugged by night. They sprawled across the filthy living-room rug and torn-up couch, half-comatose even with the sound of doom ringing all around them.

The big man in the long coat grabbed the nearest homeboy by the ear, yanked him up, and stuck the barrel of his semi-automatic into his mouth.

"Grimsley," Mick Prince snarled. "Where?"

Drool had been leaking down the homeboy's lips. Now his eyes bugged and he started to convulse and choke. The man in the long dark coat pulled the gun out of his mouth to let him speak.

"Dunno," said the homeboy, rank with sweat and urine.

Mick jammed the barrel down again, breaking off a tooth.

"Know."

Tears and blood flowed. "Toilet, man." Muffled. "Think I saw him headed for the john!"

Mick heard the click of a weapon. He didn't wait to check the direction. He let his reflexes bounce his gun up, pull the trigger, and spray.

The first rounds caught a long-haired white boy sleeping on the couch, who jerked awake just in time to die, two short bursts taking out fist-sized divots in his chest, kicking up skin and blood. Mick yanked the bullets up higher, catching the cowboy who'd drawn the gun. Two of the rounds went wild, smashing a pink plastic bong and an ohaus triple-beam scale on the table into pieces. The next bullet smashed into the black man's skull, drilling a neat hole and slamming out brains and red. The gun hand slew off, hammering a couple of bullets into the wall. Plaster spilled.

The three other drug-heads woke up amid rotting pizza boxes, coke pipes, discarded needles, and a fine mist of blood and bones that gentled down through the cordite-laden air. One of them wore a holster top with the butt of a gun. The others seemed unarmed.

Not that it mattered.

The man in the long dark coat redirected his weapon.

Mick Prince remembered once he'd read when the forces of the Roman Catholic Church, in the late Middle Ages, had attacked the city holding the apostate Cathars. The Pope had been asked if any mercy should be shown for any of the gnostic sect, in deference to any holiness. "Kill them all," the man of the Lord had said. "God will know his own."

That Pope was not merely a wise man, Mick Prince thought. *He was one practical pontiff.*

With practiced ease, the man casually emptied the rest of his clip into the three remaining lives. The dying men jerked and spasmed, splattering blood as if invisible hooks reached down from above and played them for spastic marionettes. When the clip was empty and the gun searing hot, a trace of smoke hung above the stilled bodies like a benediction and the drab walls, ceiling, and floor had been repainted a moist, shocking crimson.

Without pausing, the man of death reached into the deep

pocket of his coat, pulled out another clip and rammed it home. He'd been hired to kill the Man in this group, and though his employers would no doubt be pleased by the carnage here and the resultant terror it would cause amongst gang leaders and drug lords, his mission was not yet completed.

Mick Prince strode toward the next room, straight and purposeful, looking for the bathroom.

Mick had spent much of his life in institutions of various sorts. All these institutions had libraries. He had read the contents of those libraries. Mostly paperbacks. If he had been much of a filmgoer, perhaps he would have thought of himself as a mercenary Clint Eastwood, grim and expressionless, performing his duty in this Wild West world. However, he far preferred to think of himself as a contemporary Parker, from the crime novels Donald E. Westlake wrote under the name Richard Stark. Parker, that cool and conscienceless pro, sleek and fast and deadly.

Here is Parker now, Mick Prince thought, *moving through barebones prose. Modern and hip, in a pre–Quentin Tarantino noir escapade, raising himself some money so that he can take some months off to pursue a postmodern dream. Here is Parker-plus. Hitman, professional criminal—*

Writer!

Earning enough money to hole up with his notebook computer and write hard-boiled stories of naked screaming horror.

Parker, though he killed people, was not a professional assassin. Mick Prince was. He worked mostly in the drug trade, since he found there was plenty of money to be had there. When he was a rich and famous writer, perhaps he would still do the occasional hit just to keep in practice. However, he intended to get away from it professionally as soon as possible.

Mick Prince found himself wondering how his Writer's Digest School instructor was doing with his latest piece. It had structural problems, he felt, and probably could benefit from a trimming. That it was horror wouldn't help it in the current marketplace—that's what the writer guy in Pittsburgh would probably say—but that was all Mick wanted to write lately.

He moved past a dilapidated kitchen that smelled of refrigerator rot. The stench turned toilety down the hall. He was getting close.

There was a puddle of water running into the hall from a closed door. All the adjacent rooms seemed empty, windows shut.

This had to be where Grimsley was making his stand.

Neo-Parker—relentless, machinelike—strides through the halls, the new post-Nietzche man. The best-read man in his prison, he is able to cite chapter and verse of philosophers, poets, and pulp writers. However, now, in this Zen moment, all has been jettisoned. He is now one with the metaphorical blade-gun, one with his mission. Neo-Parker, samurai-sophisticate.

Street warrior.

His honed mind tastes of the Now *and prepares for the future.*

The fierce Enemy awaits.

Holding his gun up and ready, Mick Prince drew in a mantra-like series of silent breaths.

Then, like a martial artist in front of an audience, he lifted his metal-soled boot and rammed it at the exact proper juncture of door knob and jamb.

The rickety wooden door splintered open.

Another kick drove it back, slamming it against the side of the wall.

Mick Prince swung his gun down immediately, about to squeeze off a short burst of bullets.

Something stopped him.

The bathroom was floored in old-fashioned black-and-white tile, half torn up. Graffiti was scrawled on the walls, the medicine cabinet mirror long since shattered, and the plumbing pipes lay exposed. A narrow window, naked of curtains, cracked, lay half open.

On a dilapidated commode sat a man in a torn T-shirt. Boxer shorts hung down around his ankles. He lay back, eyes barely open.

A rubber tourniquet was wrapped around his arm. A hypodermic needle was stuck at the juncture of his elbow. His arm was blue.

Drool dribbled from the man's lips. His breathing was shallow. He was alive. He had no firearms.

Mick Prince recognized him from the picture he'd been given.

Grimsley.

The place smelled foul.

A sudden unforeseen foreboding swarmed through the man in the long coat. There was the essential touch of *something* here. Something that reached out of cell-block nightmares.

The Other.

He'd been here.

The man on the commode lifted his head. His eyelids were so wide open they seemed to have disappeared, and the skin of the man's face had contracted so much that Mick Prince felt as though he were staring at a living skull with protruding eyeballs.

"Mick," said the Other, "the Enemy is . . . *here!* I am the Enemy!"

"No," said the man in the long dark coat.

Panic gripped. He lifted his gun and flexed his finger. The nozzle spat fire. Bullets pummeled into the man sitting on the toilet. They pushed him up like an unseen force, up and up and up, ripping him into shreds of flesh and T-shirt, shards of bone and pirouettes of blood. Still Mick Prince kept his finger tight, pumping the rounds into the body, lifting him up. A protruding eye blew out, the nose cracked inward. A few more bullets and the head exploded like a firecracker up a frog's ass. He kept firing until the clip was spent.

What was left of the drug lord's body hung for a moment as though the flesh and blood were making one more attempt to re-form. Then the body slid off and thumped on the floor, splashing into the pool of blood and urine.

The man in the long coat stood in the quiet for a moment, feeling his heart thump, listening to the ratcheting of his breathing.

The Enemy.

The fucking Other!

Here in Baltimore!

He had to find him . . . Track him down . . . Destroy him . . .

A dark form, like a pile of soot collecting into animated smudge, alighted upon the sill of the window. A beak poked through. Wings spread, balancing. Talons gripped. The head cocked and a single eye stared at Mick Prince, assaying him with dark intelligence.

The man in the long coat gawked.

A crow!

What was a goddamned *crow* doing here?

As a boy, he'd spent time on a farm. He knew that crows were scavengers, clever carrion cowards.

The crow stared at him with one eye for a moment, looking at him as though it could see through his skin and straight into his soul. For a moment their eyes locked.

It was as though the crow was saying, *I know you!*

Mick Prince felt frozen in place. He'd read his share of books, all kinds of books. A crow was never a good omen.

"Shit!"

Just because he read things didn't mean he *believed* them.

He dropped the empty machine gun and reached into his belt for his Beretta .32 Cougar semi-automatic pistol fitted with a custom-made noise-suppresser. But even as he touched the gun-butt, the bird spread its wings and leaped.

A coil of oil black and fiery eyes, it flew right for Mick Prince's face, its talons extended.

If not for his excellent reflexes, the man in the long coat would have lost an eye. As it was a claw ripped across the top of his forehead, and tore out a clump of his long hair from its moorings in his scalp.

He pulled the gun out, flipped off the safety and fired. The silenced, hollow-point rounds made a forceful *thwip thwip* sound. Plaster fell from the ceiling, raining upon him. But the black wings flapped away, unharmed.

"Damn!"

Mick Prince chased the bird, his boots hammering in the hallway. It flew quickly through the door. Mick Prince squeezed off another round, then followed it into the living room.

The drug den was a mass of sprawled dead bodies and a floor soaked in blood. At first the man in the long coat thought that the crow had gone. But then, as though to say, "Here I am!" it jumped up on the couch and stared at him again, lifting its wings as though faintly ruffled but generally going about business as usual.

"Caw!" it said, and looked at Mick Prince with defiance.

His common sense told the man in the long dark coat that he

should just walk away now. His reaction before had been automatic and understandable. He'd been a killing machine and the crow hopped in front of his wheels.

Now, though . . .

Now he had completed his mission and he should just leave the place. The longer he stayed, even in this bombed-out part of town, the more likely he would be caught. What he should do was just walk out the goddamn door and bang it closed and let the crow have a feast . . . Let it have its way.

Something, though . . . Something *bothered* him deeply about that creature. It was the biggest crow that Mick Prince had ever seen, and it had a strange *presence*, a creepy *otherworldliness* to it.

Worse, it had the taint of the *Other*.

The Enemy.

For as long back as Mick Prince could remember, he had been aware of the Enemy. He had felt him prowling in his dreams, in the shadows of the day, and in the twisted motives of those who had tortured him, those who had made his life so difficult. He felt as though his soul was older than his years, had tracked across the wastelands of time on some desperate pursuit, dogged by a dark and mysterious creature he had come to know as the Enemy.

An Enemy that wished to *destroy* him.

An Enemy that wished to *consume* him.

For years he had scurried away in fear. Now, though, he had a different tack. Now he was determined to search out his foe, confront him . . .

Kill him.

"Who are you?" he said.

The crow fluttered its feathers. It hopped down to the arm of the couch and pecked its beak into the air, as though attempting some arcane semaphore.

"Why aren't you a fucking *raven*?" shouted the man in the long coat. "Quoth the Raven . . . Nevermore, Lenore! Not some goddamned stinking *crow!*"

The crow waggled its tail, as though in a kind of shrug.

"You think I haven't read my Poe?" said Mick Prince. "That overrated hack! What a joke! Some Frenchies got a hold of him . . . and whacko! The Jerry Lewis of literature! Well let me tell you . . .

I'm of the old school. I say that Rufus Griswold was right. Edgar Allan Poe was a worthless drunken bastard." Mick Prince tapped his chest with the end of his gun. "And when I write, I certainly don't kneel at his altar!"

"Caw!" said the crow.

It stared directly at Mick Prince, unblinking.

"Fuck you!" said Mick softly. He lifted up his gun, trained its sights carefully upon the bird. In his mind's eye he could visualize the bullet blasting into its chest, shattering the entirety of the delicate bone structure into a black and crimson Fourth of July firework. Oh, the feathers would fly, the beak would soar!

He was just putting pressure on the trigger when the man walked into the room. He was wearing baggy pants, a ripped sweatshirt, and a Baltimore Orioles cap slung on backward. In his right hand was a Walther PPK.

"Mutha fu—"

Without a thought, Mick Prince shot him twice. Flowers of blood bloomed from the T-shirt. The man hobbled back two steps, then stumbled over a body, his arms spinning as if to lift him away from his impending death. Mick Prince shot him again and the man's head was nearly torn in half. Brains and blood made a rough new wallpaper.

Wings spread and flapped.

The man in the long coat whipped his attention back.

The crow flew toward the hallway.

Mick Prince fired at it, but the bullet went wide, smashing into a window.

The bird wheeled around, swinging back, keeping a jagged flight path. It dove down toward Mick Prince, then at the last moment swung away.

The crow lighted on the windowsill. It swung around and looked directly at the man in the long coat.

Something in the crow's gaze stopped Mick Prince from firing. There was something so *intense*, so *riveting* about that gaze—

He wasn't sure if it was the wind or if the plumbing was responsible. Certainly it was not the bird, because crows could not speak . . .

However, in truth, the thing's dark, sharp beak moved.

Not now, said the wind or the plumbing. *Not yet. Soon!*

And then the bird turned and spread its wings.

"No!" cried Mick Prince.

He lifted the gun and fired.

But the crow was gone.

Mick Prince ran to the window, shrieking.

"No, damn you! Come back!"

But when he stuck his head out, the crow was just a speck on the horizon above the spectral, twisted city, beneath a sky the color of a fresh bruise.

three

Once upon a midnight dreary, while I pondered,
   weak and weary,
Over many a quaint and curious volume of forgotten
   lore—
While I nodded, nearly napping, suddenly there
   came a tapping,
As of some one gently rapping, rapping at my
   chamber door.
"'Tis some visiter," I muttered, "tapping at my
   chamber door—
Only this and nothing more."

—Edgar A. Poe, *The Raven*

THERE WAS SOMETHING ON THE ROOF.

Something big and noisy, and very, very annoying.

William Blessing's writing study was on the fourth floor of his large downtown Baltimore townhouse. Late at night, when he was at work on his new novel, *Objects Dark and All Aglow*, for Knopf Publishers, he'd been hearing something strange on the small roof.

. . . clacking . . .

. . . scraping . . .

. . . beating . . .

A bird? he had wondered, looking up from his computer keyboard. Had some bird made its nest up there? It was indeed springtime, and very much spawning time for the little creatures. Blessing wished them no ill. In fact, he liked the idea of birds in the city. Robins, cardinals, jays, sparrows—all were important to nature amongst the urban landscape. Even pigeons and gulls, for goodness sake! If there was, in fact, one thing that was sincerely wrong with his beloved Baltimore in his estimation, it was the lack of trees. Often as not, when the ugly, tiny townhouses were built cheek-to-jowl in grimmer eras of the Charm City's history, trees had simply been razed, giving many neighborhoods a bleak, cheap look. Fortunately, programs had been implemented to return trees to these blighted areas and it wasn't as though Baltimore didn't have trees. Its huge parks were lush with oak and pine and cypress, the wealth of green that was Maryland's treasure that had been so terribly ransacked by industry over its history. Blessing felt fortunate indeed, not merely for the huge 1890s townhouse he owned, or for the fact that it was next to a brilliant city park, but that the entire neighborhood was filled with great, oak trees, friendly old sentinels against urban blight, a stand of nature as his front yard.

A bird then, but by its sounds an awfully *big* bird.

Now, Blessing put his galleys down and looked up on the roof.

Skitter.

Flutter.

Crackle.

Damn! How annoying. He had hoped to have a pleasant morning, and the weather had cooperated grandly, giving him one of those gorgeous spring days with low humidity, a gentle breeze, low pollen, and warm sun, gently touched with stately piles of cumulus, serene in cerulean sky.

Amy was off to Saturday classes and that new graduate student wasn't due until later this afternoon. Stephen King had messengered down his new book, hoping not just for a good review from a fellow writer but perhaps, "a caustic blurb to release some of the burden of selling too many copies from my tired back." Well, that wasn't going to be possible, because the book, a real departure for King, was truly and strikingly fine, and deserved a rave review, which Blessing hoped to wrangle space for in the *New York Times Book Review*. Worst of all, it was an accursed page-turner, and although Blessing certainly had plenty of other things to do, nothing seemed so urgent now as to get to the final page of the galleys.

Atop the highest part of the townhouse, as part of the refurbishing that Blessing himself had done on the house after the success of his third dark fantasy novel *Black Soul Descending*, had been built a balcony of sorts, which connected to a small cupola, done in grand nineteenth-century Gothic style. Together with the gables the old house already sported, this created a wonderful little retreat to take tea or beer with his friends and colleagues and view the rooftops of Old Baltimore. In fact, you could see the delightful Victorian buildings comprising the better part of Johns Hopkins University, where Blessing was a full professor in the English department. Here on this balcony, on this splendid day, he had taken his Kenyan coffee, white with fresh milk, his toast and marmalade, and had intended to have a relaxing and entrancing total immersion into Stephen King land.

Scrabble.

Scutter.

Scrape.

On principle, Blessing approved of birds.

But on the other hand, a bird making all this dreadful noise when he was trying to write or read . . .

Well, that was another matter.

He sighed, got out of his chair, and went up to the space where seasoned, carpentered wood became shingles, and the roof angled up to the several chimney pots and enclosures that lined the top of the roof. Leaning on a post, he craned his head to catch a glimpse of whatever was up there. *Must be on the other side*, he thought. He couldn't even see a hint of twigs or brambles or whatever birds used to build their nests with these days. It was tempting to just give up his place on the rooftop, go down to his library, put on some Bach or Chopin and, enclosed in a chamber of music, read. However, he intended to have a party here next week and this area was a beloved place for friends to cluster. Having a bird on the roof might or might not be a bad thing, but certainly if there *was* a bird, he'd want to be able to lecture folk about it. Besides having a fine intellect and wide knowledge on a large variety of subjects, William Blessing prided himself on his *curiosity*. He enjoyed talking at length on the wonderful oddities, academic and otherwise, that curiosity uncovered. No doubt Lincoln Holmes would be at the party and, should this bird make noise, he'd ask what sort of creature would have the effrontery to nest atop the great William Blessing's house. Blessing, without a detailed answer, simply wouldn't be Blessing, and not only would his friends be worried, but his more dangerous and jealous colleagues would whisper behind his back. "Oh, dear. Poor Bill is losing his edge!"

Blessing knew birds. He would only need a glimpse of this one to tell what kind it was. Also, if it were merely *starting* a nest, it could be chased away. Blessing surely didn't wish to chase it from eggs or babies if that was the case; but the sooner he knew what was up, the better.

Although he was forty-seven years old, he kept in relatively good shape and was able to easily clamber over the fence and then up the crease in the roof centered by an aluminum gutter. The shingles were fairly new and gritty, and the grade, though steep, was not prohibitive to climbing. He was careful though, and occasionally leaned over to steady himself on the rough shingles.

At the top of the roof, he hoisted a leg over to the other side of the arch and straddled the central point, lifting himself up to a stand. From here he could see all the way down to Camden Yards where the Baltimore Orioles played, to the large office buildings and hotels of downtown, clustered around the central point of Baltimore's renaissance in the seventies and eighties: the Inner Harbor. Mayor Scheafer had dredged the thing, then hired an architect to give it just the right look—and then proceeded to create a huge tourist attraction and centerpiece for a run-down and exhausted city. Blessing could see the restaurants of Little Italy off to the east, the Aquarium and, on the other side of the water, the Science Museum. It being Saturday, dozens of paddle boats were inching around in the blue-gray, below the masts of the old colonial warship, the U.S.S. *Constellation*, restored and polished and ready for Kodak flashes and the scampering of children's tennis shoes.

There was a puff of breeze, the smell of cherry blossoms and honeysuckle and tar. Blessing looked down to the street. The house was seventy-one feet tall, six stories including attic and roof; and while this did not sound that high, when actually staring down from the top onto the hard concrete of the sidewalk, it seemed a great height indeed.

Blessing suddenly experienced a wave of vertigo. He felt dizzy and had to crouch down to steady himself. He took a deep breath. *Maybe this wasn't such a good idea after all*, he thought. Why had he even bothered? That's what money was for: to let other people risk their necks. Get a handyman to come on up here and take a look. Experienced roof people with a decent sense of balance.

However, the dizziness passed.

Well, he told himself. *As long as I'm up here . . .*

Just ahead reared the chimney, a brave, old, brick thing with the faded original ceramic, red chimney pots, proudly tilted against the elements. And on the other side, a rustle, a clatter, a scraping.

Blessing inched forward. If he could get a little bit closer, he could peer around the chimney and get a look. At that point he would know whether or not there was a nest. If there wasn't and it was just a bird perched there for a bit, or even in the beginnings of a nest, he could scare it off immediately and be done with all this. He wouldn't even have to call the handyman and he could proudly tell Amy of his valiant exploits.

He reached the chimney. It smelled of soot and ash. Blessing still couldn't see a thing around the side of the chimney base. It was as though the damned bird had intentionally occluded itself from view.

If he could just poke his nose around the chimney, there was no way the bird would be able to hide itself. At the very least he'd be able to see the twigs and whatnot of a bird's nest and that would be all he needed to make a judgment. He could creep back down and finish the Stephen King book knowing exactly what was going on.

Suddenly, in his mind, a picture flashed: Stephen himself through a fish-eye lens, peering into his life, black horn-rimmed glasses huge.

Don't go in the cellar, Bill!

"I'm on the roof, dammit." Blessing laughed through gritted teeth. "And life is not a horror movie!"

Using the crevices in the masonry of the chimney, he pulled himself slowly up toward another stand.

Peripherally, he noticed someone walking up the sidewalk. There was a chuff, chuff, chuff of feet mounting steps.

And then an angry clang, clang, clang of the doorbell.

Blast it! thought Blessing. *Who could that be?*

Distracted, he reached to the top of the chimney for the topmost brick, not noticing that years of rain, wind, snow, and sleet had eroded it.

Blessing gripped it, pulled on it to regain his balance.

Ke-rack.

With a sickening crumble, the brick gave way.

Blessing found himself hanging in the air, wildly windmilling. He let go of the half brick and it tumbled down the side of the roof, clanking off the gutter and bashing into the top of the gas barbecue before falling off the edge into the backyard garden.

William Blessing fell the other way.

He made a desperate reach for the tin top of the roof with his right hand. Missed. His body pounded hard onto the shingles, and bounced. And he began to slide. The angle was even steeper than the side he had scaled and he well knew that there was precious little hope that the flimsy aluminum gutter that ridged the edge would hold his weight, even if he could grab it.

With all his strength, he kicked upward with his legs. His Rockports caught the rough shingles at a sufficient angle to cause friction and a temporary stop to his nasty plummet.

His left hand flung out and snagged the edge of the top aluminum strip. His left Rockport skittered off the shingle, and the fall yanked at his left arm hard, but he managed to stop his fall at the last moment.

Blessing gripped with all his might, realizing that the fall had pounded much of his breath out of him. He managed to take in a ragged gasp even as he swung up with his right hand to grab hold of the edge. His first effort failed—but the second hooked onto the aluminum firmly.

Blessing hung on, not moving for a few moments, trying to regain his breath and his strength. Once that was accomplished, he knew he could use his feet (*Thank God for Rockports—good ridged walking shoes. Yes!*) and his jeans to edge on up. Then he could wrap his arms over the edge and get a decent hold onto the roof. Then he could start edging his way back down to the balcony—not exactly a study in gymnastic competence, but at least assured of a platform of wood to prevent him from falling seventy feet.

However, just as Blessing was beginning to get his wind back and start thinking about making the effort, there was a flutter and flap.

And a "caw."

Startled, he looked toward the chimney.

From behind it emerged the largest bird that William Blessing had ever seen in the wild.

His first impression was simply of black, as though some piece had been cut out of the darkness of last night, and been hidden behind the chimney until now. Its wingspan must have been at least a yard or more as it flapped toward him. It settled on the top of the roof, just inches from his fingers, and it cocked its head at him, as though to inspect him at close quarters.

A crow.

Blessing could see that it was a crow, of the sort he would normally see winging over Maryland horse farms or perched on telephone wires in the country, scanning the fields for prey—but not in the center of town.

This close, Blessing could see that it was not all black. Its feet were gray, its talons were white, and its eyes were crimson.

"Shoo!" said Blessing. "Come on! Shoo!"

Instead of winging away however, it sidled closer, its sharp talons scratching along aluminum.

It opened its sharp beak and stared down at Blessing as it stepped toward his hands.

four

But see, amid the mimic rout,
A crawling shape intrude!
A blood-red thing that writhes from out
The scenic solitude!
It writhes!—it writhes!—with mortal pangs
The mimes become its food,
And the seraphs sob at vermin fangs
In human gore imbued.

—Edgar A. Poe, "The Conqueror Worm"

WHEN BAXTER BRITTLE AWOKE AT SEVEN MINUTES AFTER NOON, he found himself half-covered in blood that was not his own.

The blood was sticky and sweet smelling. It clung to his long hair like a gypsy curse. The pain of his hangover doubled as he sat looking at his hands, dazed, wondering what the hell had happened. It couldn't be real blood, he knew. Had they been spraying around some sort of homemade Halloween dye in imitation of an Insane Clown Posse concert?

Droning in the background of the "Dungeon," the salon in Le Salon des Gothiques, were the ominous sounds of Lustmord. *Fuck me*, thought Baxter. *I gotta stop putting those damned CDs on repeat.* The unnerving vibrations echoed throughout the dim recesses of the basement. Although he'd made every effort to clean the place up and decorate it after inheriting the building from his parents (*I told them they needed new tires*), and despite the gang burning incense and censer pots like crazy, the place still smelled of fungus and damp and Baltimore. Feathers and posters and chains and swords and daggers and swaths of white muslin hung everywhere, and huge candles (the next best thing to torches!) burned in sconces, giving the area great atmosphere and depth. Hallways led to a mysterious, unfinished subbasement, an abandoned relic from the last days of Prohibition. But the ceiling was too damned low, and the altar was something out of a shot-on-video horror movie. *Garish and wretched, really, all of it*, Baxter thought. If he could ever scrape together a decent amount of cash, he'd either do this den up right—or just move away and ditch the whole Goth business. Just retire to the south of France, drink red wine, eat snails and truffles, and listen to Chopin.

He groaned and got to his knees. He was wearing his long coat, silken black on the outside, silken red on the inside. Part of his pain wasn't the throbbing hangover but from the inside of his mouth. He pulled out faux fangs and placed them on a nearby antique mahjong table he'd bought at Goodwill. *Damn!* He didn't remember putting in his Drac chops last night.

On the other hand, he didn't remember a whole lot of anything. Barney and Wilhemina had taken over the bar about nine. He'd hung around with some of the early arrivals of the gang at one of the back tables. It had been "old school" Goth night, with lots of Bauhaus, The Cure, Sisters of Mercy, and The Mission making up the spin list. He was competing with Orpheus and Hepburns, two club bars uncomfortably close by, for the city's meager Goth crowd, which included everyone from curious students and RenFest Celtic fans to confused metal-heads and old punkers. His two main DJs also worked local music shops, Modern Music and Soundgarden, and were beginning to build a following, though it was the weekend New Wave and Disco nights that did the most business.

He recalled vaguely drinking something green with streaks of blue—some sort of melon shooter, doubtless. Oh, right—there was this newbie there—a cute teenager with so much mascara and eye shadow she looked like some Gothic raccoon. Blond dye job with straggly spiked hair, torn Siouxsie and the Banshees T-shirt held together with safety pins. Obviously under eighteen, but she was so damned cute, he didn't have her carded and booted. In fact, when the gang adjourned downstairs for a meeting of the Salon, he'd instructed Baron DeBaskerville to make sure she came along. However, this was the point where memory began to shred into smoke, mirrors, throbbing electric guitars, and sonorous chants.

The rest . . .

The rest was darkness.

Baxter Brittle hoisted himself up. Damn! He had to open the bar. Hung over or not, he pulled the Saturday afternoon shift, and if he didn't let the daytime regulars in, they might switch to one of the other myriad bars near the Little Italy area of Baltimore. This was not a good cash flow time for that to happen. No, not at all.

Baxter's actual living quarters were above the bar. (The gang called the Dungeon the "Dying Quarters.") Baxter would have to take his shower there. But there was a laundry sink off in the corner, so he went over and splashed himself with some cold, brackish water. His head was pounding. His eyes were bleary. He went back to the mahjong table, and stared down hopefully. Yeah! Sure enough, there was a little vial. Just enough for a snort.

The single skinny line through a plastic straw cleared his head a little. He just wanted to get out of this hole for right now, deal with the spilled "blood" or whatever it was later. But there was a bottle of good French Napoleon brandy that should be in the Cabinet of Dr. Caligari by the Chamber of Naked Horrors altar and a swig would surely ease some of the claws digging into his neocortex. He struggled over to it, stopping a moment to put a sock in Mr. Lustmord's cavernous rumblings (oh, sweet, sweet silence) and opened the fake-walnut cabinet door. Sure enough, there was the bottle. Close to empty, but he didn't need a lot. He grabbed the bottle by the neck, pulled out the stopper, and tilted it back.

Fire and condensed wine.

The liquid burned down his throat, exploding into gentler warmth in his stomach. He could feel the raw alcohol spread its feathery fingers of comfort through his torso and up to his head, easing the throbbing pain somewhat. The comfort was so great, that he swallowed another gulp. Less impact, but still . . .

He put the bottle back, weaved around, a little unsteadily, and started back across the rug in front of the cheesy grade Z movie altar and . . .

. . . almost tripped over the body there.

It was a naked woman.

He hadn't seen her before, because she was half under the table holding sacramental dishes, goblets, and all that black magic gobbledegook. She was stretched out, spikey-haired head poking out like a bit of fading flesh amidst ceremonies of the grave.

"Oh, come *on*," said Baxter Brittle. "Hey! You're not supposed to be here . . ." God, he could get in a lot of trouble for this! "Look, wake up!"

He reached down haltingly and pulled her over toward him.

She flopped back.

The mascara and makeup looked as though it had melted down her cheeks and temples, and her red lips looked like a pile of mashed cherries.

She no longer looked like a sexy punk-tart.

She looked like a dead little girl.

From between her small, banal breasts jutted a silver-handled blade. Even through his stunned horror, Baxter recognized it as one of the gang's ceremonial knives.

It too had come from the grade Z movie, but its origins had apparently been, like many of that movie's props, through some of the less reputable downtown Baltimore pawnshops. Before, it was one of the few items down here that Baxter had taken genuine pride in. Some of the Gothiques and he would play for hours at speculating on the true origins of some of their ghoulish, macabre collection. The pearl-and-gold-handled knife had been one of their favorites. It was from the torture chambers of Torquemada's Spanish Inquisition, surely! No—it had once belonged to one of the soldiers of Vlad the Impaler of Transylvania, fighting off the barbarian hordes! No—it was stolen from an old Buddhist Monastery of Mysteries in Nepal!

Now, though, it was just a piece of sharp metal stuck into a naked girl.

There was blood everywhere.

This, Baxter Brittle realized, was where the stuff on him had come from.

Beyond here, in fact, was a large pool, already congealing.

Hoping against hope, woozily, Baxter felt for a pulse in the neck.

Nothing but cold, dead flesh.

He drew his fingers away as though he had touched something hot. His head buzzed and for a moment, he felt faint. He staggered a bit and had to fall against the table. A goblet fell over, and thick, cold blood oozed out onto a pentacle emblem on the cloth there.

He swung around to the cabinet, grabbed the bottle of Napoleon brandy, and swallowed the last few ounces of the stuff. He let it drop from his fingers, and then he staggered away from the scene of blood, death, and more blood.

There had to be better ways of waking up.

five

And the silken, sad, uncertain rustling of each purple curtain
Thrilled me—filled me with fantastic terrors never felt before;
So that now, to still the beating of my heart, I stood repeating,
"'Tis some visiter entreating entrance at my chamber door—
Some late visiter entreating entrance at my chamber door;—
This it is and nothing more."

—Edgar A. Poe, *The Raven*

DONALD MARQUETTE LEANED AGAINST THE DOORBELL FOR THE
third time.

He could hear the buzzing sound going through the house
again. Loud enough, he thought, to wake the dead. So where
was Professor William Blessing, anyway? He said he'd be available at noon and here it was . . .

Donald checked his watch.

Twelve oh seven!

Marquette felt nervous. He'd made sure he'd gotten there on
time. Although he'd corresponded with Blessing and spoken to
him on the phone, he'd never actually *met* him in person and he
wanted to make a *good* first impression and lead this literary and
educational journey off on the right foot with William Blessing,
famous writer; William Blessing, brilliant scholar; William Blessing, Edgar Allan Poe expert; William Blessing, "the only truly
fine writer and academic entering the fields of popular fiction"

according to no less an authority than *The New Yorker* and . . . and . . .

"You're no good!" he seemed to hear his father say. *"Worthless! All you do is stay in the stinking cellar and read. God! I don't think you're my son at all! You're just . . . just a mistake!"*

And when his father said that, he'd wanted to kill him.

When bad things happened in horror stories, often Donald would imagine them happening to his father.

Marquette took a moment to steady himself on the railing. He realized his pulse was rising and that his blood pressure was probably going nuts. This was the moment he'd been anticipating for months and months, and he really was letting things get out of hand, really. *Steady, guy. Twenty-eight years old is too young an age to blow out a heart valve. So you're excited . . . Blessing gets his pants on one leg at a time, and probably forgets to put the toilet seat down like all men. So he's brilliant! So he could be the ticket to literary fame, fortune, and academic majesty for a humble corn-fed boy from Dubuque, Iowa! So you worship his novels, his short stories, his criticism, and his great "History of the Gothic Tradition from* Castle of Otranto *to Stephen King and Beyond"! He said he was really looking forward to working with you, and meeting you and that he'd take you for a drink (a drink!) this afternoon to Fells Point, where Edgar A. Poe himself had fallen flat on his frothing face and died.*

Donald Marquette was a tall, gangly young man who looked as though he might be more at home taking the road from Iowa to Congress with Jimmy Stewart's Mr. Smith. He had long, dark hair that he tied in the back with a bit of rawhide strap and deeply earnest eyes above a sensitive nose and thin Midwestern lips. His ears were a little too large for his head, and his hairstyle emphasized this, making them appear to stick out rather like Howdy Doody's. Marquette was grateful when his youthful freckles had passed on a couple of years ago. He wore a mustache and dark, wire-rimmed eyeglasses to counteract his distinctly innocent look and cultivate a more serious literary air. Neither a pipe nor cigarettes had appealed to him much; however, he'd long since abandoned his teenage habit of chewing bubble gum (and started watching his weight) from his first fantasy convention onward.

Now he stood on this lovely Baltimore avenue, lined with freshly bloomed tulips, bushes, and other aromatic vegetation—a block of buildings steeped in the colors of history that his hometown so sorely lacked. A breeze played with his hair and butterflies fluttered in his stomach and bees buzzed amongst dandelions in the rich green grass the bordered that old, red brick.

A twig suddenly dropped onto the steps beside where he stood.

Then, a piece of shingle fluttered down, just missing his head by a breath.

He looked up, shielding his eyes from the sun.

Nothing more descended.

His eyes lighted on his Timex, which now declared, digitally, twelve oh nine and . . .

Oh, jeez.

Noon had been the original time. Blessing had suggested that he make it at one instead.

And he'd totally blanked out on that.

Man, what a gaffe!

He was about to turn and skedaddle, get the hell out of there before Blessing (probably wearing a towel and dripping) scowled out of a window, yelling down, "Marquette, you're too damned early. Go back to the sticks, you stupid hick."

However, before he could even get one step down and away from the landing, the door opened.

"Yes?"

Donald turned around.

He recognized the man standing at the door immediately from the book-jacket photos. However, William Blessing looked a good deal more professional and focused in those pictures. Now, his hair was ruffled, his flannel shirt was untucked, and he looked . . . well, *askew* both mentally and physically. There was a bit of dead leaf on his shoulder. He was about five foot ten and, though not overweight, he clearly didn't exercise much more than his walking to school, which he was so proud of. He had light-colored eyes and a bland, even face—but even now, in his disarray, Donald could see he was a mild, friendly sort. Not angry at all. This put him at ease a bit. Marquette swung around and offered his hand.

"I just realized . . . I'm early! I'm Donald Marquette and I'll come back later in the afternoon and I'm really, really sorry to disturb you and—"

"Oh, Donald!" said Blessing. The puzzled frown became a light smile. He pushed the door open and reached out an open hand. "You are a bit early, but that's all right. Actually I'm glad of company. I'm not much good for anything else."

Donald happily grabbed the hand and pumped it. The hand-shake was firm and heartening, and suddenly Donald felt as though a burden had lifted from his heart.

"Are you all right, Mr. Blessing?"

"Donald . . . please . . . I told you. Call me 'Bill.' I know I'm going to be your graduate advisor . . . but we're also fellow authors, eh? Colleagues." Blessing pronounced "author" with satiric self-importance. "And we're going drinking this afternoon. God knows I could do with a beer pretty damned soon. Come in, come in, though. Would you like some coffee? Tea? I've got a pot of Kenya mix on and I'm going to pour myself a bracing cup of hot joe. Oh . . . I'll be all right. Just a bit shaken up. Come on up to the kitchen, Donald. Come right this way."

Donald found himself being led into the foyer. He'd been impressed by the house from the outside, with its newly painted front door and beautiful flower boxes and its red Victorian brick. Inside, though, it was something out of *House Beautiful*. The townhouse immediately gave the impression not so much of wealth, but *taste*. It was decorated with immaculate antiques. Fine art hung on the walls, and beautiful Oriental rugs covered gorgeously refurbished wood floors. Silver fixtures and mirrors sparkled, and, past the front parlor, in a large dining room was a chandelier that glittered above a large, highly polished waxed table. Everything smelled of Endust and carpet cleaner and furniture polish—all in all, a far cry from the drab and funky houses that Donald had lived in back in Dubuque.

"Really . . . nice place!" he found himself saying.

"Thanks. Wife keeps it shipshape . . . And I must say, before my ten-year overnight success, I really couldn't afford the army of housekeepers we put to work. Too much for me to take care of, I'll tell you. So, would you like some coffee as well?"

"Sure. Thanks."

Blessing led him back to the large modern kitchen. He pulled open a cabinet and got out a couple of fresh mugs, then poured coffee from a Braun coffeemaker sitting on the tiled sideboard.

"Milk? Sugar?"

"Just milk."

"Yep. That's the way I take it. Great minds think alike. I'll tell you, though, Donald. Before the wife moved in, didn't have all these modern appliances. I had the house and lots of the antiques but I never bothered to put them all together into a semblance of order. Amy's first project was to do the full Martha Stewart, get it all fixed up into the way you see it. Impresses other women, I suppose, and it's damned nice and convenient. But I kind of miss the scattered way it used to be. Had a kind of . . . individualistic flavor before, you know what I mean?"

"Well, being not exactly wealthy, I've lived in my share of individualistic dwellings."

"Ha! Well said, well said! But Donald, don't ever tell that to Amy. She despairs of my office, which is a disaster . . . But it's my territory and I won't let her in. Am I bad for that?"

"I think the psychological term is 'boundaries,' . . . uhm . . . Bill."

"Oh. Psychobabble terms! Love them! I've got a psychobabble talk show hostess in my new book." Blessing grinned. "Gets hung by a phone cord and electrocuted. And who says my popular fiction doesn't have literary value!"

Donald found himself laughing. He felt much more at ease. Plus, the coffee was absolutely delicious. Generally, he was an instant-coffee drinker who only took the stuff to jolt him awake in the morning, or as a stimulant while he was writing, a time when he often let his cup go cold and nasty. This coffee, though, was rich and smooth with a complex and excellent taste.

"Do all bestselling writers brew super coffee?" he asked.

"No, that's not a qualification, but thanks anyway. I like it. And God, I need it now—and maybe with something more in it. Would you come round this way?"

Blessing jerked his head and then proceeded to go through the kitchen toward the dining room. At the far end of this very large room replete with antique walnut sideboard, an amazing French-style table capable of seating twelve, was a full wet bar, obviously designed to fit exactly into the formal qualities of the room. Blessing clunked his cup of coffee onto the tabletop and opened a cabinet. The array of bottles inside could have stocked a decent-sized cocktail establishment. Blessing plucked one of them out and swung round toward his coffee, displaying it for his guest. "Just a little Irish whiskey, Donald. Bushmills. Care for a squeak of blarney?"

"Uhm . . . no . . . I'll have some beers with you, but I don't drink the hard stuff."

"Good for you." Blessing unscrewed the top and poured himself a healthy dollop, filling his large mug to the brim. "I generally don't drink this early, but I have to tell you, Donald, my nerves need to be numbed down a bit."

Blessing took a sip, smacked his lips, shivered. He looked, thought Donald, like someone who . . . well, someone who'd just had some kind of spectral visitation.

"Are you all right?" That would explain his slightly disheveled appearance.

"I will be in about one more gulp," said Blessing. He lifted the cup again, drank, put it down. "There. You know, you'd think an expert on Poe would stay away from whiskey." The man looked a bit haunted and distracted. But then he focused up again and looked at Donald Marquette. "There was this crow up on the roof."

"A crow? Not a raven?" said Donald.

"No. A genuine farmyard denizen . . . The sort scarecrows are for, only lots bigger. Well, I was up on the balcony, taking in a little of this spring sun and reading the galleys of the new Stephen King book, when I hear something up near the chimney. So me, being a total dope . . . Well, I climbed up to have a look. I slipped, and had to grab onto the top or I would have come tumbling down . . . maybe on you!" He chuckled, took another sip of his Irish coffee.

The bit of shingle, thought Donald.

"So while I'm hanging there, this crow hops out and he looks at me. Big red eyes, too. Damned scary thing! He hops over to my hands and for a minute I think, Jesus! He's going to peck my fingers with that sharp beak of his."

"Yikes!"

"Well, I think stronger words were going through my head at the time! But that crow . . . he looked me over. He *examined* me. It was like he was making sure that I was somebody. He looked . . . intelligent. He just stared at me for a few moments . . . and those moments seemed like an eternity. Then he gave a caw, spread his wings, and just flapped off. I still don't know if there's a nest or anything up there. I guess I'll get someone to go up there and check.

"But not me," concluded Blessing. "I'll tell you. Not me!"

After another drink of coffee there was a moment of silence while Blessing examined him.

The professor suddenly smiled. "Oh no, Donald. No roof climbing for you. That's not a part of the deal here." He put a fatherly hand on his shoulder and patted. "You're here as my graduate student assistant. And sub-anthologist!"

Blessing's forefinger smote the air with mock-authority.

"You're not here to chase avians marauding from my gables."

"I guess that's a relief. But if that's part of what it takes to work with a man like you . . ." said Donald. "I'd do it!"

"No, no, you just read and write and research. A little grim clerical work is about all that's going to get your hands dirty. By the way, I take it you're all settled into your new digs?"

"Yes sir. The boardinghouse you got for me is just fine!"

"I thought you'd like it. Graduate students should have someone to cook and clean for them. The ones I've had who have to do daily nuisance chores too much . . . Well, they just don't get the time they need. And with you writing your novel . . . And maybe teaching an undergraduate class! No, no, Mrs. MacDonalds's is the place. And within walking distance of the university—and here as well!"

"I really appreciate you finding it for me."

"Good, good. Now then. I'm going to pour myself a little more downer and splash on a little more upper . . . and then we'll go up and I'll give you the cook's tour."

"You'll show me where I'll be working?"

"Your place at the oars of this fine galleon, cutting its way across the choppy seas of literature? Why, yes. All my slaves have their own little cubicles in the computer division!"

Blessing immediately laughed at Donald's expression. "Just

joking of course. I've got a few students I hire part-time to do files, secretarial work, and such. Amy does quite a bit as well. As they say, the writing business can certainly generate a great deal of paperwork."

"Why, yes sir!" said Donald. "You must employ a full-time helper for your fan mail alone!"

Blessing chuckled good-naturedly. "Ah, yes. The man knows his way around good, old-fashioned flattery. Always a rather exceptional quality. Come, come, lad!" Blessing cocked an eyebrow. "Enter through the gates of Edgar Allan Poe and William Blessing. Abandon all hope, ye who enter here!"

Eagerly, Donald followed, feeling very much a most fortunate fellow indeed.

Who would have known that those short stories he'd written in that creative writing class in college would have brought him *here!* He'd always loved literature, whether from the racks of used bookstores or the stacks in libraries. Being a voracious reader and enthusiast for the thrills and purposes of fiction, it was natural that he'd try to do something with it in his life. This led him toward a degree in English at Iowa University, with a side degree in education so he'd be able to teach. After college he'd gotten a job with the Dubuque school system, teaching high school English. Nights he worked on a masters degree in American literature. However, he also worked on a hobby that had started to pay: writing short stories. He'd written some mystery and science fiction, but he found his natural bent toward the horror genre. Most of his stories had appeared in smaller journals such as *Cemetery Dance*, *Bones of the Children*, *Frights* and other semi-professional magazines (several, like *Inquities* and *Midnight Graphitti*, now out of business). However, a few of his stories had made it into the *Magazine of Fantasy and Science Fiction* and other higher-paying markets (including a short-short in *Rage*, his first men's magazine sale). He'd even written one of the books in the perennial horror line based on the popular Gothic TV series, *Dark Sunset*. Unfortunately, it had been severely rewritten by the in-house editor of the series, while his own serious novel had fallen victim to the industry-wide retrenchment in mid-list category fiction. Translation: it had never sold because it wasn't "high-concept" enough and he wasn't a name-brand writer. *At least not yet*, he'd tell himself.

His masters thesis had been called "William Blessing and American Gothic." He'd been thrilled when Blessing had actually answered the questions he'd sent in a letter. When Blessing had received the final thesis, he'd been so pleased with the results that he'd helped get it published as a monograph by a small university press. They'd stayed in contact through e-mail, and when Donald had started wondering whether he should get a doctorate, Blessing had been more than supportive. Having read and admired not just Donald Marquette's critical efforts but his short stories as well, Blessing suggested that he come to Johns Hopkins to get his doctorate and had arranged for financial help, including a scholarship. Blessing was also assembling a huge collection of Gothic fiction in three volumes: one from North American writers, one from British writers, and one from writers from the rest of the world. In addition to other editing work, Blessing thought that Donald might be interested in helping to assemble these volumes with him.

Naturally, Donald had jumped at the chance.

Teaching on a high school level was getting to be a drag. Getting a Ph.D. from a prestigious school like Johns Hopkins would make it possible to get a position as an assistant professor at a university somewhere. Also, being associated with a person on the level of Blessing, both academically and in terms of popular fiction, could do nothing but good things for his writing career.

With Blessing's help, he was accepted at the Baltimore university. He'd arrived before the beginning of the next school year in order to get settled and start working seriously with Blessing on the ambitious multi-volume series.

Now, the notion of seeing Blessing's famous library with its amazing collection of the memorabilia, not merely of Edgar Allan Poe but of many other writers in the Gothic tradition, gave Donald a thrilling buzz.

Except for this strange business with that bird, it looked as though it was going to be a banner day, he thought. Blessing, though obviously troubled by the crow incident (and, naturally, by his brush with death) was a genuinely fine fellow and, although Donald was still a little nervous, Blessing's politeness and enthusiastic reception made him feel very good indeed.

What treats awaited him upstairs!

Blessing made a quick detour back to his bar.

"Come, come, then," said Blessing, pouring another drop of whiskey into his cup, this time without diluting it with first-rate coffee. He smoothed back his hair and pointed upward. There was a manic gleam in his eye. Clearly he relished showing off his home and his treasures—particularly to someone like Donald Marquette, who would appreciate them. "Let's go up to the lab and see what's on the slab."

"Lots of books, I'd imagine," said Donald.

As they passed into the hallway, approaching the staircase, the door opened.

"Ah! It's the wife!" said Blessing. He quickly downed the whiskey and wiped his mouth on his sleeve. He handed the mug over to Donald. "Do me a favor and hide the evidence, eh?" He pulled out a cough drop from his pocket, unwrapped the paper, and popped it in his mouth.

"Okay," said Donald. He thought for a moment and then walked back to the kitchen. He went to the sink and ran the hot water, washing out the dregs of the whiskey.

When he turned the water off, he heard voices from the other room: A man's. A woman's.

"I'm just glad you're all right!"

"I'll tell you one thing. No one's getting me up on that roof again! But come on up, dear. Donald Marquette's here!"

"Terrific! I've been looking forward to meeting him!"

The woman's voice was rich, sweet, mellifluous.

Marquette stepped out of the kitchen, quickly drying his hands on his shirt, anticipating an encounter with a strong, friendly woman. Probably with a touch of gray but strongly built with a gentle, mature smile and the kind of steadiness that gave a great writer and scholar like Blessing foundation and anchor in this rough world.

"Donald! I've heard so much about you," said the woman as she saw him.

Donald Marquette blinked and stopped in his tracks.

Amy Blessing was one of the most beautiful, striking women he'd ever encountered in his life.

And she was no more than twenty-five years old.

six

Out—out are the lights—out all!
And over each quivering form,
The curtain, a funeral pall,
Comes down with the rush of a storm,
And the angels, all pallid and wan,
Uprising, unveiling, affirm
That the play is the tragedy, "Man,"
And its hero the Conqueror Worm.

—Edgar A. Poe, "Ligeia"

THERE WAS A GIRL WITH A KNIFE IN HER CHEST IN THE BASEMENT.
Somehow, Baxter Brittle managed to keep his hands from shaking too much as he poured himself several ounces of good French cognac into a glass of Coke.

A very, very dead girl.

Brittle drank gratefully, allowing the carbonated varroom of alcohol to separate him just a little bit more from the problem.

The familiar environs of his bar helped him as well, the touch of the field of bottles, the smell of last night's beer and cigarette smoke in the air. Fortunately, Ed the janitor had come in early as he was paid to do and swabbed the place down after last night's bacchanalia. He and the other bartenders could pretty much take care of it through the week, but on Saturday and Sunday mornings, they needed a professional.

Now the beer cans were in a black sack along the side of the road outside, with the rest of the Friday flotsam and jetsam. *Too bad the garbage collectors don't take dead bodies*, thought Baxter.

Outside it was a beautiful spring day, unfortunately. The nice thing about his bar was that it was equipped with shutters as well as windows, so he could pretty much control the lighting. Most of the time, he kept them tightly shut. Baxter took pride in the fact that, in his bar, he could create perpetual night. Right now, in fact, those shutters were closed. The only light in the room was provided by the dim overheads, a few lights in the bar, and an EXIT light to the rear of the place. However, even *this* was too bright for Baxter Brittle's delicate condition, so he was very happy that from time to time he wore shades, inside and outside, and no one would wonder why he was wearing them now. (Not just to keep out the light, but to hide his puffy, bloodshot eyes, as well.)

He tilted back the rest of the Coke and allowed the cognac entrance into his system. Then he poured himself a little more, neat, and put it upon the bar. And surveyed his domain.

Thank God no one is here, he thought.

He knew that customers would be straggling in eventually, but every moment of peace he got he needed to get his brain back in gear.

After his intimate acquaintance with blood and death, he'd managed to hobble to his upstairs apartment. The shower had been hot and welcome, going a long way toward getting him back on the road to something at least approaching sanity. A scrubbing, some shampoo, and lots of steam had led him to a conclusion.

Whatever had happened last night, there was time to deal with it.

Enough time had passed to allow certain key memories into his brain pan, the most significant of which was the fact that the girl was from somewhere far, far away; was, in fact, a runaway, if memory served, who'd just arrived in the area and knew practically no one. The others of the Gothiques, Baxter felt, were probably having a similar morning as he had. Even if any of them remembered what had happened last night, he was pretty certain that no one would go to the police. No, he had enough on them, enough power, that they'd just come in here, check things out, talk it over. That this had not happened yet did not surprise him. Many of the gang didn't even rise before the sun set. Baltimore vampires! Just as well.

After his shower, he'd put on some fresh clothes, padlocked the cellar doors, and then opened the front door. He'd pretty much figured that if he kept the bar closed today, that would be a pretty damned suspicious thing. No, better to get through today, another Saturday-as-usual, and then deal with the horror below late tonight or tomorrow. To that end, he'd padlocked the door to the cellar. Cops could hack their way through, sure, but he'd deal with that if it happened. Right now the main thing was to put on a good face, get enough drugs and alcohol into the system to appear normal, and just get on with slinging the good old booze.

He'd just about started thinking normally, without the spike of terror and anxiety rammed up his butt, when the door opened and the man all in black walked in.

He was a tall man with a muscular build, tightly wound around a large frame. He had a V-like torso and wore tight blue jeans. An expensive coat hung down from immense shoulders all the way to the heels of his black leather boots. Long hair in loose ringlets highlighted a face that could have been something chiseled out of stone. His eyes were deep-set and looked at Baxter with an amazing intensity.

"Hey, Brittle," said the man, showing strong white, wolflike teeth in a predator's smile. "How about a nice vodka martini. Shaken, not stirred. Just like you."

The smile turned into a grin.

Baxter stared at the man.

He knew this guy.

Yeah, he *knew* this guy . . . and things started falling into place.

Last night.

This man was at the bar last night!

But had he been below?

Baxter Brittle's mind churned hard, but that was all that he could come up with. It was enough, though. There was something about this man that was important. *Vital.*

Exactly what was hard to say, but making the guy his martini would buy him some time.

Baxter grinned. "Hey, man. First customer. You get a big one, small price."

"You always pay more than money for martinis," said the man. He had a resonant precise voice, rich in irony.

Baxter forced himself to chuckle. "You bet. But oh, they can go down so smooth."

He pulled out the stainless-steel mixer, dug up some shaved ice. Mucho vodka, a whisper of vermouth. Affix top. Shake, shake, shake. Quickly, before too much ice melted, he set up one of his classic martini glasses on a napkin in front of his customer. A strainer affixed to the top of the tumbler kept the ice back as he poured the clear mixture into the glass. It was a focused ceremony, and the traditional moves gave him an odd kind of familiar comfort.

"Olive or twist?"

"Didn't Charles Dickens write that book?"

"What? Oh, yes. Right." He winked at the man, cocked a finger at the man. "Good one. I'm a bit slow this time of day."

"I would think so . . . after what happened last night." The man leaned forward on the bar, his teeth going into a Jack Nicholson sort of grin. "I'll take both the lemon twist and the olive. Please."

Baxter pulled open the condiment tray, selected a nice fat Spanish olive, and squeezed a toothpick through it and the pimento inside. Then he pared a bit of lemon zest and gingerly placed it in the drink. Cautiously, he said, "I'm not sure I know what you mean."

He studied the man's face, tried to get some memory back, but there was nothing there but a vague certainty that, in fact, the man had somehow been involved with last night.

The man picked up the toothpick, waggled it for a moment in the drink, then sucked off the olive. He chewed this methodically for a moment, then drank off a half inch of the martini, still staring at Baxter with those penetrating eyes.

"I hope you won't think of me as anything but an ally, Baxter. In fact, I want to make sure you know that I absolutely harmonize with everything in your life. Only I believe I can take you in the directions you desire."

"I'm sorry. You lost me." Baxter was frightened, but he was also annoyed. "Look, I admit I drank too much last night. I don't remember a damned thing that happened after about ten."

"But you recognize me."

"Vaguely."

"Good. That's all that's necessary. Oh—and help yourself to some of the mix if you like. On me."

"Don't mind if I do."

Baxter grabbed some normal crystal, poured himself the drink, and took a swallow. The chill bite gave him a bit of relief. "What's this about—blackmail?" He sighed. "If you're after money, I'm afraid you've got the wrong guy."

The man sipped at his martini, still intently staring at Baxter. He looked like some gigantic snake, its prey in the corner, sizing it up, getting ready for a strike.

"Oh, I think we're both after money, but that might come down the line, if we can get in synch." The man leaned back, looking relaxed. "If you woke up as I imagined you did, it was to a bit of shock, Baxter Brittle. I'd like to help you with the situation that you're in."

Baxter knocked back the rest of the drink. "I'm tired of beating around the bush. What are you proposing?"

"Ever see that movie *Pulp Fiction?*"

"Sure."

"John Travolta and Samuel L. Jackson accidentally blow a guy's brains out in the backseat. The result: one messy backseat. They take the car to Quentin Tarantino's garage. The mob boss calls in Harvey Keitel, who figures out what to do before Tarantino's wife gets back. He's called 'The Cleaner.'"

"What are you saying?"

"Just call me *Harvey*." The man smiled. "You've got yourself a situation. I can take care of it for you. It's that simple."

Baxter shook his head. "If you know I've got a situation, maybe you can tell me what happened!"

"Maybe it's just as well you don't know, Baxter. Maybe you'd sleep a lot better in the future if we just get this little matter behind you. And I'll take care of the . . . uhm . . . dead weight in your life. No one else knows, Baxter. No one really cares about the victim. I have the talent and the power to erase just about everything that might lead anyone looking for her here."

Baxter was just damned grateful there was no one else in the bar. His entire being had shut down from the moment he'd seen that knife stuck in that girl. Now something very much like hope glimmered at the back of his mind. He knew very well that this man could be some strange kind of informant. Maybe an investigator into cult activity, looking into the warped world of the Goths, and coming away with a lot more than he'd bargained for—trying to nail the heinous slaughter of a poor innocent.

No. As Baxter studied the craggy face of this man, he saw nothing but a different kind of ambition. An ambition that had already etched itself into his own heart.

Baxter pulled out a pack of French cigarettes. He took one and stuck it in his mouth. He felt a little more powerful just completing this ritual.

"Tell me your name. I need to know your name first," he said, offering the stranger a cigarette.

The man took the Gauloise and fitted it into his mouth. He pulled out a cigarette lighter from a voluminous pocket. He lit his cigarette. As he held the flame out to light Baxter Brittle's tobacco tube, Baxter could see that the lighter was made of wood and metal, carved to resemble one of the famous gargoyles of Notre Dame.

"Prince. The name is Mick Prince."

Mick Prince. Yes, he had heard that name before. Last night . . . Yes, definitely last night . . . but also elsewhere.

"You're a subscriber! A subscriber to *The Tome*. And—"

And you've sent in stories and poetry . . . The sickest, nastiest prose and verse I've ever seen in my life . . .

And I've rejected every single one.

He caught himself.

". . . and you've submitted material, I believe."

The man glowed with a kind of infernal pleasure. "That's right. Nothing that fit your purposes, I think. But that's one of the things we can talk about. You see, there's a whole new dimension awaiting you and Tome Press." A cloud of smoke billowed up past his face, obscuring it. "And I would like to show you the way."

Immediately, Baxter saw it. He bought himself some time by sucking in some thick aromatic smoke and blowing it out slowly, very slowly, through his nostrils, examining the burning end of this Gallic cancer stick.

This guy was some sicko. One of the unfortunate side effects of the various fringe groups that read the magazine he published and edited, that bought the various books Tome Press released. These were the sort of sad unfortunates Baxter had known were out there, but had always endeavored to avoid. Now though, apparently, one had managed to insinuate himself into the scene.

What had happened last night?

If only he could remember! Then he'd be able to judge better how far he could trust this dark creature.

Brittle tried to reconstruct the scene in his mind. He could imagine the Salon's sybaritic revelers, stoned and drunk both, dancing with Mr. D . . . The ceremonial knife, a lethal plaything, somehow burying itself in one of the participants, and that little slip, whether intentioned or not, could very likely spell the end not only of Le Salon des Gothiques, but to the freedom and joi de vivre of Baxter Brittle.

Had his hand been on that knife?

Had he cried out in joy to penetrate that girl so?

No. There was far too much at risk. If nothing more, the stranger knew that there was a dead body in the basement and not only didn't seem to be inclined to run for the authorities, but in fact wanted to *help*. Wanted to take away the little problem, dispose of it under the fresh pourings of some expressway on-ramp or deep in the Chesapeake Bay, weighted down by anchors, food for the crabs.

So why not? Why not let him?

A deal with the Devil?

No. Of course not. There was no devil, just as there was no God.

As Brother Crowley, dear old Aleister, said: *Do what thou wilt shall be the whole of the law.*

Well, this thou here wilt that his butt not be parked in some state institution or prison, prime young meat for predatory fudge-packers!

"You'd do this? Why?" he asked.

"I want to move to Baltimore. I want to be part of the Goth-iques salon."

"Why? Anyone with any ambition gets the hell out of Balti-more. If I didn't own this bar I'd be long gone."

The agate eyes in the man glittered and twisted. "Because I think you have . . . potential. And I believe with all my soul that I can be the heart of that potential."

Again, the lips parted and he showed that strong, hard grin.

Baxter Brittle shivered at this. The darkness in the man was astounding. He tried to slip back in his memory and recall the poetry and stories the man had sent to *The Tome*. Vague recollec-tions of twisted viscera, decayed corpses dripping, flayed chil-dren, imploring chants to forgotten gods . . . the usual litany of adolescent death-worship. But this guy's material had been dif-ferent; there was a freakish intensity, an unfettered ferocity that had been, well, startling. Frightening. And if a hint, a breath of literary value had invested the work, Brittle most certainly would have published it. However, it was fairly puerile, showing no real sense of structure or rhythm or character or just about *anything* that distinguished it . . . except of course for that brutally assaultive, weirdly confessional *intensity*.

Yes indeed, this ferocious man gave Baxter Brittle the creeps.

But he also intrigued him.

And if he wanted to pull Baxter Brittle's posterior out of the crack into which it had lodged . . .

So be it.

He had no illusions. It was pretty clear what this was going to cost him. The man wrote like a fiend and valued his writings; he wanted to get published. Pure and simple. Ah, yes, literary ambi-tion! What a charming state! Yes, yes, Mister . . . Why these poems in fact are quite fine. And the stories . . . well, I suppose they could do with some editorial polish, minor revisions for tone and consistency. However, that can be arranged. Why yes! And while I don't think we'll be able to squeeze *too* many into *The Tome* . . . let us see, there must be other possibilities. Of course! A collectors edition, signed and numbered! With illustra-tions by . . . who? Why, yes, Alan Clark or Harry O. Morris would be superb for the dustjacket, with one of those hot young horror artists from Chaos! Comics or Verotik for the interiors. I believe, sirrah, that we can do business . . . Oh, and again, thanks so much for hauling that spitted naked girl out of my closet. No more liquor-fed home-surgery sessions for me . . . uh-*uh!*

"Hmm. Yes . . . well, the gang is always looking for new blood!"

The man extended his hand. He wore leather gloves with the fingers cut off. Small chains twinkled.

Baxter shook the gloved hand. "Welcome to the club."

"No parties tonight, Baxter," said the man. "Stay as sober as you can. You're a lucky bastard. No one else remembers what happened last night either."

"How do you know that?" said Baxter. That was only a slight concern, as the gang had blood oaths and even if several had been present at the unfortunate, inadvertent "sacrifice," they'd pretty much all be in Baxter's state of murky amnesia. Certainly none of them would be so foolish as to go to the authorities.

"Just take my word for it, brother." He looked around. "You get any customers this time of day?"

"Yes. They just haven't straggled in yet."

"That's what I thought. Just keep the basement shut tight. I'll deal with it tonight, after you close." The man's long coat shifted and swung like curtains hiding mystery. "I'll come into the bar at midnight. Be here." He strode to the door. There he swung about and again showed that manic grin to Baxter Brittle. "It's nice to be a part of the Gothic tradition, isn't it, Baxter?"

Then he was gone, a blur of black against the Saturday morning glare.

seven

True!—nervous—very, very dreadfully nervous I had been and am; but why *will* you say that I am mad?

—Edgar A. Poe, *The Tell-Tale Heart*

SHE TOOK HER HAND IN HIS GENTLY AND GAVE HIM THE SWEETEST handshake he'd ever received in his life. That hand was soft with long, elegant fingers and a touch that he'd wanted on his body all of his life.

"Uhm . . . Oh. Yes. It's really nice to meet you too, Mrs. . . ." Oh, gakk! No. Donald Marquette's flustered mind flailed about for the right term. "Amy. Yes, Amy."

"I was about to take Donald on the nickel tour," said Professor Blessing.

Amy Blessing's eyes twinkled and her smile lilted mischievously. "Oh, I think you should charge him at least ten dollars, Donald. All that old wretched stuff is pretty hard to take."

Donald laughed and reluctantly let go of her hand. "Oh, you don't realize how much I've been looking forward to seeing that old wretched stuff." How he'd gotten back hold of his speaking facilities, he wasn't sure. Inside he still felt like an awkward teenager, tongue-tied and stunned. "And to being here, to meeting you both . . . to being in Baltimore at the university. It's all like a dream."

She giggled with almost childlike joy. "Oh, good. How nice to be in someone's wonderful dream."

DAVID BISCHOFF

Donald Marquette had never met a woman quite like Amy Blessing before. His first sight of her was like a physical blow—a blow wrapped in velvet, reaching every part of him. She was not a tall woman, perhaps five-five, but somehow her vitality seemed to make her physical presence overwhelming. She had long blonde hair, perfectly cut and resting just-so atop a simple black blouse grazing breasts sweetly poised between big and small. She wore blue Guess jeans that wrapped around a narrow waist but gave a pearish posterior room to express itself. She made her simple black Reebok shoes seem utterly feminine. A minimum of makeup managed to accentuate her pert nose, her chin was just short of sharp, and she had high cheekbones. Perhaps her most amazing feature, though, was her eyes. She had large hazel eyes filled with spark and crackle, innocence hot for experience. Every jot and lilt of the woman bespoke a bright, *alive* personality. She was simply so pretty it was almost painful to look at her.

And her eyes looked at him with frank interest, saying, Who are you? I'm very interested. I really want to know. I *care*.

Care.

Something Donald Marquette had not known much of in his life.

"Hmm. Well, no dreams are allowed here," Professor Blessing said gruffly. "Only nightmares. That's the way to riches, fame, and wealth!" He laughed with obvious irony.

"Did you find your boardinghouse all right?" asked Amy. "All settled in and everything? We've got guest rooms if there's a problem."

"Oh, no. I got here yesterday and it's been very easy. The landlady is already spoiling me," said Donald. "I guess I'm just not used to people making breakfast for me."

"Oh, such a hardship," said Amy. "Well, you'll have to get used to having meals over here, because you certainly will be invited. This project that you're working on with the Good Doctor here is just *so* exciting." Her eyes shone with delight. "I'm going to help as well, you know. I mean, as much as I can fit in . . . I'm pretty busy."

"Amy's doing some writing of her own these days, when she's not working on a masters in music. I guess you'd be out of a job if she didn't have a life," said Blessing.

68

"I'm afraid you'll have to put up with my practice while you work," said Amy, playfully. "I do try to keep my instrument in tune, though. As for the playing itself . . . and the compositions . . . Well, I make no promises."

Donald lunged at the opening. "Oh! What instrument do you play?"

"Piano," she said.

"Concert piano," explained Blessing. "And sometimes I think she married me just for my Steinway." He put his arms around her. She eased into his embrace with a kittenish languor, looking up at him with love, admiration, and something else even more intimate.

"Actually, darling, I prefer your organ."

Suddenly, she blushed and put her hand over his mouth, giggling as she looked at Donald.

"Oh, dear. He does actually have a very nice organ, you know, a pipe organ, like in church . . ."

Blessing blushed a little bit. "All you have to do now, darling, is to describe proportions and my male ego will be properly confirmed for our guest." He smiled ruefully.

Donald blinked with mock-bafflement. "I'm sorry. All this banter is flying right over my head!"

Both Blessings laughed. Not only did all embarrassment disappear, but some other slight rind of ice, of formality, disappeared as well.

William Blessing reached over and draped an avuncular hand over Donald's shoulder. Donald did not notice his closeness as much as the impact of the subtle flowermusk scent of Amy's hair. "Don't worry, lad. Just stick with me. You'll be able to banter with the best of us. Now what about that tour?"

"Which is my cue to go and make lunch," Amy said. "You will stay for lunch, won't you, Donald?"

Professor Blessing blanched comically and placed the back of his hand up against his forehead in melodramatic malaise. "Sigh! My secret is out. My politically correct status is kaput! I force my wife to make lunches."

She cocked an eyebrow and placed her hands on her hips. "Just as long as you don't keep me barefoot and pregnant, I guess that one will pass. So do say you'll stay, Donald. The Professor can be so very dull at lunch."

"Sure. Thanks," said Donald.

"Brilliant!" Amy tossed them both a toodle-loo wave and then strode off to be about her business. Donald had to force himself to turn away from the sight of her. He had to work hard to focus back again on what Blessing was saying as the professor led him up the old-fashioned banistered stairs. The scent of her, the feel of her in the air seemed to linger like a pleasant haunting.

"You two really are too kind. If I report this to the world at large, everyone will want to get a Ph.D. at the Johns Hopkins graduate school."

"I do believe our previous interactions have something to do with our ease with you, Donald," said Blessing convivially. "You're an intelligent, talented, hardworking young man with great promise in the field. I pride myself on being able to discern that. What's more, you have something that's perhaps just as important as all those other qualities. You have drive."

Donald found himself nodding. "I would characterize it as *relentless ambition*."

Blessing stopped at the top of the steps and turned around, obviously struck by the intensity and sincerity and conviction with which his new associate had said that.

"Well, then! Far be it from me to do anything but facilitate the rise of our new literary star!"

Donald smiled with the fanciful irony. But a little smolder of anger touched him.

Just you wait, you smug bastard.

I'll show you.

I'll show everyone.

"I believe," Donald said mildly, "that even when he was a teenager, Edgar Allan Poe thought he would become a great poet. And I think I remember a few words in your early work, talking about your mission in life. That's why I'm here, Professor Blessing. Bill. To be in such good, aspiring company."

"Again, flattery is always welcome when honesty is involved." He pursed his lips with mock chagrin. "Hmm. I believe you're referring to that essay I wrote in graduate school, 'On the Wings of Poe.'"

"That's right."

"I was quite young and foolish then. As certain of my opinions as only the young can be. Now, I'm just foolish."

"I understand, but where you invoked Poe as your muse, saying that sometimes you felt as though you were his reincarnation. And if not—then you invoked his spirit. You almost invited possession. It was a bravura performance. A really amazing piece. Power and passion—yet in artful control. God, it made the hairs on the back of my head stand up." Donald shook his head in frank and total admiration. "Literature can just be so powerful."

"Yes. You're right about that last part. Beyond spirit. Beyond art. Beyond space and time and the petty things that weigh us down," said Blessing.

There was a moment of shared seriousness.

Donald Marquette found his new mentor looking at him in a strange and serious way. Assessing, judging, joining . . . And a shiver of dark brightness brushed across his heart. He felt a *connection*. And yet also, a *danger*. And the combination was as thrilling as the thought of Amy Blessing's lips gently touching his earlobe.

Blessing grinned again, and broke the spell. "Ah, yes, Poe! Poe! Let us now more than invoke his spirit. Let us invoke his glorious spoor!" Eagerly, he gestured his guest to follow. He took out a set of keys. Upon the next, large-framed door was an alarm box. Blessing punched in a number in the sequence of keys. The light atop the box switched from red to green, and something clicked.

Blessing inserted one of the keys from the twisted, jingling set. As he opened the door, Donald felt a soft rush of cool air.

"Uhm . . . Are you sure this isn't the H. P. Lovecraft room?" asked Donald.

"Oh, my. The witticisms keep on coming. No, no. It's just best to keep the room at a lower temperature—to preserve the collection, you understand." Blessing gestured and affected a Vincent Price imitation. "Won't you come in, honored guest. Please excuse my lack of a candelabra, but it's being cleaned."

Blessing reached in, clicked on a switch. Soft light flowed. He beckoned with a manic gleam to his eye, and thus ushered his guest in.

Incredible, thought Donald as he entered the room.

What struck him first was not so much the content of the room as its orderliness. The room itself was large, with Victorian filigree but modern tables, bookcases, and glass showcases, all immaculately lit with track lighting or underlighting to throw things into something a little more profound than three dimensions. There was clothing, spectacles, pens, combs, glasses, bottles, shoes, furniture, sketches, paintings, photographs, and daguerreotypes, all immaculately presented and labeled.

Mostly, though, there were books.

Books, magazines, manuscripts. Letters, chapbooks, writing pads.

The room was simply filled to bursting, its principal subject matter centrally indicated by a bust of Pallas, crowned by a stuffed raven; and above this, a large and beautifully framed portrait with the familiar domed forehead, the thin lips, the mustache, the dandy's clothes, and the night eyes staring out, barely surviving their own darkness.

EDGAR A. POE, was lettered in the plaque below the remarkable portrait.

"You'll have plenty of time to inspect everything closely, at your leisure," said Blessing. "Various items of clothing and artifacts of the man and his time—" He walked along, letting a finger gently stroke along glass tops. "Letters. Signatures. What have you. All the evidence of a great man's time on Earth. And also, of course, all the editions extant of all his publications, including all foreign editions of note, pirate editions, and bootleg translations. *Tamerlane. Al Aaraaf. Tales of the Grotesque and Arabesque. Collected Tales. Eureka.* First editions all."

He spoke with a dramatic enunciation, but Donald was barely listening. He went up to the glass-enclosed cabinet Blessing was indicating and simply stared. The books here were modest-looking enough, and certainly old. However, they seemed to glow with some inner light to the writer and student.

The first editions of Edgar Allan Poe.

Had he held these in his own shaky hands?

Had he signed them for admirers? Had he spilled wine on them accidentally? These were the children he'd been able to actually witness in their infancy. Even in his wildest cups, had the man ever realized how great they would become, how much they would be esteemed?

"Of course the rarest copies are protected in custom slipcases, most from Baltimore's great private libraries of the time. Specialty binding was quite the thing back then. It was common for publishers to make available uncut sheets for wealthy book lovers to take to their favorite bookbinders. Quite the status symbol back then. Exquisite craftsmanship.

"Also, I managed to track down every known appearance by Poe in all the magazines of his day. Not only in *The Southern Literary Messenger, Burton's, The Mirror, The Broadway Journal*, but all the other magazines he appeared in or edited. I generally even have representative runs of other magazines where he may well have contributed under pseudonyms, something we know he did often. I think I may have even found a few tales and poems previously not attributed to Poe." Blessing's eyes simply glowed with enthusiasm. "I'm preparing an article on that very subject now in advance of a small book. Imagine! New stories and poems by Edgar Allan Poe."

Donald Marquette was stunned. This, of course, was unheard of. Enough scholars had pored over Poe's life and times and magazines to have found such if they existed long since, surely! Half of him still disbelieved. However, the Poe enthusiast was ecstatic at the very possibility.

"What you see here, Donald," said Blessing, "is the largest private collection of its kind. It is the reason I don't have a summer home in the Hamptons!" He smiled. "I have spent far too much time and money on all this, but then, such are the fruits of being a scion of old-school money. And I mean that literally. My family has found a home in academia since before the Civil War. Many elements of my collection, and of course this house itself, come from the farsightedness of my scholarly forebears. Even with all the funds now available to me, I don't believe it would be possible to build such a collection."

His eyes grew distant, unfocused, as if gazing on some private vision. After a brief moment, Blessing turned back to Donald, smiling. "I find it . . . inspiring . . . to have so much of Poe here. I find it equally invigorating to know that I need but drive a short way to be in the presence of his gravestone, his earthly remains. It's as though all of these are parts of some arcane microphone, through which his spirit speaks to me, becomes me, serves me, as I serve the voice that found its throat in his grim and sorrowful delivery."

Blessing grinned wryly.

"Of course, it's also damned good equity."

"No. I understand," said Donald in a soft, encouraging voice. "That's not why you collected it. You collected it because it was in your blood."

"And because I could. The Blessing blessing, you might say. I've got other manuscripts and books throughout the house. And heaven knows, stored elsewhere, safely, or else even this large house would burst its seams." He walked up to the bust, and touched the excellent example of taxidermy that graced the top of it. "The collection is a hobby of mine. I used to be much worse about it—until I met Amy."

"Worse? Seems like it's a worthwhile thing to do . . ." said Donald. "I mean, you said yourself you've got the money and the time—"

"The money, anyway. No, Amy appreciates my collection. She's just put a great deal of sanity back in my life." Blessing shook his head and smiled. "Not that I was insane before. Perhaps just a little monomaniacal at times." He lifted his hands up to the image of Poe. "Oh, God, I am *so happy! So very happy*. I cannot imagine what I did to deserve to be *so content*. No. Content is not the right word. *Happy, Donald!* The word is *happy*. Thank the heavens Zeus and company aren't knocking around Olympus. They'd be jealous!" He caught Donald's eye, swung around, and pointed a finger at him. "Oh. Of course. I can see what you're thinking. How exactly *did* a crazed bachelor professor and scholar meet a delightful creature like Amy?" His eyes brightened. "A delightful, *young* creature. She's twenty-five years old, you know. Twenty-five!"

Dead on, thought Donald to himself.

"I met her when she was twenty-two, at a World Fantasy Convention in Providence, Rhode Island. She was in town, visiting relatives and she heard I'd be signing. She wasn't particularly a fantasy fan, and at that time I was better known as a critic and short-story writer. *Black Soul Descending* had just come out, with very little fanfare I might add, so at my publisher's behest I was there to help it along—even though the convention is limited to only 750 attendees. But somehow she'd been exposed to my work and was intrigued enough to come see what I was like." He smiled wistfully. "I instantly adored her, of course. Who knew she'd adore me, too?"

There was a bit of dead air between them as Blessing lapsed back into pleasant memories, his eyes unfocused. Donald found himself flailing about for something neutral to say. Even now, the impression of Amy Blessing hung about him, gently yet insistently. "She was a pianist then too?" He finally ventured.

"Hmm? Oh, yes. Yes. A very good one, but what impressed me most was that she was also composing. Creativity! God, that is the greatest gift we humans have. That, and the ability to love."

"And collect!" said Donald.

"Oh, yes. Well, Amy was pretty fascinated with all this, I can tell you. But it was she who suggested that maybe I should spend more time on the creative part of my career. Try to make a serious go of it." He grinned. "In fact, after next year—in which I hope to get you all settled and at least one of our anthologies completed—I have a sabbatical. Perhaps a permanent one. We're going to rent an Italian villa on the Mediterranean where Amy will devote herself to composing—and I to writing *two*—" Blessing flung up two fingers, "—count them *two* novels. I have a new three-book deal, you see, and I'm almost finished with the first. Should have it done this summer. Then three seasons of intense academia . . . Then bliss."

"This is a year where fortune is smiling on us all," said Donald. "I can't say I've ever been more thrilled with where my life is headed."

"Then we're a fine pair, Donald. A fine pair." He looked around happily at his treasures, then rubbed his hands together. "But let's show you where we'll be working together before we go down for lunch, eh?"

"That sounds great."

Across the hallway was a sitting room. Donald glimpsed the interior as he went past. Chiffon curtains, pleasant wallpaper, antique chairs, and a couch. To one side stood a Steinway grand piano—black, shiny, elegant. The room smelled of fresh cut flowers.

"The music room, I take it?" said Donald.

"Oh, yes. I was going to leave it to Amy to show you that one. Tinkle some keys for you. You'll hear her many times, I'm sure. But come on. I've had our secretary make this space up for you especially, and I'm very eager for you to see it."

Donald followed him up another set of stairs. "How many floors does this place have?"

"Five, not counting the basement. Our rec area and bedrooms are on the fourth level. My study is on the fifth. Going up and down contributes to my exercise. That, and walking to campus."

They reached the landing of the fourth floor. "Here we have our business office and two guest rooms. This is where you can crash on heavy work nights if you like." He pointed to one of the rooms. "Or simply if we carouse too much and you can't wobble back to your boardinghouse."

Donald smiled congenially. "That's always good to know."

Blessing led him into a large room filled with desks, cabinets, bookcases, filing cabinets, and computers. Again, the smell of cut flowers (lilies?), this time mixed with the smell of laser printer toner and fresh paper. Donald could almost taste work—and accomplishment—with the aftertouch of stamp glue, in the air.

A waggle of a finger and Blessing was leading him toward a corner of the room. Donald couldn't help noticing a pile of paperback copies of *Black Waiting Room*, Blessing's second Gothic novel, sitting by a desk.

After years of toiling in the anonymous world of "serious" fiction, producing well-crafted, intellectually challenging but emotionally dry works that consistently sold in hardcover in the mid-teens, Blessing had begun to write short stories that interpreted Poe's core creative principles. Initially a self-made challenge to see if it was possible (those who can not do, teach), he gained enough confidence to try for the big leagues. *Black Soul Descending* would encompass everything he believed about the Gothic tradition. It would be his breakout book, his *Rosemary's Baby*, his *Exorcist*, his *Shining*, his *Ghost Story*.

And so it had come to pass, much to his amazement, and often time consternation, due to the demands of "the business."

Something about William Blessing's work had kicked off new mainstream interest in the Gothic tradition of suspense and horror. Not since Stephen King had the marketplace been so excited about a new writer. And, unlike King, the critics worldwide had fallen over themselves to praise Blessing's novels and short-story collections.

When asked what he owed his books' success to, Blessing had simply answered, "Accessible literary values."

Man, thought Donald Marquette. *Seven million copies in the U.S. alone! That's worth ten years any day.*

"Here you go," said Blessing, breaking the spell. "What do you think?"

The question immediately knocked Donald out of his reverie. He turned and looked at what Blessing indicated.

In a corner of the room was a brand-new desk, featuring a sparkling new Compaq computer, filing cabinet, bookcase, printer, plus an office chair obviously ergonomically designed for comfort.

On the wall was a tastefully framed picture of Edgar A. Poe. Beside it was a Picasso poster. On the desk was a bouquet of flowers, beribboned, with a card set beside it, reading: "Welcome Donald, to the hall of high literary endeavors . . . and any silly computer game you wish to play. William and Amy Blessing."

"I'm speechless," said Donald, moving forward. "Computer games. Wow!"

"Indeed. We've got you all set up. If I recall you characterized yourself as a disorganized soul. Even before Amy, I knew that a properly organized office was absolutely paramount in importance to freeing the creative soul. So we took the liberty of providing you with what you need. You may even, if you like, use this office to do your own writing. Naturally, we don't want that to interfere with your work for us, but if you're inspired . . ." Blessing shook his head, as though seized by some intense muse. "Creativity. Inspiration. We worship them here, Donald. They are our guidance, and we revere them. Do you understand? *Revere* them. So many people think that writers merely sit down and string together words and *poof!* a piece of writing. Not so!"

"Whew!" said Donald. "I can't agree with you more. And furthermore—" he said, wishing to continue the thought, but then suddenly halted in his tracks with what he saw. Set neatly between leonine bookholders was a familiar stack of magazines, and a single paperback novel. He recognized them only after a moment of shock, but then was so touched that he didn't know what to say.

"Writing is very hard," said Blessing. "You have to keep on looking at the evidence that you can do it. Hmm?"

"My published stories!" Donald laughed. "My stupid *Dark Sunset* novel. You got them all!"

"I told you I was a collector. I have my sources. You must realize, they are for viewing only. They still belong to me." Blessing smiled warmly. "And I hope, during your tenure here, that you might find time to autograph them for Amy and myself. All except that one piece in *Rage*. I'm afraid my wife might get the wrong idea." He laughed.

"You're so kind. Thank you! Of course," said Donald.

Blessing reached over and thumbed through the collection of publications. He pulled out a neatly printed magazine, with clay-coat paper, looking rather like a cross between a literary magazine and a quality trade paperback.

"*The Tome*," he murmured. "You've got a few stories and a couple of poems with those people," he said softly.

"Yes. And there's some interest in a collection of my work, too, I think," said Donald.

"And they're right here in Baltimore," said Blessing.

"Yes. I thought it wouldn't hurt to go down sometime and say hello. You know, fraternizing with the editors and all that."

Blessing looked down at the magazine.

On the cover was a beautifully rendered medieval-style print of Satan as a goat, squatting in a pentacle decorated with Barbie and Ken dolls in various angles and combinations of copulation. The Satan goat wore vampire fangs, shades, and a velvet Dracula cape. In one hand was an electric guitar. The other held a huge cigar-sized *ganja* spliff, the mother of all reefers.

Donald felt vaguely uncomfortable, sensing disapproval from Blessing.

"These are the folk I see all dressed up as vampires and such at some fantasy conventions," he stated blandly.

"Well, sort of," said Donald. "I'm not sure these guys really go to conventions at all. But I suppose you can call them a Goth offshoot."

"Goths. I'd always thought them rather harmless. Rather a fascinating subculture as a matter of fact." Blessing started paging through the magazine. "Spooky British rock 'n' roll. European affectations. Layers of makeup. Attitude. Leather. Oh, no, let's not forget leather. And . . . uhm . . . decadence. That's the word I was looking for. Byronic decadence."

"It's all just role-playing."

"Oh, of course. Problem with American subculture I suppose is that it doesn't provide enough variety. So young people invent their own as they define their individualism through group rituals and behavior," concluded Blessing quickly, realizing too late he had strayed into his didactic lecture-mode. "Hope they pay; the magazine, that is."

"A few cents a word."

"Hmm. Better than most of the literary magazines." Blessing looked bemused. "Interesting. Might give me an idea for an article and—" He was looking at the masthead. " 'Editor and Publisher, Baxter Brittle.' " Some new realization seemed to flit over Blessing's face. He frowned. "I recognize this name . . . Oh, yes. I got some calls and letters from this fellow. Wanted me to talk about Edgar Poe's influence on Aleister Crowley and modern-day Paganism. Well, of course, that was absurd! I told him that politely. He sent a nasty reply back, and I haven't heard from him since, thank God." Blessing shuddered. "Something about these particular Goth fans."

"What do you mean?"

"They strike me as rather creepy. Unduly so, by my lights. Maybe you should be careful if you go to meet them. Nothing wrong with literary markets, but you've got to be careful. There are some strange people out there. My secretary fortunately handles the letters from the crazies that are attracted to me, so my paranoia factor is still very low. All the same—I'd give this Baxter Brittle wide berth if I were you, Donald."

Donald shrugged. "I guess that's not the reason I came to Baltimore."

"No," said Blessing. "No, of course not. But come on up and I'll show you my *sanctum santorum*. We've just time before lunch."

"Your office!"

"Yes! I do believe that you mentioned in a letter once that you'd like to see it sometime."

"Right. I guess . . . Well, I guess I've got this feeling I'd feel inspired."

"Well, thank you . . . Sometimes I wish it inspired *me*."

Blessing laughed and started walking away enveloped in musing haze. He'd left the copy of *The Tome* on the desk. Donald picked it up, feeling grateful to this generous and vastly talented man . . . and yet, at the same time, oddly angry.

Patronizing bastard! a voice seemed to say deep within. *I'll do exactly what I want to do, meet who I want to meet here!*

He slotted the magazine carefully back into its place and followed his mentor.

eight

The old man's hour had come! With a loud yell, I threw open
the lantern and leaped into the room. He shrieked once—once
only.

—Edgar A. Poe, *The Tell-Tale Heart*

ABOVE THE DREAMING BUILDINGS, THE CROW CIRCLED.
Clouds were boiling over the half moon while darkness
slipped through the streets and alleys of the Baltimore neighborhood, flowing like liquid fingers, touching and erasing all.

The crow blinked its piercing brown-black red-flecked eyes.

It wheeled and fluttered, like a piece of the sky cut out from
between the constellations, a section of destiny scissored from
reality's fabric, lost and looking for a perch.

Down below its heady spin: movement.

The wind whirled past its ears as it flapped down. Atop an
old church, half in ruin, it settled. The place stank of pigeon
droppings, but the crow paid no heed.

It cocked its head, its senses ethereally alert.

There.

Figures.

They moved amongst the shadows, half shadowstuff themselves.

The crow leaned down, like a gargoyle, watching as the figures weaved and spun through an alley. A trash-can lid clattered
off. Drunken laughter echoed against broken windows.

A current of cloud moved and the moon peered down again, silken light washing over the crow.

It cawed with alarm.

"Hey!" cried a voice. "What the hell is *that?*"

"Bad luck."

A whistling.

An empty can clanked against the rusted gutter by the crow's perch. Alarmed, ancient instinct overriding indistinct mission, the crow leaped back into the air, its large wings grabbing hold of the air and pushing up, pushing up, flapping back into the sky, and back between the stars . . .

. . . for now.

"Fucking sky vermin!" said Mick Prince, clapping his gloved hands free of any muck they might have collected.

With a half-aware chuckle, Baxter Brittle watched as the big bird exploded into flight. A feather floated down, backlit by the moon. The empty can clattered onto the cobblestones of the alley, rolling over toward Count Mishka's foot.

"Kick the can!" said the figure in dark leather, eyes black with makeup and long hair flowing in tangles about his narrow face. He booted the can toward the Marquis de la Cinque, who caught it on one of his black jacketed arms.

"Hey! Have a care!"

Count Mishka lifted his pale face toward the moon and laughed wildly. Wracked by this amusement, he wobbled, finally having to fall against the alley wall for support.

That bastard is somehow more fucked up than I am, thought Baxter Brittle.

"A crow!" he repeated, looking back up. The bird had been swallowed up by the darkness. "What's the problem with a crow?"

Mick was standing stiff, like some romantic statue. His hands were clasped together into fists, held up against his chest as though preparing for the first part of some arcane martial arts move.

His huge coat billowed up in a breeze, filling up like the sails of some phantom ship.

"I despise crows," he whispered through clenched teeth.

The man's intensity was a gas! Baxter could feel the drugs dialing in harder, and his brain seemed to be swelling up like some hot-air balloon billowing, gently flowing upward toward the skies to look down upon this grand jest called Earth.

Cool it, man, he told himself. *Don't puncture yourself on the stars!*

"I wish," said Mick, "I had my gun. Would have blasted it right off that fucking spire." He spat the words like pieces of ripped flesh. His stillness was rapture. His presence was catharsis. Baxter Brittle suddenly felt surging drugs kick *through* . . .

Something.

The detritus of the destruction drifted up high, higher, highest, spinning his brain up into a vortex of consciousness. He felt as though he was rising up and up on the wings of the crow, up past the planets, past the constellations, into the arcs of Olympus and Valhalla, up through the dizzying verandas of the Cosmic . . .

All to the delicious smell of rotting orange rinds, the scent of whiskey in the litter, pounding and thrashing to a Nine Inch Nails soundtrack.

He could taste the blood of delirious pleasure/pain in his mouth and it was, oh, so grand.

Like the crow he soared, to the industrial pulsebeat, to the Ecstasy-meth-morphine-cognac cocktail in his brain, to the rhythms of his heart, this ratcheting soundtrack. He gazed at the gang, the roving Avengers des Gothique at three-thirty A.M., a touch of fall chill in the air, Baltimoring.

Guided by Mick, the Arch Deacon himself, the Cleric of Chic.

Hovering so, in Mick's rock 'n' roll presence and yet somehow apart, Baxter felt he could look back at the past months with absolute clarity and see the crystalline *rightness* injected into the veins of night.

What a spirit!

What a dark and powerful spirit was Prince Mick, oh Royal Fellow!

Good to his word—that unfortunate girl's body had been thoroughly "cleaned," never to be heard of again. Baxter knew.

He'd scoured the papers for weeks afterward. Nothing. Zilch. Brittle was a stone-free man, and the truth was, he hadn't had even the *foggiest* notion of how to deal with that *knife*, much less the body that held it to its bosom.

However, more than a deliverance, Mick the Man had been a godsend. Exactly which dark god, Baxter hardly knew or cared; he didn't have to. All he knew was that suddenly the salon was stocked with the best drugs, and business in the bar was up so much he'd hired new people, including a manager. Now he could devote his full time and attention to writing, editing, and publishing. *The Tome* and Tome Press were prospering like never before. The first new book had been Mick's *Hatescrews in Your Corneas, Baby*, a collection of the prose and poetry he'd so stupidly rejected before (its print bill subsidized by Mick himself). The deluxe limited edition (illustrated by T. M. Caldwell) had sold out and the trade edition was moving along quite well. True, no mass market publishers seemed particularly inclined to take it on, but then Baxter didn't really expect them to, didn't really *need* them to.

Next step would be a trade paperback anyway, and he'd already contracted with Publishers Group East to handle that for him. Mick was finishing his first novel, *Decapitation Nation*, and with the new funds from the expanded publishing efforts, Baxter would be able to produce even more fine works.

Now that Tome had a real publishing program up and running he'd found the independent specialty bookstores more responsive, stocking his backlist and some even paying on time! He'd made sure to get on-line listings with Amazon.com and the web-stores from the major chains, and now his press was getting reviews and notices in the college papers and alternative journals.

Also, he was able to do his first favorite thing.

Party down, Beelzebub!

Oh, the glorious times they'd had in the cellar. No more dead naked runaways, uh-uh. But lots of other kinky stuff, real Anton Levey action. Mick had introduced strange (and messy) new rituals based on the *Golden Dawn* material. It had been a bit hard to accept it initially. Oh, yeah. First some chickens, then rabbits, a pig here and there, then up to goats and sheep. There had been some accidents along the way, but hey—whatever words Mick was intoning when he did the slicing and dicing (oh! bright!), they were for sure working some kind of major juju on the fortunes of *The Tome*, the Cork'd Sailor, and life in general.

Dark angels!

Finding that young stiff in the middle of his hangover had been the low point of his life. (And what a waste of perfectly good pussy, he'd later concluded.)

Now he was arcing up toward the high point.

And, ah! What a ride!

"Baxter!" snarled Mick.

Baxter Brittle, wobbly-hobbly and adrift in his trance, managed to tug his consciousness back in, plant his billowing gray matter back into his brain pan.

"Yo!"

Baxter turned toward the Prince and blinked. The man's thick, strong face was startling in its present visage. The eyes bugged. Veins in both temples bulged. The teeth ground audibly. The neck cords bulged. Without warning the dude's right hand shot out and gripped Baxter's shirtfront, pulling him into the stink of garlic and French cigarettes.

"I can feel him. I can feel him near, Baxter." Even in the dim light of the moon and the halogen bulbs, Baxter could see how bloodshot Mick's eyes were.

"The Enemy, Mick," cried Count Mishka.

"I sense him. He would devour my soul—I must tear out his heart first and split its sinews. I must snap it up in my mouth and gnash the ventricles and spit them into the dust. I must be sure that his spirit is shredded and sinks into the netherparts of creation."

Baxter suddenly remembered.

Oh, yeah. That was why they'd gone out on the town in the middle of the night. Lying about in the cellar, blasted on drugs and drink, speakers thumping with Usherhouse and Sleep Chamber, Mick up and hollered: "He's *out* there!"

He, of course, being the Enemy. The Anti-Mick. Whether Mick's obsession was delusion or not, there was in fact some other *something* out there freaking him bad. Following him. Making him swear he'd get it before it got him. Now, paranoia was fine, of course. Baxter Brittle had always thought, even in his idealistic days before the Bad Thing with his parents (he'd *told* them to get new tires, he was almost sure he had), that just because you weren't paranoid didn't mean people weren't out to get you. But Mick . . . Jeez, Mick would go just bugfuck crazy sometimes, feeling that presence . . .

"That's why I came here, man," he'd admitted once, wild-eyed. "I felt Him all my life. All my life I've been running. I don't know who or what he is. I'm tired of running. I'm making my stand. I'm here and I'm going to get the bastard! I'm facing up to him. That's my wall I have to get through. Get through to get to my destiny. Do you understand, Baxter? And you're going to *help* me. You *do* understand, right?"

Sure Baxter understood. He understood that when Mick was happy, things went well. When Mick wasn't happy, things got real ugly. So when Mick decided it was time for a little jaunt, a hunting in the supernal night, zapping along on dope-fueled dreams, Baxter Brittle figured it was best to go along with him.

"There!" gasped Mick, angling a finger across the street. "Over there, beside those castle ruins. I *feel* him. Dark knights under my liege. *Avaunt!*"

With a billowing of that great coat of his he leaped out and across the street.

Baxter motioned the attendant members of the gang forward after their Prince, hoping that not much would happen. He could feel himself starting to spiral down, a headache taking deep root, and he hadn't brought the proper medications for a soft landing. *Well, get this over with*, he thought. *And then back to the opium pipe . . .*

With uncommon speed, Mick had dashed across the street and was now stealthily slinking along a brick wall, a shadow fading into darkness.

Huffing and puffing, Baxter and the others found themselves at the edge of the alley.

They peered into the murk. Baxter found apprehension beginning to crawl up his spine on fat spider legs. Something was wrong here. Something was *real* wrong.

"Here!" cried Mick's distinctive gravelly voice. "Come here!"

There was a rustling, a clanking of boxes.

"You!" The voice was harsher now, edged with broken glass. "I found you!"

An electric light beam flicked on. The strong spike of light stabbed across the alley, bounced, steadied. There was a grunt, a clatter of cans and bottles.

A groggy voice growled from a pile of refuse. "Hey man! I'm just tryin' to get some goddamned sleep. Leave me the hell alone!"

"Sleep?" cried Mick. "MacDuff hath murdered sleep!"

"Wha—"

"You have persecuted me long enough, you foul cur! Get ye back to the Hades where you belong."

Baxter and company were now close enough to see what was going on. Mick was holding a flashlight on the intersection of ground and adjacent wall, a bunch of cardboard boxes. Huddled there amongst rags and newspapers was a bum in an overcoat and beard that reminded Baxter of every other home-less schitzo he'd ever seen passed out on the streets. Christ, why couldn't they ship them all off to D.C. where they be-longed?

"What the shit you talkin'—" the rheumy, smelly man was saying. He got up to his feet, an empty bottle of Thunderbird rolling away from under his legs.

"Mick!" said Baxter. "This is just some derelict!"

Too late.

Mick stepped forward, and kicked.

The toes of Mick's black thigh-high boots were silver with reinforced metal that flashed in the bouncing electric torchlight. A sickening thunk and an *"Oof!"*

The tramp gagged, gasped—then blew chunks all over the diseased alleyway.

Wine and bile and rotting Wonder bread . . .

. . . and blood.

Something in Baxter clicked. He stepped forward and put a restraining hand on Mick.

"Hey man! Chill!"

Mick pushed him back, pointing down at the retching man. "You see. He attempts to spit poison at me! Do not under-estimate the wiles of the Enemy. Now you must help me. You must help me *remove* my Enemy! Now. Hold this!"

He handed Baxter the flashlight.

Then, from the folds of his coat, he drew something out. Something that gleamed harder and sharper in the shaking light.

A black, eight-inch tensile butterfly knife.

"Begone, filth!" said Mick.

Before Baxter could say or do a thing, the knife blurred in Mick's hand, the blade diving in, doing its wet, messy work. The bum managed to get off one gurgly scream before red gushes burst from his neck and torso.

Mick stepped back, his blade and hands dripping with blood.

The bum twitched and splurged and shuddered.

"Now," said Mick, turning toward the gang, "prove your loyalty to me. Send him off! Stomp him, trample him, kick him so hard he'll go soaring off through the other side of the afterlife, never to return."

"Mick . . . Mick . . ." said Baxter. Head spinning, reality chipping. "I can't . . ."

"Sure, Mick," said Count Mishka.

"Cool, man," said the Marquis.

They stepped forward and started playing soccer with the bum's bloody head.

Baxter couldn't move. He just stood there, frozen.

"What's wrong?" said Mick. "What the fuck is wrong with you!" The butterfly's blade waved about wildly, splattering blood onto Baxter. "Do it. *Do it!*"

Fear wrapped its prickly thorns about Baxter's viscera. He wanted to run, get away from this far-past-madness.

He dare not, he knew. For Mick Prince would just as soon bury that knife in *his* spine. Baxter could almost feel the blood-hot shaft touching his nerve stem now . . .

Clearing the way for him, leering in the light, the Count and the Marquis stepped aside.

Separating his sanity from the rest of him, Baxter allowed his body to step forward and kick the prostrate body.

It squelched and oozed. Dead meat.

Baxter stepped back. "To the butt of the netherworld, Mick. And shat into oblivion," he made himself say.

Mick grunted. "Bastard!" he cried. Hawked up phlegm. Spat on the just-dead meat. Then he stood back, taking in great, victorious gulps of air. "Yes! Yes! Freedom. Freedom at last!"

Silence.

Ponderous silence, broken only for a moment by what seemed to be a flap of wings.

"Give me the light!" said Mick.

Baxter gave it to him. Mick took it and flashed it onto the gory mass on the alley floor.

Mick sighed with disgust.

"Tricked!" he said. "Tricked."

"What?"

Mick shrugged. "Not him. Not the Enemy." He plunged a fist into the air. "I'll get you yet, you bastard!" He turned. "Come on. I need a drink."

He swung away and stalked off.

Giggling, the Count and the Marquis followed.

Reeling, Baxter Brittle could do nothing but follow.

Wings seemed to beat softly in the air above him but he dared not look up into the night sky, blackening again.

nine

I dwelt alone
In a world of moan.

—Edgar A. Poe, "Eulalie—A Song"

. . . WINGS BEATING SOFTLY IN THE NIGHT SKY . . .
Away from the alleyway, the crow flaps.

It flies toward the harbor, where boat lights glitter. Fog is rolling in, thick, creeping on catarrh feet, smelling of the sea, smelling of dead fish.

. . . wings beating softly in the day sky . . .

The crow wheels and caws, flying into another date, dipping down through sunlight. It perches atop a chimney pot, above the smell of tar.

It watches as the man named Marquette enters the bar known as the Cork'd Sailor. It blinks and stands a lonely vigil. The sun sets, the stars wink on. Traffic snarls and jerks in the streets and laughter and music wax and wane.

After the full moon is set, at the bottom of night, the writer known as Marquette leaves the Sailor, books in hand . . .

. . . weaving ever so slightly.

The crow caws and leaps toward the stuff between the stars.

. . . wings beating softly in the summer sky . . .

The crow dips and swoops.

The black bird flies past the Washington Monument, past

Johns Hopkins University and the smell of hot dog and pretzel vendors and the rustle of oak leaves.

It flaps down and lands upon the roof of a townhouse. It peers down upon a balcony and a table. The young writer named Marquette and Amy Blessing sit across from each other at a table, eating salads and drinking wine. They talk intently for a bit. Then the young woman laughs and puts her hand across the table and touches the young writer's hand. He clasps her hand, smiles and lets go.

With a caw, the bird leaps up for the stuff between the clouds, moving forward, forward . . .

. . . *wings beating softly in the autumn sky* . . .

The buildings of Johns Hopkins poke up, venerable and sturdy, from the coloring leaves. A cool current carries the crow as it sails down toward the sidewalk.

There, holding a large briefcase, warmly wrapped in a cardigan sweater, puffing on a pipe, strides the man known as Professor Blessing.

The crow flaps down and sits on a park bench—staring intently through one side of its face, brown eye on the professor.

The professor stops, looking intently at the crow.

"You!" says the professor, stopping.

The crow says nothing.

"You're the one that's been hanging around my house, aren't you? Ever since spring."

The crow says nothing.

"Well, all I can say is that I'm just grateful you aren't a raven!" He laughs and shakes his head. From his case, he pulls out a half-eaten bag of Chee-tos. The crow cocks its head, almost inquiringly.

"Okay, okay. So I've got some bad habits. Look, let's make a deal. You take the rest, you don't tell my wife, okay?"

He dumps the Chee-tos onto the pavement.

The crow regards them for a moment.

Then it hops down from its perch and begins eating the Chee-tos.

"You know, if I was more of a believer in such things, I'd say you were trying to tell me something, Crow. You are a mythological symbol, did you know that?" He folds his arms. "Well, you don't seem to want to kill me. If you wanted to do that you could have just pecked my hands when I was hanging so stupidly on my own roof, hmm? Got something to say, Crow?"

The crow does not say anything. It merely eats another Chee-to and peers up intently.

It is not time.

"Well. Have a nice day, chum. Hope you have as good a life as I do."

Laughing, the professor turns and, whistling, proceeds on his walk back to his hearth and his home.

The crow eats more Chee-tos until the man disappears around the corner.

Then he flaps up again into the stuff between the Victorian spires of Johns Hopkins.

. . . wings beating softly on the winter air . . .

Dusk has come to a snowy January. Ice crystals twinkle below streetlamps. The smell of roasting chestnuts rises up from street vendors.

The crow flies to a townhouse. Lights glimmer warmly from a window. The black bird settles down upon a window box.

Inside, in a large office are three people: Professor Blessing. Donald Marquette. Amy Blessing.

They are talking.

The crow watches intently.

. . . wings beating softly on the air of otherwhere . . .

Soon.

Soon.

ten

And travellers, now, within that valley,
Through the red-litten windows see
Vast forms that move fantastically
To a discordant melody,
While, like a ghastly rapid river,
Through the pale door
A hideous throng rush out forever
And laugh—but smile no more.

—Edgar A. Poe, "The Haunted Palace"

THE FIST POUNDED INTO THE MAN'S FACE.

Mick Prince could hear teeth break. A spout of spit and blood gushed. The man's head snapped back and the wooden chair in which he was tied creaked as it tilted, then thumped back onto the floor. The bound man whimpered and moaned. Mick could smell his sweat, could sense the pain and fear. His nostrils widened, taking in the sensations.

However, this was merely peripheral to the main subject of his attention. The man with the knuckle dusters. The torturer. Something about him . . .

A black man in an Italian suit held up his hand. Brass-knuckle guy took a step away as the Suit leaned in toward the prisoner, careful not to get his nice clothes soiled with blood.

"So, homeboy. Hear you been messin' on other turf."

They were in an abandoned warehouse. Night hung outside,

like protective padding. A boom box spat up Mack 10's latest west-coast gangsta rap, alongside the five other gang guys who served as audience. Mick had wondered why he'd been brought here. Now he knew why.

Homeboy's eyes bugged, livid with pain. His face had already begun to swell. "Shit. That's a lie, Cobra!"

"Oh?" The sleek, short-haired man in the Italian suit stepped back to where a table had been set up. He pulled a forty-ounce bottle of Cobra malt liquor from the ice and poured the amber stuff into two long-stemmed wineglasses. He handed one to Mick. Mick hated the stuff, but he took the glass from the Suit. You want to do business with the Man, you drink what he drinks. "Oh, yeah, sucka! You know, that could just be real true. But you know, that don't mean, though, it couldn't be true. Money, man . . . Money has a way of fuckin' up a man's mind. Makes him forget his bloods, huh?"

"I don't forget you, bro!" said the man tied to the chair. "Man, we go back a long ways."

"Yeah. A long ways. So I won't be killing you."

The man whimpered a bit, as though with relief.

"Just gonna fuck you up a bit, see." He looked over at the big white man. "Theodore. Give the man a little more metal, please."

Then he nonchalantly lifted the glass to his lips and sipped.

Theodore stepped up.

Mick figured him to be late twenties, early thirties, but with a face that had a lot of life's hard road ground into it. A face that looked forty. The man had an ex-Marine vibe to him, a blond jarhead feel. He was wearing black chinos cinched tight over a narrow waist and a knit shirt that showed off rock-hard abs, a large body builder's chest, and thick ropey triceps and biceps. *Must've kept up his exercise routines from prison*, thought Mick.

The man appeared Nordic. Maybe, when he was younger, he looked like the sort whose pictures Hitler yanked off to. Now, though, he seemed wizened and grizzled. An experienced pro. His eyes were not dull, though. They glistened with intelligence. They did not seem to be taking any particular pleasure in this task.

Theodore pulled the steel-clad fist up and slammed it into the sitting man's abdomen. The man jerked over. He coughed up blood and gasped and wheezed. Theodore lifted his fist again, clearly targeting the face. This time the other side.

"No!" screamed the man. "No more. Okay, okay, I sold a couple bricks on the side. Shit! But it was DelRoy . . . DelRoy, he told me how to do it. DelRoy's on the take from the D.C. Crips!"

"Shee-it!" One of the young men in oversized pants, oversized sweatshirts, and floppy-tongued tennis shoes stepped back and pulled a gun. "I ain't gettin' my fuckin' face smashed. None of you assholes move an asshole hair, I'll make holes in you, I swear. Big muthafuckin' holes!"

"DelRoy, man. I was wonderin' about you," said the Suit. "Shit, man. Why?" The Suit seemed calm, as though this happened all the time.

Mick's adrenaline was spiking though. Hell, he just wanted to make a deal for the Tome boys with the homeboys, not get his shit blown up in a family gang fight.

"You gettin' weird, man! You gettin' big-time shit. You bringin' in white trash. You bringin' in Mob shit. Man, I'm thinkin' about gettin' my black ass outta Baltimore. Maybe down to Miami. I ain't done nothin' to hurt you, man. So leave me the fuck alone and let me—"

The sound of the gun echoed through the warehouse.

A fat hole appeared in the black rebel's forehead. Brains and bones and blood sprayed out the other side, leaving a fine red mist to settle onto the floor's sawdust. The man's semi-automatic tumbled from his fingers, clunking onto the floor. The black dude buckled, folded. Went down. A basketball shoe spasmed off a foot.

Mick swung around.

Theodore stood, holding a smoking Coonan .357 Magnum in his left hand.

"Ambidextrous," he said.

"God *damn!*" The Suit smiled, then let out a good-natured laugh. "Man. You expensive, but you *worth* it."

He went over, pulled a bottle of malt liquor from the ice. "Shit with this." He tossed his glass away and it smashed into a distant wall. He upended the bottle and glugged down a few swallows. When he was finished, he offered it to Mick.

"No, thanks. Still working on this," said Mick, holding up his half-full wineglass.

Cobra shrugged, pulled out a fresh bottle. "I figure you ain't here to have a gun waved at you. Maybe a little nervous, eh?"

"I don't get nervous."

"You a stone man, huh? You Clint Eastwood."

"The Man with No Name."

"Yeah, that's why I don't put names on my bullets. Shit, yeah. You white boys, always gotta show what a big pair you got. What do our Latin brothers call them? *Cojones? Huevos?*" He took another sip of the malt liquor, then nodded at the others. They hurried over and dug out the remaining bottles for themselves, looking decidedly uneasy, despite their street faces. "So Mr. Eastwood, what you want from the Cobra?"

"Peace, brother—just like that old song says. You see, I'm contemplating a career enhancement, having just recently relocated to your fine city. The group I'm working with is expanding, part of which includes some light dope trafficking. I heard you were the Man in Baltimore so I came to pay the Man his proper respect."

"You got that right, and I likes how you say it. You honest, but what's this group you're talking about?"

"A start-up entertainment company. Small press publisher. Magazines. Books. Get into music and movies down the road."

"Say *what?*" The boss man shook his head, as though to realign his hearing. "What kind of magazine? What *kind* of books? None of that kiddie stuff, right?"

It took all of Mick's self-control not to laugh. "No," he said patiently. "Dark fantasy."

"What?"

"You know, horror books, like Stephen King. Vampire stuff. Noir."

"Far out!" said Theodore, though not part of the conversation.

Mick turned.

The big man was smiling. The smile looked strange on that big face.

"You're kidding me, right?" said Cobra. "Really running a front for porno and blow. I got no problem with that, we can deal."

Mick tried it once more. "Sure, there's some dope on the

side, but just club stuff, party favors. Basically this is a legit operation, with great opportunities for moving cash around, clean it
up, hide it from the Feds. Then we'll move on to the top dollar
side of the street: music, movies—show business."

"A Death Row Records thing I can understand. But books,
man," said Cobra, shaking his head. "Where's the money in that?
Unless they hollow, got something else in 'em."

"I take your point, but as the good reverend doctor said, I
have a dream. I see a real growth potential here, which no one
has had the vision to exploit yet." He smiled. "And best of all,
we're not going to be in the street, carrying guns and shooting
people." He gave a quirk of a grin. "What we've got is a real
peaceful operation. All legal—" He tapped his chest. "Except my
part. Which is why I'm here—"

Cobra shrugged. "Hmmm. The money cleaning sounds interesting." He gestured at the fallen hoodlum. "You gotta know
though—I don't take no shit."

"Wouldn't have it any other way," said Mick, grinning.

"Okay Clint, my man. We'll be talking. Come on up to my
crib. Tomorrow. And like the Thelonious Monk song says:
'Round Midnight.'"

"Cobra!" said the man tied in the chair. "Hey man. I'm cool
now, right?"

Cobra held up a finger toward Theodore.

Theodore took off the brass knuckles.

Then tossed his gun to his right hand, aimed, and fired.

The bullet *thunked* straight through the bound man's heart,
crashing out the back of the chair, splattering the floor with torn
fleshy debris.

"Yeah," said Cobra. "You cool like that, bitch." He turned to
the others, who stared, trying not to be affected by the sudden
carnage. "Looks like we got ourselves the human wreckage of a
turf war, people." He snapped his fingers. "Get these traitors out
to the right place and maybe they'll lead the six o'clock news
tomorrow night, make their mamas proud."

Mick watched all this without flinching or reacting. It was
rather interesting, observing without participating. Mick always
enjoyed it.

Cobra patted him on the back. "Later, Clint." He waved

toward the hired gun, Theodore, who holstered his weapon and followed his employer.

However, the big man stopped by Mick.

"Horror, huh?"

"That's right."

"I like horror books. Horror movies. Crime fiction and all. This kind of job . . ." He shrugged. "Relaxes me."

"I know."

"Maybe we can have a drink or somethin'. After Thelonious Monk time, ya know?"

"Trade some used paperbacks?"

"Yeah. Sure."

Mick shrugged. "Nothing better to kill time in prison."

"Nothing I found."

Mick nodded. "Okay."

The muscular man nodded and gave a strange smile.

Then he trooped off after Cobra.

Mick checked his pants and shoes, making sure no blood had splashed on them.

Then he walked casually toward the other exit of the abandoned warehouse. *Books*, he thought. *They sure can bring people together*.

eleven

I presume every body has heard of me. My name is the Signora
Psyche Zenobia. This I know to be a fact. No body but my enemies ever calls me Suky Snobbs.

—Edgar A. Poe, *How to Write a Blackwood Article*

"THIS IS THE MOST LUDICROUS IDEA I'VE EVER HEARD!"
Professor William Blessing stared down at the letter and
slapped it, as though to knock some sense into the thing.

"I don't know, dear," said Amy, smiling brightly. "Donald's
talked to me about it and I . . . well I think it's rather an *interesting* idea." She laughed with a naughty gaiety. "Of course, I guess,
I'm prejudiced—being bought off and everything."

Blessing glanced up at Marquette. His assistant and protégé
was smiling too, but uneasily. "Exactly what have you got to do
with this, Donald? I know you're associated with these people.
Obviously they know you're associated with me . . . but I'm still
confused."

"Uhm . . . Bill . . . Perhaps you haven't read it properly," suggested Donald. "I've only looked at Amy's copy, and briefly. So
perhaps if you read it again . . ."

"Okay," said Blessing. He was feeling very odd about Donald
and this letter just added to the load. However, as Amy had
often told him, he had a tendency to fly off the handle.

One breath.

Two breaths (deep).

101

"Very well," he said, utilizing his full professorial plumage to prevent any sign of weakness or fluster. "I'll just read it out loud, then, shall I?"

"I think that's an excellent idea, Bill," said Amy. She bounced over and put an arm around him. "And just remember, you always promised to help make me famous."

"Famous!" He had a strong urge to say "Balderdash," but bit his tongue. Too much nineteenth-century reading was infecting his vocabulary. Instead of commenting further, he reached over to his office desk, grabbed a set of the numerous reading glasses he kept around the house, fitted them on, rattled the letter, and began reading:

Dear Dr. Blessing,

I'm sure you've heard of me—or at least the line of books I edit. My name is Roscoe Mithers.

Yes! That Roscoe Mithers, the editor of the *Dark Sunset* series of books for Paperback Gems. Ah, yes! Based of course on the television series and movies (which you doubtless watch, since I can see much influence in your own very excellent writings, although I honestly think you should watch the vampires closer on *Dark Sunset* for better lessons on that particular creature of the night!) and regularly ranked on the Walden and B. Dalton bestseller lists right along with your worthy efforts.

One of our authors, Donald Marquette (*Flowers of Torture*, number twenty-two in the *Dark Sunset Extreme* line) has informed me that not only is he under your tutelage in matters of the Gothic and supernatural, but he is assisting you in editing a new series of anthologies of horror greats.

As you no doubt are aware, the *Dark Sunset* TV series, its spinoffs *Dark Dawn*, *Dark Day Dawning*, and *Ricardo the Vampire Lover*—along with the top-grossing movies—over the past ten years have kept the horror field alive in the world's mind. How else would your well-deserved popularity have found its right audience?

Naturally, you were one of the first people I thought of when we were able to convince the Dark Powers That Be (heh heh) of the potential efficacy of this project:

The Dark Sunset Anthology.

This would be a thick trade paperback volume (which will doubtlessly be immediately snapped up by book clubs and thus see hardcover release) containing original stories based on the most popular characters of the series: Rupert the Zombie, Hilda the Sorceress, and of course, Ricardo the Vampire.

We'd love to see a story from you. In fact, I have even made the arrangement with the Dark Powers That Be that if you were willing to write a story for us, you could place it in the universe of one of your novels. (Rather like King having Ricardo visit Castle Rock, true?)

Naturally, we're looking forward to Donald's story as well. However, he tells me that you have a charming wife who dabbles in fiction. We would most certainly welcome something from her. Or, since we understand that you're a busy man, perhaps a collaboration!

We who work with *Dark Sunset* have always been amazed at the power it has for millions of readers and viewers. Just the other week I was at a *Dark Sunset* convention and once more, I was astonished at how this phenomenon so well-embodies the fruition of the Gothic and horror tradition in modern culture!

We hope you'll join our growing throng!

Fangs!

Roscoe Mithers

P.S. For your reference (and collection) I am enclosing under separate cover the latest batch of our *Dark Sunset* books, including the exciting launchbook of a new Young Readers series, Backbone Shivers, *A Monster's in My Lunchbox*.

When he finished reading the letter, there was silence for a moment.

Finally, William Blessing chuckled half-heartedly. "Okay. I understand now. This is a joke! A kind of preemptory April Fools' Day guffaw."

He couldn't help noticing the hurt look on Donald's face. "No, Bill. It's not a joke. That's the editor who bought my *Dark Sunset* book. And he's talking about me doing more, at twice the money as before."

"To say nothing of a story as well," said Blessing, unable to keep a barb out of his voice. "Hmm. All right, I was just hoping it was a joke. That's all."

Amy had started to frown. "Bill, really. That was a very important step for Donald, that book. And it's not like he's been able to sell the other novel he's written. It's given him the confidence to forge ahead. You don't have to be so negative!"

Blessing checked himself.

Invective had been on his tongue. He held himself in, leashing the words "puerile," "asinine," and "joker." However, he had to make one small comment.

"It would seem that this ... Roscoe Mithers ... is ... uhm ... very involved in his occupation."

"Oh. Right. Sorry about that!" said Donald. "Roscoe's been a fan of the show since day one. This is like a dream come true for him, editing these books. He really sinks his heart and soul into the job!"

"To say nothing of his fangs." Blessing shook his head sorrowfully, reigning back his anger totally. He just felt vaguely depressed now. "I apologize. Of course you can write a story for the collection, Amy. You're getting very good. And naturally, Donald, you're going to. You are already becoming a very fine writer. This whole experience has clearly just propelled your abilities even further than I expected. I guess I had hoped that you'd have set your sights a little higher than *Dark Sunset* material."

"Aren't you being just a little bit pompous and elitist, Bill?" objected Amy, hands on hips, not at all pretty in her miff, but rather beautiful instead. "I mean, come down from your ivory tower! This is a fun series, fun books. Bill, I watch the show and we've seen the latest movie together!"

"Purely because you dragged me to it!" said Blessing. He could feel his ire rising again. He couldn't believe that his own wife was challenging him on this matter, right in front of Marquette. "Look, I teach popular literature! I know all about popular literature. Do you know how many novels and stories were published in the nineteenth century that are forgotten now? And better fiction than anything in the *Dark Sunset* series. In my opinion, this rush of commercial books, cashing in on dubious trends by publishers, and now the corporate puppeteers of modern publishing, is helping along the gradual desiccation of Western culture. Decline and fall, people. And you want to join in the madness? Well, that's jolly good for you, but the very notion of someone having the nerve to ask me to write something of . . . of . . . this . . . this . . . *drivel* . . ."

"Uhm . . . maybe I'd better not bring up that other thing, Amy," said Donald, looking sheepish.

"No," said Amy. "You have every right. And you promised you would."

"But—"

"Very well. I will."

"What *are* you talking about?" demanded Blessing.

"Mr. Mithers suggested that if you weren't interested in writing a story for the anthology, that maybe you'd do a blurb for it, Bill."

"What?"

"You know, Bill. A little something nice about the book . . . or even the series. You do it for your other friends. Dean and Peter and Stephen and Clive all get blurbs from you. What about one for Donald and your wife. Hmm?"

Blessing saw red.

He turned around and walked to a bookshelf. He leaned against it, breathing slowly and deeply, trying to get his composure back.

Finally, he turned.

"You know, one of the things I've always commented on concerning the life of Edgar Poe was that although he wrote a great deal in his life, he was only able to do a comparatively little amount that he really cared about: his poetry and his tales, *Eureka* . . . maybe some of his criticism . . . The rest of his time was spent doing magazine hackwork. Oh, the torture the man must have felt in that alone, along with the other miserable parts of his life. Can you imagine what he might have accomplished if his horrible foster father John Allan had believed in him? If he'd gotten a really fine education, if he'd found a nice teaching position like Longfellow? Or even if some moneybags had seen his value and simply become a patron? No, he had to work in a pathetic and squalid industry full of sentimental bullshit fiction and formulaic emotion and style.

"Well, Poe had to do that. And what little he was able to write in his short life *triumphed*.

"But now the hackwork, the silly sensationalistic nonsense of popular taste, of puny capitalist minds has perverted the goals of the tradition that he so well modernized. And what do we have? *Buffy the Vampire Slayer*? *Xena*? And God help us, *Dark Sunset*."

He sighed.

"And you think I would affix my name to the kind of stuff which I abhor!"

Blessing could feel his blood-pressure rising. *It was like a sacrilege! A defiance of everything he stood for!* However, there seemed nothing that he could do to stop himself. He had to vent. *This point was central to his existence. Didn't they know that?*

Amy rolled her eyes. "Oh, for heaven's sake, Bill! No one's trying to compromise your integrity when you can do it so much better yourself. So just forget it, okay? Forget it."

She looked at him, and the anger flashing in her brilliant hazel eyes startled him.

"Sorry, Bill," said Donald. He looked stiff and pained, obviously feeling awkward and upset to be in the middle of this kind of conflict.

Anger control, man. Count to ten.

He did so, quickly, moving his shoulders within his cashmere sweater, loosening his tie, letting the blood flow a little better. "I guess you struck a sore point."

"I'm really sorry. I didn't think you'd like the idea much," said Donald. "But I guess, well . . . we figured it was worth a try."

The look on his face said, *We sure didn't realize you'd blow a gasket.*

"I suppose I do have strong feelings on the subject," Blessing said. "But I'm afraid that I have to stick to my principles." He cleared his throat, hazarded a look at his wife. "Look, dear. I'm sorry. You can do what you like. You have the right. I just don't want to be roped into something like this. I have far better things to do with my time, and I have better uses for my good name and what I have achieved in academia and literature. Mainstream success doesn't mean a person had to stoop to the lowest common denominator to get it."

"But it usually does, that's for sure." Amy fumed. "God, Bill.

You can be such . . . such an *asshole* sometimes!" Amy threw up her hands. She turned around and stalked from the room, clomping down the hallway and then the steps.

Looking startled, Donald seemed about to follow.

"No, no," said Blessing. "She'll be all right. She's probably just gone to take a walk or call one of her girlfriends and talk for a couple hours. I'll make it up to her."

Marquette seemed uncertain.

"Look, I'm sorry to be such a jerk, eh? Stick around. There's something I need to talk to you about anyway." Blessing could still feel the adrenaline coursing his veins like razor blades. He stepped over to his desk, pulled open a drawer, and yanked out a half-full bottle of Johnnie Walker Red and two glasses. "Join me for a drink?"

Marquette, for once, did not seem hesitant about hard liquor at all. "Sure."

"There's the lad." Blessing poured unhealthy amounts of Scotch into both glasses, slopped one over to Marquette.

"To Poe!" he said, repeating the toast he and Marquette would use when they went out drinking beer.

"To Poe," said Marquette, without quite the gusto.

Then Blessing tilted a good two ounces down his throat. The liquid dragged raw, tasty fire with it and splashed into the sour cauldron of his stomach. Immediately, he could feel the warmth spread out on little feelers of calm and hinted oblivion.

Oblivion? Was that what Edgar Poe had sought? A surcease from the overwhelming agony?

If he truly was the reincarnation of Poe, then he would know that, wouldn't he?

He looked over to his assistant and protégé. Donald was handling that liquor as well as he. It was already half gone.

A little shiver of dread touched him.

A little too close to what I want to talk to him about . . .

These nine months with Donald Marquette had been good ones. The man learned incredibly quickly. He absorbed like a sponge, and worked hard. The first volume of the anthology was almost put to bed, Marquette's doctoral work was going well, the articles he was writing on the "Manifestations of the Gothic Tradition in Modern Prose" were not only well-researched, but contained keen insights. Plus, he was churning out fiction as well, as though inspired by listening to Blessing's rambling seminars and actually watching him write and then revise. When he lectured, Marquette was always close and focused and extremely attentive.

He reminds me of a younger me, thought Blessing. *Only slightly off, a bit askew . . .*

And then, there was that latest story.

Not only was it very good indeed but its style and comprehension of tropes and allusion played against its taut and powerful plot, and was very much like something that William Blessing might write.

This was a little startling, but rather gratifying in most ways. No, what was disturbing was another matter entirely.

Blessing took another sip of his drink, then put it down. Marquette clutched his, however, as though anticipating something unpleasant approaching. It still had a jigger or so of Scotch left, but Donald eyed the bottle, as though he was thinking about asking for more. Blessing could already see the alcohol in his eyes.

"Donald. Tell me again about that ambition of yours!" said Blessing, affably.

Donald's eyes burned. "What? You mean literary immortality?"

"Yes. That's not such a bad goal, is it? It was Poe's, you know. Even when he was far younger than you, he thought he was great. Of course, *Tamerlane* is hardly the greatest of poems, but it showed huge ambition, no?" Blessing regarded his drink. Set the glass down and sighed. "You're good," he said, getting up and walking over to his thick, leather bag. "A damned good writer. And getting better. Much too good to waste your time on juvenile stuff like *Dark Sunset*. I mean, if you need money . . . Well, I'd increase your wages . . . Hell, I'd pay for your room and board and computer supplies, if that's what you need. But *Dark Sunset* . . ."

"I guess it gives me confidence," Marquette said tersely. "It stretches me, exercises me, and to see my name on the bestseller lists . . . That's part of the dream."

"Hmm. Well, we can talk about that later, I suppose." Blessing unlatched the bag, pulled out a hardcover book. "Oh, by the way, congratulations." He put the book down. *Dreaming Demons*, proclaimed the title. *Stories Dangling on the Edge*, by Donald Marquette.

"The Tome Press, I see," said Blessing.

"Oh. Yes. You got one. It's just come out. I was going to give you and Amy a signed copy," said Donald, still looking a little apprehensive.

"You've been down there. Haven't you? You've hung out with them."

Marquette shrugged. "Sure. I went down for a few business meetings."

Blessing shook his head. "Okay. I just wonder why you didn't think about some other press."

"Well, frankly, no regular publisher is taking horror short story collections."

"Why not another, more reputable small press? Why *this* press?"

"They wanted to publish me." Marquette finished his Scotch. "Simple as that, Bill. Plus they're local. I can be more involved. And they're no less reputable than Necro, Subterranean, or Terminal Fright. The small press scene for horror is not like it was in the eighties, when Scream/Press, Underwood/Miller, Dark Harvest, and a dozen others were fighting the good fight. There's just not a lot of options now."

"Well, I hope it doesn't hurt your reputation." Blessing took a deep, pained breath. "And I hope that it doesn't hurt mine since we're associated together."

"I don't understand. Tome is doing extremely well lately. They've already shipped half their first printing, and a trade paperback is in the works. What's wrong with that?"

"The same thing happened to the horror field last time," responded Blessing. "Some warped writers thought they could use it to hype their own private psychopathology. And some editors thought that what people liked about Gothic literature— which is the term, as you know, that I far, far prefer—was the pure nastiness of it. These disturbed, misguided people simply wanted to screw with readers' brains, foist off their private hells of pornographic violence as some kind of statement. That's my take on the Tome people. And I might add that I've been hearing disturbing things about them from other sources. Whispers of Satanic blood rituals. Evil stuff, Donald. We, as serious writers, have a great deal of license but we need to carefully watch our lives—for many, many reasons."

"Hmm," said Donald. "They seem all right to me. A little way out, perhaps. Extreme Goth, they call it, but they do care about literary quality. They're really quite serious."

"I don't doubt it. But seriousness of purpose alone does not ensure good intentions." Blessing folded his hands, placed forefingers to his lips. "These people—I've got a bad feeling about them."

"Just because of what you've heard from some wimpy writers without lives!" said Donald.

"Donald," said Blessing firmly. "I suppose your appearances in their magazine and this book won't do a great deal of harm. To either of us. However, your association with this Baxter Brittle can cause me a great deal of damage. My reputation is very important to me—and because of the nature of some of my material I have to be very careful who I affiliate with. I guess what I'm saying is, that as much as I like and respect you, if you continue to be involved with these people, we'll just have to go our separate ways."

Marquette looked as though he was about to say something in defense of his actions, in defense of Tome Press—but stopped himself.

He nodded. "Okay. Yes, I'm sorry you feel that way. I think maybe you're being slightly paranoid, but I guess I can understand." Marquette smiled lightly. "Do you still want me to sign that copy for you and Amy?"

"Please! That would be a great honor."

Feeling great relief at Marquette's acceptance of his request because he didn't particularly care to part with someone of his caliber (and someone who was almost becoming a part of the family), Blessing relaxed.

In the corner of the office, by a bookcase, were two Eames chairs with foot rests and a coffee table. Blessing grabbed the bottle of whiskey and his glass and gestured Donald to follow. "This is a real relief, I must say, Donald. Because I don't want to lose you. And I'm certain that Amy would be very unhappy with me if that happened."

"I'd be unhappy, too."

Blessing went to a stereo unit and turned on the radio, which was permanently tuned to a classical station. Soft strains of Bach gentled over the office. He poured Donald another little bit of whiskey and then motioned him to sit down.

"I've been working on a brand-new project. Now that this difficulty is behind us, I feel I can talk to you about it," said Blessing.

"Oh, really!" Marquette brightened with enthusiasm.

"Yes. It's quite startling and no one has done it before. If it succeeds, and I can make a case, it will be very controversial. It could really make a great deal of noise not only in the academic world, but in the world at large."

"Sounds juicy. This is about Poe, then?"

"Absolutely." Blessing leaned back in the comfortable leather chair. "Donald, we've discussed Poe's fascination with encryption and puzzles, haven't we?"

"Oh, sure. Like in 'The Gold Bug.'"

"Yes. Precisely. Well, let me take this into the Twilight Zone. Are you familiar with the theories about Jewish mysticism and the Old Testament that have been espoused lately; this so-called Bible Code business?"

"No. I'm not really familiar with it." He took a sip of his drink. "Sounds fascinating though."

"Oh, as Hollywood cocktail chatter, it is. Faddish pseudo-science of the highest order. However, it made me think about some aspects of Edgar Poe's work."

"But this code or whatever it is, we're talking esoteric knowledge here, going back thousands of years. How does that relate to Poe?"

"Hidden messages, Donald. You see, supposedly there's a mother lode of messages and prophecies embedded in the original Biblical texts, which this researcher's computer program was able to ferret out by reading the pages up, down, backwards, like a diagram word puzzle. The fact that such arbitrary elements as page margins are necessary for the decoding to work has been conveniently ignored by the theory's proponents.

"I could go into it more, but it's really irrelevant. All esoteric groups from the Knights Templar to the Rosicrucians have claimed to have secret teachings, just read *Foucault's Pendulum* by Umberto Eco. But according to a book on the theory, recent current events, things like the assassination of Israel's prime minister in '95, are encoded in these ancient writings. Ridiculous of course, but like I said, it made me think about Poe's own fascination with that kind of thing."

"So I take it you've been doing similar research work with Poe's work," prompted Donald, trying to get Blessing to make his point.

"Yes, yes. I downloaded a version of this decoding program, customized it a bit, and have since come up with some fascinating possibilities. Once I do a little more work, I'm going to publish an article that could turn eventually into a book."

"You've discovered something? Secret messages from Edgar Poe?" asked Marquette, now fully attentive.

Something cold and serpentine seemed to uncurl in Blessing's gut. He shivered, unable to help himself.

Then he leaned forward and told Donald Marquette.

twelve

One night as I sat, half stupified, in a den of more than infamy, my attention was suddenly drawn to some black object, reposing upon the head of one of the immense hogsheads of Gin, or of Rum, which constituted the chief furniture of the apartment. I had been looking steadily at the top of this hogshead for some minutes, and what now caused me surprise was the fact that I had not sooner perceived the object thereupon. I approached it, and touched it with my hand. It was a black cat—a very large one—

—Edgar A. Poe, *The Black Cat*

"PRAY FOR ME," SAID DONALD MARQUETTE. "FOR I AM A SOUL damned as no soul has been damned before."

The group exploded with laughter.

Donald grinned, took another drink of his beer, and shrugged. "That's the message the good professor believes he found buried in the works of Edgar Poe."

"Kinda like a Captain Planet secret decoder ring, huh?" said Count Mishka. The Count wiggled his fingers, displaying the numerous baubles he wore himself, more colors amongst his long, lavender, sparkle-encrusted fingernails.

"Or Batman!" said the Marquis. The Marquis was in a retro New Romantic phase, aping the looks of Gary Oldman's Dracula and Alan Jorgensen of Ministry. Tonight he wore a purple velvet coat, flowery dress shirt (only a few wine stains so far), and the requisite black crushed-felt top hat, wire-rim glasses with purple lenses, and shiny black nail polish. He was seriously considering going for hair extensions next week. The look seemed to be working for him.

The group around the table snickered at these remarks.

"Pretty damned loony, if you ask me," said Baxter Brittle, at the head of the table in an elaborate Victorian high-backed chair. He lay stretched out along the arms, legs a-dangle on one side, snuggled up to a goblet on the other. Baxter had effected an Oscar Wilde persona lately—lids drooping, dark hair winged over his forehead, baggy Edwardian topcoat and black pants above spats. "Love old Oscar's fashions all right, it's that cocksucking business I don't go for," he would say routinely, lest anyone get the wrong impression about his bedroom orientation.

The murky odor of wormwood drifted up from a jewel-spangled goblet. Baxter had been drinking absinthe lately, having found great success in concocting a homebrew version of it for the bar. Thanks in part to Trent's *The Perfect Drug* video, the exotic liqueur, with twice the potency of vodka, a mild hallu-cinogenic property, and a coolness factor hyped by association with such artist types as Hemingway and Rimbaud, was making quite a comeback with the young Goths.

Donald Marquette scowled into his British-style imperial pint of Old Peculier beer, another new addition to the Sailor's distilled fares. He was getting very fond of the high-alcohol brew with the strange, rich taste.

Damn the bastard, he thought. *I'll show him! I'll show the arrogant asshole!*

"Yes, it's going to be the subject of a new article," he said, after another dark, yeasty quaff. "And the funny thing is that he's so high up in the academic and literary and *popular* pecking order, that people are going to take him *seriously*."

"Here's a chap," said Baxter, sloshing his absinthe lightly, then pinging the side with a fingernail so that it rang like a little bell, "who should be taken down a peg or three!"

"You might say he puts the *Poe* in *poseur*," quipped the Marquis, going for a droll George Sanders tone (having given up on doing Peter O'Toole or James Mason with any credibility).

Donald smiled, then sighed.

Yeah. Exactly. The Poe in poseur.

He could feel the beer murmuring around in his veins, and the dope they'd done before down in the basement turning his brain into an Escher study. It felt good. Damned good. *Down a peg. You bet! Arrogant jerk!*

"There's more," he said.

It was a Wednesday night at the Cork'd Sailor, "lounge" night, and not terribly successful with the irony-deficient crowd Baxter was forced to cater to. (*Cocktail Nation, my ass!*) But still the air was bluish-gray with smoke. It smelled of cigars and the cordite of matches, and of bar rags. Donald liked it, though. It was dark and comforting, with all manner of Victoriana and pictures cluttering the walls. The rows of spouted liquor bottles against the bar mirror looked like a lovely glass garden, glittering in the muted lighting. Though closer to Little Italy, the place tasted of the exotic funk of Fells Point, and Donald Marquette had fallen in love with it, almost as much as he had fallen in love with Amy Blessing.

"More?" drawled Baxter, blearily looking up at his author.

"Yes. He hit the roof when he saw my collection from you. He's pretty much figured I've been down here, hanging out. He wants me to cut off all relations with you guys. No more stories in *The Tome*, no more books from the press . . . And I suspect that if he finds out I even drink at your bar anymore, he'll boot me."

Even as he said the words, Donald steamed.

Like he had any other outlet!

With his workload, he had to be able to blow things off with friends once in a while! Professor Adolf Hitler Blessing was acting like Donald was a teen, and Blessing his dad!

In fact, Donald only came down here, generally, on weekends. It had all started innocently enough, with a few business meetings. But when the contract for the story collection had been signed, Baxter had started inviting him down to the bar on weekends and giving him free drinks. Donald had gotten to know his clique, who had all read his stories and *adored* them. He seemed to be somewhat of a celebrity amongst them. They hung on his words, especially when it came to literature. Initially, Baxter had wanted him to be an associate editor, "To get some kind of class into this rag, dear boy!", but Donald had demurred. No, far too much *else* to do. However, he *had* been honestly flattered, and the respect they gave him had made him feel not only good about himself, but more at ease with all the . . . er . . . *flamboyant* aspects of Le Salon des Gothiques.

In fact, he'd rather developed a taste for their liquor. And even a few of their drugs. He kept that intake down. Just for special occasions, actually. Party time and all that. However, with his heavy workload, he sometimes found himself taking a tab or two of the more stimulating items they provided him with. And damn, if it didn't rev him up, allowing him to work a great deal and sleep little. In his opinion, it also actually *improved* his writing. It cut something open inside him, allowing his raw creativity, yes, his *genius*, to flow out.

Cruising with the Goths.

It was great, great fun. True, that Mick bothered him sometimes—something in his eyes, and manner and dress. *And the man's stories.* Donald had to admit that Blessing hit the nail dead center on that one. Both Mick and his prose were hard, driven, strange, and resonant with menace. Yes, Mick had even inspired a couple of his better recent stories. He was just kind of grateful now, in what would probably be the last visit here for a while, that Mick wasn't around.

"Oh, goodness," said Baxter. *"How very annoying."*

Yes. Annoying enough, Donald noted, for the bar owner and publisher/editor to actually rouse himself for his torpor of world-weary dissipation.

Something, in fact, was sparking in his eyes, like the end of a broken power line.

"No," Baxter said. "I don't think I care for *this* bit of news one bit."

Donald found himself not merely flattered, but moved at Baxter's response. He often thought that the Goths merely patronized him, because he amused and diverted them. If he had to go, he'd pictured them saying, *Well, au revoir, baby.*

Now though, a little *frisson* of connection touched him.

They actually valued *him.*

Actually liked *him.*

Donald Marquette had always been a bookish sort, never

very successful with girls or other people. He even still felt stiff with the very friendly, but pompous and somehow too formal William Blessing. His bonhomie with the scholar and author he often had to fake. Basically, the main reason he was there was to advance his knowledge, training, and above all, his career.

Certainly, he'd never been associated with people who had been anywhere near as self-possessed, self-assured, and hip.

These Gothiques, though. They were . . . well, *cool*. And he liked the fact that they thought *he* was cool, too.

That was, as they might say, a major *buzz!*

Baxter Brittle stroked his chin. Then he got up, stuffing his flask of absinthe in one of his oversized pockets. "Come, Inner Core. This is a serious matter indeed. We must descend to the *sanctum stinktorum* and cogitate."

With a casual air of consummate presence and mastery, he rose. The Count and the Marquis followed. Presuming that he also included, Donald got up and followed.

However, halfway to the door they were stopped by the arrival of a young man and woman, attired in elegant Gothic vampire attire—save for the fangs.

"Baxter Brittle," said the young woman, holding up a hand gloved in black silk.

"That is, indeed me," Brittle said, giving a polite half-bow. "How may I be of service, Lady Jessica and Prince Knowlton?"

The young woman, a spunky, almost punky sort with multi-colored hair, stepped forward in front of Baxter. "Something weird is going on with your people, Baxter."

"Pardon me?"

"Look, I like the Goth scene as much as anyone. Maybe more," said the slender girl. "But there's stuff going on here that we're not very happy with."

"Oh? How so?"

"Some perfectly straight people I know have turned into drugheads in the past six months," said Lady Jessica earnestly. "I'm not some naïve, 'Just Say No' hypocrite either, but this is getting too serious. It's not fun anymore. And the Prince came home last night with blood on his cape!"

"Mercy!" said Baxter Brittle. "A vampire with a little blood on him. Dearie me." Brittle wobbled a little, obviously the worse for his absinthe habit.

"I don't remember a thing about the whole night!" said Prince Knowlton. "Man, that scares the *shit* out of me!"

"This salon thing used to be cool decadent fun, not just degenerate drinking and drugging," stated Lady Jessica, accusingly. "Most of us get up on Monday morning and go to work or school or whatever and deal with the normal world. I'm sorry about your parents and all, but we don't have inheritances to live off of. That's fine, but you guys are digging down too deep in the darkness." She shook her head. "Too deep."

"Please," said Baxter. "Brevity is the soul of wit. I'm afraid you're not being very witty."

"We're leaving the Gothiques," said Lady Jessica. "We're starting up our own group. Me and Knowlton and a few others. We're getting *out* of this scene and away from *you*."

Baxter held a spread hand to his chest. "Gasp! You've cut me to the quick!" he said, sarcastically. "Am I really so bad, mad, and dangerous to know?"

"Come on, Prince," said Lady Jessica, taking him by the arm and leading him away. "Let's get out of here."

"Ooooooh!" called Baxter after them. "Going to have a vampire tea party, are we? Make sure to hold your pinkies out!"

Donald found himself laughing along with the others.

"Couldn't stand the heat, then," said Baxter, gaily. Suddenly, however, a hard cast came to his face. He looked at his core group, at the Marquis, at the Count, and at Donald Marquette, and he said, "You guys can, can't you?"

They all nodded. Yes, they could stand the heat.

Yes, thought Donald. *I can stand it. These are my friends. These are the kind of people I've been looking for. And if they play with darkness . . . well, so do I.*

So, really, do we all, in our heart of hearts.

That was a line from one of his stories, and he knew deep down it was true.

The group jangled through the bead curtain at the back of the bar, through the kitchen, as Baxter drew out his keys from his pockets—then down into the Dungeon.

Even though Donald had found the cellar "salon" ornate,

clever, and well, rather kinkily mystical the first time he'd been down some months before, now . . .

Well, now, with the financial state of Tome Press improving by leaps and bounds, so was the opulence of this den of dissipations. Baxter Brittle had purchased a number of spectacular Oriental rugs which now draped over the floors, adding richness and luxury. Elaborate antiques had been added to the mix, and beautifully framed artwork. Necklaces and crosses and symbols from the darker side of the esoteric and the occult dangled hither and thither, sparkling and shiny in the glow of flame from thick aromatic candles. The dense, rich smell of incense, along with the ruminations of Baxter's French cigarettes, lingered. Tallow and tobacco and frankincense—and the aftersmell of exotica and alcohol.

Baxter led them round a large and gorgeous old teak table with elaborately curved chairs. He fluttered his hands. "Sit! Sit!" He pulled his bottle and goblet out and placed them at the head of the table before him. "Libations, my brethren?"

They all chose beer. Baxter blithely pointed to the icebox. "You may retrieve your own."

Donald pulled out another bottle of Old Peculier.

They settled back.

"Cosmic think tank, gentle people!" said Baxter. "We have a dilemma. On the one hand it is very good indeed that some of our members are leaving. However, we must watch carefully to be sure they keep their mouths shut." His eyebrows waggled a bit at that one. "However, we have a friend here who does not wish to disassociate yet finds he is professionally being forced to by his mentor."

"William Blessing!" said the Count.

"A powerful figure to cross!" noted the Marquis.

"Perhaps we should invite Blessing to join!" suggested the Count.

"I have long since made overtures," said Baxter. "The good professor lives in an ivory tower, it would seem. He scoffs at us. He despises us. So easy to do when you have barrels of money, cauldrons of success. And yet, brethren, do we not drink from the same well? The literature and the philosophies and the emotions that travel through our gray matter, through our very veins—it travels through William Blessing's. Our friend Donald Marquette acknowledges it. We acknowledge it. Others acknowledge it. And yet, clearly Blessing is a necromancer who denies his spells stink of sulfur. He believes himself impervious, powerful, and aloof from the delightful vapors of night that cloak us."

Baxter was silent.

The candle flames beside the table flickered as though a phantom wind whispered through the room.

"Perhaps," said the Count, "someone should wake Blessing up."

"Yes," said the Marquis. "He should wake up and smell the tea!"

Donald was about to correct the elaborately attired and coifed fellow, but one look at his three-quarters dazed expression changed his mind. "That's all very well to say," he said. "But at the moment, all the people I'm meeting, all the publishing ins I'm getting . . . I mean, New York publishing, that is."

"Nothing to sneeze at, chum," said Baxter. "But there's the *Dark Sunset* stuff! Remember."

"I'm afraid he wasn't thrilled with that, either."

"Hey!" said the Marquis. "That's my favorite!"

"I admit to being partial to it myself," said Baxter. "But let's face it—they could get *Star Trek* writers to hack out that stuff and it would still sell to the *untermensch*."

"Hey," said the Count. "I *like Star Trek* books!"

"Well," said Baxter. "We can't all have good literary taste." He leaned over, stroking the bridge of his nose as though coaxing out inspiration.

Donald sipped at his beer. It seemed very bleak to him. He'd have to just throw himself harder into his work. It was damned tough being around the household, suffering Blessing's eccentricities. God, the man liked to talk, and all the talk was generally pompous and self-absorbed. Smile and scrape, Marquette. Kiss his hairy ass! Lo! The Great Authority pronounces and exposits. Pay heed to another tedious rumination!

Worse, though, was being around Amy.

He'd fallen hard for her the moment he'd seen her, and it just got harder as time went on. Man, it was *so* difficult to get near her, and not put his arms around her and kiss her forever. She was such a *tactile* person. She loved to touch him. Lately, she'd hug him from time to time. The touch of her breasts against his chest or arm was electric. The warm scent of her perfume was ecstatic. At Christmas, she'd actually kissed him under the mistletoe. On the cheek, true, but still . . .

She's so hot for me, he thought, gurgling down more amber liquid. *Maybe she doesn't realize it yet, but she most certainly is!*

If only he had more *power* in the situation.

If only . . .

Suddenly, footsteps began to trudge slowly down the steps.

Baxter Brittle looked up from his mire of thoughts. "Now whoever could that be?"

The swirl of a long coat.

The pound of leather boots.

The coat lengthened into the long and black frame of Mick. He carried a bottle of Courvoisier in one hand. The other one gripped a fancy riding crop. He slapped the banister with it as he descended.

The candle flames guttered. It somehow seemed colder— with the touch of the bay fog and the stink of rats and seagulls arriving with this man.

Behind him came another set of boots, this time not touched by the edge of a coat. The scuffed black of the boots rose up into a fluid transition to black leather pants. As these legs descended farther, Donald could see that the pants were ridged with silvery studs. Up and up they went to powerful buttocks, tight across a codpiece crotch. Up further to a tight belly, open past the navel to show ridged abdominals. A leather shirt, up yet farther to huge pectorals and heavy shoulders and a football player's face, heavy and dull. Hooded in more black leather, more studs.

"Come, Theodore," said Mick. "Don't dawdle. I can't guarantee this crowd won't bite—" He smiled grimly. "—but I'm sure you'll like it if they do."

Mick turned to the others. "Gang. This is a new recruit. This is cousin Theodore. He wants very much to become a Literary Light. Hmm, Theodore?"

The heavily muscled man grunted.

"A brew, Theodore?" said Mick.

"Becks."

"Why surely—go and help yourself. The refrigerator over there is very well stocked."

The big man lumbered over to the icebox, while Mick sauntered over to the table. He slapped his riding crop down gently onto the tabletop and then sat down in a chair.

"Council meeting without me?" he asked, slowly and suspiciously. "Something the matter?"

Baxter fell back and laughed with a maniacal edge. "Not any more."

Mick's brow knitted. "What the fuck is that supposed to mean?"

"Your arrival is a solution," said Baxter. "I believe I have an idea. Indeed, a *wonderful* solution!" His face, previously dark and unfocused, now simply beamed as he turned his gaze to Donald. "And not only will it further you in the estimation of our dearly beloved Dr. Blessing, and allow you to continue your frolic with us—but it shall further our cause—immensely!"

At this point, Donald was willing to listen to anything.

He took another drink, folded his hands together, then leaned over to listen.

thirteen

Open here I flung the shutter, when, with many a flirt
and flutter,
In there stepped a stately Raven of the saintly days of yore;
Not the least obeisance made he; not a minute stopped or
stayed he;
But, with mien of lord or lady, perched above my
chamber door—
Perched upon a bust of Pallas just above my chamber door—
Perched, and sat, and nothing more.

—Edgar A. Poe, *The Raven*

WILLIAM BLESSING HAD ALWAYS HEARD ABOUT THESE KINDS OF evenings. However, in his bachelor life, he simply had scoffed at them. Foolish sentimental prattle, he'd thought. Nonsense and humbug and general propaganda conjured up by society to strike down independence, stick the bit in the male mouth and keep it hauling those genes across the dismal fields of time, toward certain, total winter.

Now, though, sitting here, Blessing realized that not only was this business rather pleasant, not only did he feel content in a way he'd never felt before.

But he felt happiness.

Pure unalloyed happiness!

The glow of the crackling fire in the hearth cast a wavering warmth of peace over him. The rich smell of the burning cedar blended perfectly with the pots of potpourri that Amy had gently simmering under candles. The taste of cocoa in his mouth had just the right edge with that touch of whiskey he'd put in the mix. In his hands was a very well preserved nineteenth-century beautifully illustrated and designed copy of Charles Dickens's *Nicholas Nickleby*, the book he was savoring at calm moments these days, away from the literary rapids and in a timeless backwater of magical words and eternal characters. It was a comfortable Saturday night in February, and he and his beloved were tucked away in their safe and snug house, away from the snow and the wind that puffed and howled beyond the window.

The fire popped.

He looked up at the flames, feeling a moment of alarm, then, seeing that all was well, and that only a small spark had jumped out from the fire and was now fading on the tile, looked around.

The truth was, of course, that all this contentment—no—*happiness*—was because of the person who sat across from him in the other armchair, her knitting put aside and now deeply immersed in Jane Austen's *Mansfield Park*.

Amy.

His very own Amy.

He couldn't help, now, but just sit and gaze at her. She was so very beautiful, and her beauty touched off something deep in him, something resonant and pure and . . . well, yes . . . holy. For although there was youth in that beauty, even when there was not, maturity would take its place and perhaps create even more beauty than now.

They used to joke that his Poe obsession had gone too far. That, like Edgar, who'd married his thirteen-year-old cousin, William Blessing had taken a child bride. Of course, even when they had begun corresponding and speaking on the telephone after that first weekend together at that fantasy convention (chaste! a first in such an experience for bachelor Blessing), it had become obvious that in certain emotional ways, it was Amy who was the more mature. Then, a few months after the excitement of marriage and honeymoon, constant togetherness, flowers, billets-doux, and all the other heartbeats of joy, the jokes stopped. For very quickly and comfortably they settled into a tight domestic unit of passion, love, and understanding. There was this amazing *connection* between them that transcended age or flesh that was merely celebrated by sex. To Blessing, Amy embodied all the best of poetry itself, from her beauty, to her taste, to her musical gifts—to her sweet and gentle soul. In fact, this had been something at the back of his mind since he'd first seen her shy smile, and every once in a while he would write verses about her with an old-fashioned quill pen, its feather shivering as he scratched. When the book was full, he was going to wrap it in a red ribbon and lay it upon her pillow before some journey.

God, how he loved her!

He peered up again from his book to admire her fine features, as he often did these peaceful reading evenings, and he found her looking at him oddly.

"Amy, is everything okay?" he asked.

"Yes. I think so. I think so, Bill."

"You look . . . troubled."

"Hmm. I guess I've been having difficulty reading. I'm a little worried."

"About what?"

"I don't know. Just this . . . this feeling."

He got up and put his book down. He went over and knelt by her chair, put his arm around her. She smelled of jasmine tonight and Earl Grey tea. Her hair was lustrous in the flickering flames of the fire. "Are you still upset at me about that little spat last week?"

"What? The *Dark Sunset* thing?" She laughed softly. "Why? I won. I'm going to have a story there, despite your snooty upperclass priggishness." She wiggled his nose gently. "And I have to confess, I'm not at all upset that you suggested that Donald not associate with those Goof people."

"Goth, dear. Goth."

"I know." Her eyes twinkled. "I know."

"It's not that I disapprove per se of groups getting dressed up and acting strangely, although I don't think I ever did that when I was younger."

"No, you were too busy writing footnotes."

He smiled, acknowledging the joke. "It's just that I've read these people's publications and they rather bother me. I guess

I've unfortunately managed to get myself a good reputation—though how on earth I don't know—and I have to be very, very careful. Do you understand?"

"Certainly. Donald doesn't seem to mind very much. Although I do wish he'd find himself a girlfriend or something. That's what he needs. Maybe we just keep him too busy. I've been trying to introduce him to one of my friends from the Peabody, but he doesn't seem interested."

"Is that what you're thinking about now, Amy? Donald?"

"Well, no . . . lots of things I suppose." She bit her lip, looked at him sadly, and placed a hand to his cheek. "Bill. Sometimes I think we're both . . . both just too busy. I wonder if our lives aren't just eating us up."

"You think we need a vacation?"

She laughed. "Oh, you know me. I *always* need a vacation. No." She bit her lip. "I've been thinking. The years are passing. I know I'm young . . . but you—"

"I'm aging rapidly?"

"No, no. I guess I'd better just spit it out. I know we've talked before about . . . about having a family . . . and put it off. But now I think if we wait too long . . . Well, you'll not really appreciate children. And who knows?" She smiled bleakly at him, tears glistening in her eyes. "Who knows what the future holds? I'd like to, maybe, enjoy . . . grandchildren with you . . . and all that other stupid and sentimental nonsense." She sniffed and turned away. "This is just too much. One year I'm reading Herman Hesse and listening to Kurt Cobain. The next, I want to start knitting booties for grandchildren and planning retirement cruises!"

He laughed, deep feeling moving within him.

So many of his emotions had been buried or stunted before he'd met Amy. Now there seemed a rich harvest of them—he felt as though he owned a Matisse's garden of wonder and life, the bountiful spectrum of love in all its colorings and art.

"Oh, dear. Age creeps into the mix, finally."

"I'm sorry," she said. "You know that I don't feel comfortable not expressing my feelings."

"No. That's perfectly fine," he said. "You're not just talking about your feelings. This is logical fact that you're facing. And we've got to face it together."

"I was worried you'd be mad."

"What? That I'd be so vain as to not acknowledge that I'm getting to be an old geezer!"

"You're not old. That's not the issue."

He chuckled. "No, of course not. I know." She had turned away. He reached over and pulled her head around. He kissed her gently on one cheek. "Darling, you're perfectly right. There's absolutely no reason we shouldn't have children. Immediately. I guess I've just been so very selfish. I've wanted to have you all to myself as long as I could."

Her eyes were filled with wonder and delight. "Bill! You're serious!"

"Well there is the little matter of where we'll find the money . . . But you know what they say. When it comes to kids, you always scrape together just enough."

She spoke in a baby voice. "I can write a *Dark Sunset* novel, Daddy!"

Then she hugged him.

She held him so hard, it felt as though she were trying to melt into him.

And if that were at all possible, the way William Blessing felt now, it would have been perfectly all right with him.

He held her close, and the firm softness of her, the heady fragrance and warm essence surrounded him in a nimbus of erotic sensation. They kissed, and somehow it was the sweetest, tenderest kiss he'd ever experienced.

The next thing he knew they were entangled passionately on the floor, fire hot beside them. He could feel his love for her burning hot as the coals in that hearth. And far longer lasting.

"Well, darling," said Blessing. "Even Charles Dickens pales in interest compared to you." He pointed upstairs. "And you know what? Despite what you say, I think I'm a bit too old to be rolling around on the floor. I think I'd far prefer to work toward pregnancy in our nice warm and very expensive bed."

"Spoilsport," she said, laughing.

Athletically, Amy Blessing hopped to her feet and helped Blessing get up. He mimed creaky rheumatism and then wobbled and hobbled as Amy led him, chuckling and amorous-eyed, toward the steps that led up to the bedroom.

Halfway up, the doorbell rang.

"Who could that be?" said Amy, looking vexed.

"Couldn't be Donald," said Blessing. "He's got a key and can let himself in. Besides, he never bothers us on a Saturday night."

"I think you should just ignore it, Bill. Come on." She tugged on his arm. "Let's just not be at home."

"No. It's obvious that we're home. It could be something important." He gently disengaged himself and gave her a reassuring smile. "Look, go on up. I'll deal with whatever it is and I'll be up immediately."

"No. I'll wait for you here." She crossed her arms, looking vaguely vexed at his insubordination.

"It's a snowy night. Maybe someone had an accident or got stuck outside and needs to use a phone," he said. "One has certain neighborhood responsibilities."

"In the middle of a city? I'm not so sure," she said.

Amy was a suburban girl, and she tended to be a bit nervous about living in an urban environment. This was a fairly safe neighborhood, though, and Blessing couldn't imagine street criminals out and about in the snow. Icy sidewalks and roads made for a slippery getaway!

Besides, he didn't even have to open the door to see who was out there.

At the front door, he clicked the security monitor on.

"Hello," he said through the intercom system. The TV monitor fuzzed into life, lived a moment as a flipping horizontal colored band, and then became a blur. Snow must be covering the lens outside.

"I'm so sorry to bother you, but there's been an accident out here. I need to call a tow truck and perhaps the police."

It was a woman's voice, teeth a-chatter slightly with the cold. Blessing could hear the whir of the wind and the clattering slap of hard snowflakes. He could almost feel the bite of that chill in her tone.

But no image.

Damned snow. He usually didn't mind snow, but at times like this he wished he lived in a milder climate. The east coast could be pretty damned vicious. Why this woman had chosen his door to knock upon, he didn't know. But he felt obliged to perform his humanitarian duty and help her out.

Quickly, he tapped out the off-alarm code, then twisted the door lock, unlatched the latch, and pulled the heavy oak door open.

Immediately, the cold air blasted in, hard and nasty, carrying with it a flurry of flakes.

"Exactly what hap—" he began.

Immediately, he saw that it was no woman who stood out there, but a large man in a long coat, a monolithic black form against the less-black swath of outside snow.

Before he could even think about trying to slam the door closed, the man stepped in and drove a fist into his solar plexus with the precision and speed of a veteran boxer.

Stars mixed with the snow. He gasped out a choked cry and dimness clouded his vision. He doubled over with the blow, fell into the big form. The big man walked him back into the foyer.

Blessing felt he had been split in half.

"That's right, Professor Blessing," said a voice from behind the man who'd attacked him. "Give us a little room, so we can get out of the cold."

The pain was beginning to creep from his abdomen up to his chest. He seemed to flicker in and out of consciousness as the other man stepped in from the scatter of snowflakes and slowly eased the door closed behind him.

Long, long coat.

Naked fingers sticking from black gloves.

Hard chin.

Smirk.

"There we go. That's better," he said in a biting whisper. "Now then, Professor. There's no reason for anyone here to get hurt further, although we certainly have the instruments available to sufficiently accomplish that task."

"Yeah. Like fuckin' knives and guns," snarled the man in black.

"Oh, and a few other choice items, I suppose," whispered the man in the long coat. "We're professionals, you see, and we enjoy our work. Now, we understand that you have a most remarkable collection, containing quite a few items of value. Is that true, Professor?"

The breath wheezed from Blessing's lungs, carrying no words.

"I said—" The man pulled his hair back and glared face-to-face at him. Blessing smelled alcohol, garlic, and something nastier on the man's breath. "I said, Professor, is that true?"

Blessing managed a harsh "Yes."

Enough adrenaline had charged into him now that he was focusing. The thought that occurred to him was not fear for his collection of Poe—but rather for his wife.

Amy.

They mustn't hurt Amy!

"Yes. Please. Force isn't necessary," he managed. "You may have whatever you like."

"Why, there's a smart man," said Long Coat. "All the same . . ." He nodded.

The dense, tall thug with a face like a battered Marvel comic character grabbed Blessing from the rear, yanked his arms back, and easily held his wrists together.

A jab of pain shot up to Blessing's shoulders. It felt as though they were trying to pull his arms out of their sockets. Unconsciousness beckoned, but as if he anticipated this, the big man eased the pressure.

"Excellent. Now. We can make this very quick and, if not painless, then at least not as agonizing as it might be," said Long Coat. "Please, Professor. Show us to your collection. We presume it's somewhere upstairs, true?"

"Yes," Blessing said.

"Good. Slowly and easily . . . up we go. But not too slow. We get very impatient."

Neither man wore a mask, and as his senses sharpened back up, Blessing took in every detail, every scar, every bend of nose and hair follicle he could, imprinting it on his memory.

You are making a mistake, he thought. *You will be caught. You will not be able to get away with this.*

This was the thought that kept him going, that kept his mind from snapping and rebelling. Kept it away from *This can't be happening,* firmly on *There will be justice!* and *I must protect Amy.*

They hustled him up the stairs.

"Now, show us which door and then let us in," demanded Long Coat.

Blessing thought about offering them money or whatever

valuables he had if they would only leave, but he knew that would accomplish nothing. Clearly, they knew what he had, and were intent on their goal.

He'd always known that so many valuables were vulnerable. But he'd only thought that incidental burglars might fall upon them. He'd never imagined that someone might want all those first editions and other collectibles badly enough to make it a special job. How could they hope to resell, to make any money off of that kind of heist?

Yet clearly, this was the purpose of the duo. That they, in the end, would not be able to get away with this seemed obvious. Blessing was concerned about the preservation of the items he had paid so much for and so revered; however, his life and Amy's life were far more important.

He'd do whatever they asked.

They reached the second floor when Amy came out of the bathroom. "Bill. Is everything—?"

As soon as she took in the sight of the men with Blessing, alarm registered on her face. She turned and started to hurry away.

"Amy. No!" Blessing cried after her.

Long Coat sprinted after her. There was no contest. He caught up with her on the first stair step, flung an arm around her waist, and yanked her back.

She yelped.

"Shut up, bitch!" he said. He shook her like a dog shakes a rabbit.

"Don't hurt her!" cried Blessing.

Amy stopped struggling. Long Coat dragged her back to the door.

"No one's going to get hurt if you do what we say. Understand?" He gave Amy another shake. Eyes wide and terrified, she nodded. She looked over to Blessing and showed relief that he didn't seem hurt.

"They just want the valuables in the Poe room," said Blessing. "I'm going to let them have them."

"A good liberal policy, Professor," said Long Coat. "Now please . . ." He pointed at the alarm. "Would you do the honors?"

"I would if I had a free hand."

"Of course. Just remember, we're more than capable of hurting Mrs. Blessing here. Try something and that's exactly what will happen."

The big bruiser was still hovering over Blessing as he rubbed some circulation back into his hands, then applied himself to the alarm box. A few finger-punches later, and the red light winked off.

He put his hand in the right pocket of his pants.

"Careful, Professor," said Long Coat.

"I'm just getting my keys."

"Fine."

Blessing drew the keys up. Jingling. He showed them to Long Coat, then selected the correct one.

Inserted it.

Twisted it.

Pushed the door open.

A cool draft pushed out of the room as the door opened, with it the smell of old leather and paper. He reached in and turned on the overhead light.

The group walked in.

As soon as Long Coat stepped into the room and looked around something changed.

Previously, he'd been wearing a self-satisfied smirk. Now, though, he looked vaguely confused. Disoriented. Troubled. Perhaps even frightened.

"Oh, man," he whispered.

"What gives?" said the other man.

"Hold the woman," said Long Coat.

The bruiser immediately obeyed, stepping over and grabbing Amy. "Hey, she's a babe. Smells damn good, too."

Absently, Long Coat reached into the pocket of his coat. His hand came out, holding a gun.

"Son of a bitch!" he said.

He started quivering. He turned around and looked at Blessing, his eyes had turned red and bloodshot.

Up came the gun. The bore was the blackest, coldest thing that Blessing had ever experienced.

"You!" said Long Coat.

"What?"

"No!" cried Amy.

Instinctively, despite the fear that ran through him, Blessing turned to his wife.

The big man had been distracted from the proceedings. His proximity to comely female flesh had apparently triggered more immediate desires than the need to rob. His bullish nostrils were wide, and he had his mouth buried into Amy's neck, a thick hand over her right breast, kneading it roughly.

"Get away from her!" Blessing cried. With no regard for his own safety, he stepped over and swung his fist into the big man's face. The blow hurt Blessing more than it hurt the man, though he did attract the fellow's attention. He looked up and glared defiantly, raw lust in his eyes.

Despite the pain in his fist, Blessing was about to punch again, when a hard blow smacked him on the back of the neck. Reality jumped and jarred. Blessing popped in and out of consciousness as he stumbled over to the other side of the room then bumped into a set of books.

He crumpled to the ground, trying to cling to awareness.

Stay awake! Stay alive!

For Amy's sake!

The next thing he knew, Long Coat was standing over him, straddling him, gun out and brandished.

"You!" he snarled through clenched teeth. "You are my Persecutor!"

"What?" said Blessing.

The cords on the man's neck stood out, and veins bulged on a sweating forehead.

"Finally, I confront you!" said Long Coat. His eyes wobbled wildly. "You shall trouble me no further—"

"Get that beast off my wife!"

Blessing started to get up.

Two bullets put him back down.

The pain was sharp and blunt and radical.

Darkness came swiftly.

And it was no friend.

fourteen

Then this ebony bird beguiling my sad fancy into smiling,
By the grave and stern decorum of the countenance it wore,
"Though thy crest be shorn and shaven, thou," I said, "art sure no
   craven,
Ghastly grim and ancient Raven wandering from the Nightly
   shore—
Tell me what thy lordly name is on the Night's Plutonian shore!"
Quoth the Raven, "Nevermore."

—Edgar A. Poe, *The Raven*

IT WAS A BRILLIANT PLAN!

Absolutely *brilliant!* thought Donald Marquette as Baxter Brittle's Volvo chugged through the frosty streets. The snow was coming down so hard now it blurred the streetlamps. Marquette wore no gloves and so he kept his hands warm at the car's hot-air vent as he sat in the front seat.

The Marquis had been ordered not to drink that night, so he negotiated the street, with the help of the car's heavy-duty snow tires. Baxter Brittle and the Count were in back. The whole interior of the car smelled of the sickly sweet scent of the absinthe that Baxter had insisted on drinking, despite Marquette's request that he remain sober. He wore a Victorian-style fur coat, and seemed fascinated just watching the dance and swirl of the snow as it rushed down out of the sky.

"Nice night for peace and joy, eh?" Baxter slurred. He started crooning, "I'm dreaming of a white post-Christmas!" in an off-key warble.

"This is the place," said Donald. He pointed. "And that's the house."

"Park! Park!" said Baxter. "This is going to be a lark!"

"Sure," said the Marquis, peering around through the nearly opaque air. "All I have to do is to find an empty spot, okay?"

Donald shot his cuff and examined his watch. "Well, don't be too fancy about your parallel parking. We're just about at the meeting time."

He himself, though not drunk, was not entirely sober either. Although he'd suggested that sobriety was best in this particular situation, he found his excitement and nerves had been a bit much to take, while waiting back at the Sailor. No one seemed to mind that he'd had a few beers, or that he'd slipped a bottle of vodka in his pocket. Just in case, he'd told himself. He could always chuck it.

A fabulous plan!

Even as the Marquis fought with the wheel to back the Volvo into a space, snowflakes battering the windshield only to be swept off by the swishing wipers, Donald Marquette could hear Baxter Brittle's voice drawl, back in the basement below his bar:

"A simple plan, indeed!" he said, waving his cup of drink about happily in one hand and pointing toward Mick and Theodore. "We have before us the solution. Here: two rather large, rather frightening men. Aforesaid men bust into the Blessing establishment with a maximum of menace but a minimum of actual violence. I trust that you two are up to this so far," he'd said, eyeing the guys in black.

"Sounds like fun," Mick said, mildly.

"Yeah. Cool," said Theodore.

"Excellent. So far, so good," Baxter Brittle had continued. "Now then. Along comes our hero, young Donald Marquette. Why has he arrived on the doorstep of the Blessing residence on the fateful Saturday evening? Why, to mend a rift. To prevail upon the Blessings to directly deal with the subject of controversy! The illustriously bad influences themselves! The Gothiques! To that end, representative members—to wit, myself, the

136

Marquis, and the Count—have accompanied him, carrying with us offerings of peace and perhaps books to be signed."

His finger smote the air melodramatically.

"But wait! Wait. There seems to be trouble! Yes, the Blessing homestead, with its wonderful collection of Poe artifacts, is in trouble! And, being brave and valiant citizens, and very, very *good* Goths, we come to the rescue.

"Bam! Pow! Whack! Out you baddies! Take this, take that!" Baxter Brittle had become so enamored of his scenario, that he arose and started whacking the air with fisticuffs.

He huffed and puffed as he shadow-boxed. Then he gave one climactic whack, whirled around, and spread his arms in glorious celebration.

"Behold, the villains are vanquished. Off they go, escaping into the night. But the Poe collection and the brilliant Professor and his Missus are safe and sound, thanks to our valor. Our heroes, they shall say." He picked up his absinthe. "Thank you, Donald! Thank you, Gothiques. Clearly, we should reconsider our stand concerning you. Let's reconvene at a peaceful time, have a few drinks, and be pals!"

Baxter had turned to Donald.

"And you, Mr. Marquette . . . why, we value you so much now, that we have no problem at all associating with such fine people!"

He'd grinned.

"So you see! Very simple but very effective. And who knows what value Tome Press might receive? An exclusive edition of an obscure William Blessing work? Why yes! What a good idea, Baxter Brittle. You are a genius." He bowed. "Thank you! Thank you all so very much!"

They'd all had a few more drinks to toast the proposition.

To Donald, it was perfect.

Not only could he consolidate his position with the Blessings, he could also still hang with his friends—perhaps even gain status with the gang. Perhaps his own line of books! Anything was possible! The only limit in this kind of situation was imagination, and his imagination was . . . well, literary and therefore limitless.

The banging of the wheels against the curb, the squeak and squeal of rubber against ice. They were parked. He pushed his way out, into the blast of raw cold. He pulled out his bottle. Nothing like vodka to warm the soul. He took a bracing swallow, another, and then placed the bottle back into his pocket.

"This way."

He led them up to the front stairs of the townhouse.

The street was a winter wonderland. Icicles hung from the branches of trees in a bizarre imitation of fangs. Snow was piled high on cars. The large range of townhomes squatted under the burden of ice and snow, like frozen giants.

From somewhere above in the darkness from which the snow materialized, a sound emerged.

A caw!

Donald looked up. A piece of night seemed to flap away up there. Then the smashing of snow on his face made him look back down.

Baxter Brittle had a bit of difficulty navigating the snow, but with the help of the Count and the Marquis he managed not to slip and slide. A sorry bunch of saviors. Fortunately, the villains were in on the game and would fall and flail and then fly away. A minimum amount of force would bring a maximum amount of effect.

Donald led them up the icy steps. He had to grab the railing to keep himself upright. The door was closed and locked, of course, and presumably the alarm system was off. He didn't bother to knock. He could claim that he'd tried to knock and, upon getting no response and being concerned, had simply brought out the keys the Blessings had given him and used them. "Thank goodness you did that" they'd say, and that would be that.

The lock clicked.

The door squeaked open.

Donald walked in and was surprised at what awaited him.

Silence.

He held up his hand to the others. "I don't hear anything."

"Look, this is a pretty solid house," said Baxter. "If they're ransacking the Poe room by now, we wouldn't hear it. Let us in! I'm dying of cold."

Donald walked in farther and the others followed. He walked toward the steps that led to the second floor.

Thumps.

A muffled cry.

More thumps.

"Okay. We'd better go up," he said.

He swallowed and found himself nervous and frightened, even though there should be nothing to be frightened of.

"Look," said Brittle. "We hear bad noises. We grab weapons. Boys! There's a kitchen. See what you can do." The Count and the Marquis scurried off into the kitchen, while Baxter Brittle looked around the room. He pointed toward the fireplace. "Yes. We hear noises. We grab fireplace utensils as weapons. Perfect!"

Baxter got the shovel, and Donald the poker.

The Count and the Marquis emerged from the kitchen with a cleaver and a chopping knife. Fortunately, they were in normal clothing tonight, looking like nervous young men dealing with burglars extemporaneously, and that was exactly the impression that was needed.

They made their way upstairs.

The door to the Poe room was open.

The thumping had stopped though.

"You first," Baxter whispered. "You're the hero."

Donald nodded. He raised the poker and proceeded into the room.

In the middle of the room, sat Mick, coat and legs flailed. He was staring at a gun he held in his hand. Upon sensing an approach, he looked up. Glazed eyes focused. He smiled at Donald like one possessed.

"Mine Enemy is Dead!" he whispered harshly. "Finally! Dead! I can rest at night! No longer pursued!"

Alarm filled Donald. He stood transfixed, staring at Mick, not knowing what to do.

Then Theodore arose from behind a table. His face was flushed, and his eyes looked sleepy and slaked. His pants were halfway down his powerful thighs. "Man," he said. "What a gas!"

Donald stepped over to him. Behind the table lay Amy Blessing, clothes half torn off, bloody and unconscious. Donald didn't have to ask what Theodore had been doing to her.

"Oh, my God!" he said.

He lost control of his grip on the poker and it dropped from his hand, thunking onto the rug.

Baxter Brittle staggered in, looked at Mick. "Dear me," he said. "Mick! Mick!" He made a naughty-naughty gesture with his fingers. "This was not in the plans, Mick!"

"He's dead! The Enemy is dead!" repeated Mick.

"What?" asked the Count, breathlessly. "He *killed* Blessing!"

Killed Blessing?

The words reverberated in Donald's mind. Part of him simply walled up, denied it. Another part drove him to action.

"What are you talking about, Mick?" he demanded, almost on the point of hysteria. The horror of Amy's naked bloody body was bad enough. But Blessing—murdered? "Where is he?"

"Hell! I have boosted his soul straight to Hell—away from me. An infinity, an eternity—away!" Mick leaned his head back and laughed.

Dire realization flowed through Donald like a raging fever. He instantly understood that all the uneasy feelings and dark suspicions he'd ever had about Mick were just mild doubts compared to the reality standing before him. The man wasn't a writer with a few odd personality quirks, but a true-to-life sociopath, a for real deranged killer who just happened to dabble in fiction when not out skull-fucking his latest victim.

Donald looked up and around.

Legs.

He saw a pair of legs, beyond a high-backed Victorian chair. Donald hurried over. The legs were indeed attached to Professor Blessing. His body lay half-propped by a dump of fallen books, beneath the raven atop its bust of Pallas. Two bloody holes were in his chest, and he was still and stiff and apparently quite, quite . . .

Dead.

Dead!

Donald Marquette could feel his whole world fissuring and crumbling as he neared the fallen author, looking down at the blood that dribbled down his chest, staining the floor, rendering it sodden with dark red.

He spun around.

"You *idiot!*" he screamed at Mick. And turned to Theodore, stabbing a finger. "Why did you *do* this? This was not . . . *not* in the plan."

Baxter Brittle shook his head forlornly. "Oh, dear! Oh, dear me!"

"Hey!" said the Count. "Cool stuff here, though!"

"Yes!" said the Marquis. "We may as well take it now, huh?"

"You were supposed to just scare them!" screeched Donald. His voice lowered plaintively. "And then we were going to come . . . to . . . the . . . rescue."

"Enemy . . . gone . . ." said Mick, wearing a silly grin and laughing. "Enemy . . . kaput! Enemy—*banished!*"

Donald was about to run forward and kick that damned gun out of Mick's hand. Then he had to check on Amy. Yes, if Amy was all right, just unconscious, this whole nightmare could possibly be survived. Could possibly—

Something grabbed his pants leg.

His heart jumped up his throat.

He wheeled around.

William Blessing's eyes were open. He leaned forward and was grabbing hold of Donald Marquette's pants leg so hard his nails dug into his leg beneath.

"You!" Blessing croaked. "You did this . . . Donald. *Why?*"

As he stared down in shock and horror, something went cold deep inside Donald Marquette. Glacier cold, ancient cold. The whole scene seemed to slow, to freeze, like the re-run of a winning touchdown. The frigid Donald Marquette observed, analyzed, made the logical and totally inevitable decision.

"You . . . will . . . *pay,*" gasped Blessing, inching forward, hand reaching out as though for Donald's throat. *"Pay!"*

Donald grabbed the bust of Pallas, the stuffed raven tumbling off as he raised it high above his head. His mind screamed *No Dad, you'll pay!* as he drove the bust down with all his might upon the head of Professor William Blessing.

The head made a sickening cracking sound.

Blessing issued no other sound. His hand lost its grip on the pants leg and his body splayed back onto the floor, adding a larger splash of blood to the carpet. The bust of Pallas rolled off and lay facedown upon the floor.

Stunned at what he'd done, but nonetheless still coldly convinced that he'd had no alternative, a different, deader Donald Marquette turned and looked back.

"I had no choice," he said in a monotone.

"The Enemy . . . wasn't dead," said Mick. He turned his head toward Donald, new respect and gratitude in his eyes. "You . . . killed the Enemy."

"Oh, dear," said Baxter Brittle. He took out his flask and polished off a swallow. "Oh, dear me!"

Donald walked around the table to Amy Blessing. He knelt down and felt for her pulse.

Yes. It was there. She was still alive. Mercifully unconscious, but still alive.

"Listen to me now," said Donald, suddenly feeling totally sober and in command. "Take as much of this stuff as you can carry. There's no one outside. No observers, but still we must be careful. We will all go . . . and then I will come back and discover this scene. Understood?"

The others nodded.

"Quickly now!" said Donald. "And I'll show you what's worth the most."

Mick's gun had a silencer. There was no sign of alarm from the adjacent houses. Good. They just might get away with this.

They had to.

It was Donald Marquette's only hope.

But if they did get away with it . . . if it was believed that the Blessings had been the victims of random drug-crazed burglars . . .

Donald looked down at Amy Blessing, sprawled and bloody but somehow still beautiful.

Amy's mine!

So, he thought, taking out a rag to start cleaning off fingerprints, was a great deal more.

Outside, Donald thought he heard the flap of wings.

He ignored it.

fifteen

Mimes, in the form of God on high,
Mutter and mumble low,
And hither and thither fly—
Mere puppets they, who come and go
At bidding of vast formless things
That shift the scenery to and fro,
Flapping from out their Condor wings
Invisible Woe!

—Edgar A. Poe, "The Conqueror Worm"

THE REST WAS *NOT* SILENCE.

Professor William Blessing woke up.

The first thing he was aware of was muted light, coming through tinted windows. He looked up and realized that he was in a huge room below a rotunda. In the top of the rotunda, some kind of white bird was fluttering, trapped. As he focused, he could see it was a dove. A dove flying from perch to perch, looking for a way to escape.

He looked down.

He sat upon an old wooden chair. Underneath was a beautiful tile floor. Around him were lines of desks. Reading desks, with no occupants. Upon the circling shelves were books and magazines and newspapers.

A library, then.

He was in a beautiful old library.

It smelled of that delicious combination of worn leather and paper, of silence and concentration. Dust motes danced in a shaft of light, like unbound atoms intellectual, dancing in the halls of knowledge.

He was wearing a dark suit of Victorian cut. It was silken and comfortable. As he turned around, he saw, beside a large circulation desk, still untenanted, a drinking fountain. His mouth was dry, so he got up and got a drink. The water was cold and refreshing, but brackish.

When he arose from his drink, he turned and saw that there was a man behind the highly polished wood desk. He too wore a Victorian coat along with odd spectacles, mutton-chop sideburns, and a black bow about the neck, tied with a Byronic flair. He was an elderly man, but there was something familiar about the shape of the head, the stare of the eye.

"May I help you?" the librarian asked.

"I . . . I don't know why I'm here," said Blessing.

"Surely you are here to use the library, sir," said the man. "May I see your library card?"

"Of course." Blessing checked his pockets, but found nothing in them. "I don't seem to have one," he said.

"Well, then!" said the man, still dark and ruminative. "Obviously you are here to obtain one. Allow me to help you. Step up to the desk, if you will."

Blessing obeyed, still feeling confused and disoriented. The man in the dark suit and tie and domed forehead reached underneath the counter and pulled out a piece of paper.

"Your name, sir?" asked the librarian.

"William Clark Blessing."

"Date of birth?"

"Uhm . . . December fifteenth, nineteen-fifty."

"Date of death?"

Blessing blinked at the old librarian. "Excuse me . . ."

"I need the date you died, sir. If you're going to check in or check out of the library, or even use it, I'll have to have all the proper information." The man looked faintly impatient and piqued. But there was something else in his eye: a kind of fury. A challenge.

"But I'm not dead! I don't know what you're talking about."

"No memory of death. Hmm. Not uncommon," said the librarian. "Well, I suppose there might be something in the records that could help. I have your name. Let me see what I can do." He sighed, then gestured about. "Here are the current periodicals. You're not allowed into the stacks or the other reading rooms or the crypts without a library card. However, please feel free to peruse our journals while you wait. I'm sure we can get all this sorted out, please be patient with us."

Blessing was not so much patient as bewildered. The whole experience had the skewed reality of a dream, but all the sensations and validity of reality. "Thank you," was all he could say.

"If you'll excuse me."

The clicks from the librarian's heels echoed up into the rotunda. Blessing looked up. That dove was still flapping up there. Looking for an escape. But the windows all seemed closed.

Blessing walked over to a stack of newspapers and magazines neatly displayed upon the table.

His eye was immediately caught by a headline.

HORROR WRITER SLAIN—MYSTERIOUS SERIAL KILLINGS CONTINUE.

He read the article. Dean Koontz had been killed, despite extraordinary security measures he'd taken following the deaths of Stephen King, Peter Straub, Clive Barker, and the first, William Blessing.

The paper was *The Washington Post*.

The irony! Dean always claimed *not* to be a horror writer.

Blessing felt oddly aloof.

Detached.

He felt as though his emotions were someplace distant, his brain itself not quite fitted properly into his skull but floating up above him like a helium balloon, oddly fitted with new sensory apparatus he had no idea how to engage.

Next to the *Washington Post* was a copy of the *New York Times*.

Idly, he flipped back to the bestseller lists.

There was a book at number one on the hardcover list by himself that he had never written. Number five was a novel by William Blessing and Donald Marquette. Number twelve was a novel by Donald Marquette.

Blessing turned to the paperback bestseller lists.

Number one was *William Blessing Presents Classic Dark Sunset*.

Number three was *William Blessing's Spook Nook: Goblins Ate My Shorts!*

Number five was *Soul Bite: William Blessing's Short Stories, Volume Two*, edited by Donald Marquette.

Number ten was another novel that he'd never written.

Randomly, he paged through the magazine. He noted an advertisement for *William Blessing's Magazine of the Outre* and upcoming novels by himself and in collaboration with Donald Marquette.

Slowly, very slowly, he could feel something like emotions. They trickled in from the floor, like flames slowly warming first the bottoms of his shoes and then, upward, toward his abdomen.

Next was a copy of *People*.

He paged through this. Toward the front, he recognized two people in a picture . . .

The title of the article was "The Blessing Heritage."

The caption of the photo read, "Newlyweds Donald Marquette and Amy Blessing, widow of William Blessing, relax in their Maryland estate."

There was another picture on the next page of Amy Blessing in a riding outfit upon a thoroughbred. The next page had a photo of Donald Marquette sitting near a stack of hardbacks, paperbacks, movie posters, and videos.

Blessing read the article carefully.

In it, he learned that somehow additional novels he had written had been "found" after his death. Some were stand-alones, but others had to be finished. Also there were notes for many, many series, a few screenplays, and enough jottings concerning high concepts and plots to keep several writers busy for many years. Many of his books had sold to the movies, and he was now considered to be the most popular horror writer of all time, surpassing even Stephen King, who, alas, had left no unpublished works after his untimely death and who had specifically requested that his name not be merchandised.

In the works, according to Marquette, after the launch of the Blessing magazine, were a line of William Blessing Halloween masks and William Blessing *Spook Nook* action figures.

Marquette also promised a television series, a comic book line, and the possibility of a Blessing theme park. Right now, he was working on special logos and emblems, based on ancient symbols, for a series of William Blessing designer plates and Franklin Mint mugs to be sold only on QVC.

The article said, "'I even had a paper company call me. They wanted to get merchandising permission to use Blessing logos on toilet paper.' Marquette, brushing back his long locks from his healthy tanned face, leans back and laughs. 'But I had a few fundamental problems with that!'

"Nonetheless, upon contacting Esquire Paper, *People* learned that Marquette, President of Blessing Enterprises, apparently has approved William Blessing Presents Edgar Allan Poe toilet paper, featuring illustrations and text and poetry from that famous American author, as part of their Bathroom Reading line."

The article also noted the booming success of Tome Press, associated with Blessing Enterprises, and the wild parties and antics of its Baltimore members at a popular series of conventions and concerts promoted by that organization. A new record label, Tome Records, was in development, as well as a movie and television production company.

"When asked if he thought that William Blessing, a noted scholar and academic whose bestselling dabblings in fiction were intended merely to be a side-career, would approve of the use of his name in such intense merchandising, Marquette replied: 'I don't even consider that an issue. The work of deceased great men belongs to history. As an academic myself, I see my role as making sure that William Blessing's name is firmly chiseled into the stones of literary immortality.'

"And, along with the immense wealth and fame that his present work brings him, would Marquette like to be a literary immortal?

"'Hey. Why lie? I'm just a humble scribe . . . But every man jack of us would like literary immortality. But I tell you, that's not what matters to me the most, and if it happens it's because of what Blessing bequeathed to me. What makes me happiest is my beautiful, dear wife Amy, who William Blessing left behind.'

"And if there was one thing he could say to William Blessing now, what would it be?

"'That I'm keeping Amy happy.'"

When he finished the article, William Blessing closed the magazine. The room seemed to have changed colors. He looked up and saw that clouds had passed over the rotunda, jabbed with lightning. Thunder rumbled, and spatters of rain could be heard against the glass.

William Blessing went back to the circulation desk, where the old man waited for him, holding a small laminated card. There seemed a nimbus of gloom around his head, along with a grin that seemed more rictus than amusement.

"I remember now," said William Blessing.

Above the sound of rain now was the flapping of wings. Not just the dove's, it would seem. A darker pair.

"Ah, yes. I found the records. Most unfortunate circumstances. I've already inked something in on the certificate. If you'll just sign in, you can make this wonderful, quiet establishment your home and roam the halls of books or rest in peace, as you may desire."

"There is unfinished business," said William Blessing. He could feel emotions rising up to his head, out to his hands.

And the emotion was rage, strong and pure.

"Well now, I suppose we all leave behind unfinished business, Mr. Blessing."

Blessing raised his hands and his head to the lightning and thunder. He saw the dark form, chasing the dove.

"It is me," he said. "I am the crow."

Above there was a furious screeching and scrabbling. Pain and anguish shrieked and echoed through the rotunda. Lightning flashed, showing coal black ripping cotton white.

A small body fell, flopping and spasming upon the desk, splattering blood.

With one final jerk, the dove died.

Flapping down came the bird of black, the killer.

It stood beside its victim, eyeing the librarian and Blessing, challenging. Dark crimson matted its beak and breast.

"Quoth the Crow," said William Blessing.

Intuitively, Blessing reached out his right arm to serve as the creature's perch.

sixteen

Regarding, then, Beauty as my province, my next question referred to the *tone* of its highest manifestation—and all experience has shown that this tone is one of *sadness*. Beauty of whatever kind, in its supreme development, invariably excites the sensitive soul to tears. Melancholy is thus the most legitimate of all the poetical tones.

—Edgar A. Poe, *The Philosophy of Composition*

THE MELANCHOLY STRAINS OF A BEETHOVEN PIANO SONATA DRIFTED down from the top of the large townhouse.

"Delightful," intoned Baxter Brittle, beaming up toward the roof and chandelier. "She plays so very well!"

"At this point," said Donald Marquette with a bite to his tone, "I think I'd rather hear *Roll Over Beethoven*. That's all she does. Play mournful classics. When I work here, I have to put on headphones."

"Healing takes time," said the Marquis, inspecting the place settings, glasses, silverware, and silver serving dishes one last time. "There. I believe that all is in readiness."

"Wait!" said the Count. "We forgot to uncork the wine. This is very fine wine. It needs to breathe—"

Baxter Brittle picked up the large bottle that they'd been working on, eyeing its diminishing contents analytically. "Well, tell it to take deep breaths, because we'll be drinking it very, very soon, I think."

Brittle was not wearing his Oscar Wilde outfit.

In fact, he was dressed conservatively, in a nice coat and tie and loafers. Only his long hair attested to his usual look, as was the case with the Count and the Marquis. No trappings of decadence, those sartorial affectations were tonight in abeyance. Now they were just neat twentysomethings attentively making sure that all the dinner preparations were made. The rich smells of exquisite Italian food, heavy on oregano, basil, tomato sauce, virgin olive oil, and the crisp texture of fresh-baked bread floated above all like a promise.

The wine was all red.

Donald himself wore new casual clothes: nice slacks, a faint blue shirt, a tweed jacket from Saks Fifth Avenue. They felt good, and the recent influx of money he'd bought them with felt good, too. The expensive Calvin Klein cologne he wore now gave him just a jot more welcome self-confidence, aided by the two glasses of wine he'd already consumed.

He was limiting his alcohol intake, though.

Tonight was *the* night, and while he wanted his nerves to be slightly coated, he wanted to be very far from blotto. He'd ordered the Count and the Marquis to restrict their intake as well. With Baxter though, it didn't really matter, since his tolerance was quite high and wine was like water to him, compared to his beloved absinthe. The evening would end long before Baxter Brittle's intoxication would cease being pleasant and charming.

"One question, my boy," said Baxter, looking blearily up over his vintage burgundy. "Why Italian?"

"This is Amy's favorite," said Donald. "And Blessing loathed all forms of Southern Italian food. Allergic to the spices, I think. They never had it."

"Good thinking!" said the Count. "I got it from the best place in Little Italy."

"My mouth is watering, man!" said the Marquis. "I love Neapolitan food. I've already sampled the cheese—and it is to die for!"

"Unfortunate words," said Baxter Brittle. "Cannoli for dessert, I hope."

"Oh, yes. Absolute tops!" assured the Count.

"Mmm. Lovely and decadent," said Baxter. "Well, all seems to be in place. Perhaps you should go up and fetch our hostess."

Donald nodded.

Yes. Yes, it was time.

He straightened his jacket in the living-room mirror, then ran a comb through his hair. He took a deep breath, then went up the stairs.

The Poe room was double locked and boarded up. It hadn't been entered since he'd had the inventory done, to determine what had been stolen. Since her return from the hospital, Amy had not been able to even look at the place, much less go in it. It was she who had more or less walled it up. This was unfortunate, since Donald could have used what was left in the room—quite a bit, actually—to good purpose.

But, he thought as he slowly and methodically took the stairs step by step, *assuming tonight works out, there's plenty of time for that*.

A Chopin etude commenced, lovely, but slower than it should have been. Not surprising, really. Everything about Amy was slower than it should be these days. He was just glad, though, that she was reasonably functional and not in some mental institution.

Surprisingly, despite all the death and blood and rape, things had worked out far better than Baxter Brittle's original plan.

They'd hustled boxfuls of books and letters and Poe collection items out to the waiting cars. The others had sped away to store it and lie low. Then Donald had returned to "discover" the horrible scene. He'd called 911. The cops had arrived. They bought his story, and if any evidence pointed toward him, Amy Blessing's tale upon awakening two days later immediately refuted it. A manhunt began for the burglar/killer and the burglar/rapist, but they could not be found. Tome Press had provided sufficient funds to send them off for an extended "vacation."

It was only during the aftermath, however, that Donald Marquette learned about his true talents. With the police detectives he had been perfect, the grieving student, the horrified protégé—but that had only been practice for the outstanding performance he gave for the media.

Suddenly, with the spotlight upon him, Marquette became Fred Astaire, dancing away gracefully and capturing the hearts and minds of readers everywhere. Blessing's latest books, already selling well, shot to the tops of the bestseller lists. Movie proposals turned into production deals. Rights were sold to countries that had not yet bought them. And Donald Marquette, his name now inseparable from the famous slain horror writer (and scholar!), had easily sold that languishing novel and contracted for another as part of a two book deal at a very respectable sum, a healthy portion of which he had pledged as a reward for information leading to the arrest and conviction of Blessing's killer, and the recovery of his ravaged Poe library.

Of course, considering who the killer truly was, he knew he'd never have to pay out.

Minor chords from the piano waxed and waned as he entered the room. He'd put a vase of cut flowers on the Steinway today, and they smelled fresh and nice. However, this close to the scene of death, the place still held the faint odor of old blood. Not entirely a bad smell . . . mixed with the scent of Amy's shampoo. She didn't wear perfume anymore, and had taken to dark, drab clothing, but to him it made her look more beautiful.

Now, as she sat on the bench, softly playing the keys and working the pedals, she seemed very pale and precious, a breath of weary life in a frozen picture.

He leaned on the piano, just within range of her peripheral vision, adopting an attitude of intense listening. When she finished the Chopin piece, he clapped softly. "Very nice."

She smiled wanly. "Thanks, Donald."

"Hi."

She nodded and then shuffled through the leaves of music on the holder.

"Has any chance any fragrance drifted up from the kitchen in the past hour or so?"

She blinked. "Oh, dear! Are you making dinner? I forgot!"

"Yes. Would you believe, rigatoni bolognese with some nice Italian sausage thrown in for balance? Antipasto for starters and a fresh spinach salad to get some green in. And for dessert: cannoli." He comically acted out a role of a waiter ticking off the specials. "Oh. And a fine vino rojo."

She brightened a bit at all this. Just a shade, but it did seem to light the room just a notch. Never much of a drinker before, she'd taken to consuming more red wine. In part, this was one of the reasons for the Italian meal. Red sauce needed some red wine. It would encourage her to drink.

"Sounds good." She stared off, looking remote and slightly troubled. "Wasn't there something else?"

"You've forgotten the extra treat. I've invited the Tome folks."

"Oh, yes. Your funny friends." She smiled a bit.

"It will certainly take the onus of conversation off of us. Baxter was just at a British convention, and I do believe he's chock-full of gossip."

She nodded, but just sat, looking spacey and disoriented.

She'd been like this, to one degree or another, ever since she'd woken up. It was as though the pain of her husband's death and the trauma of rape had, if not turned her socially autistic, then at least turned her partially oblique to the rest of existence. The doctors claimed she was perfectly fine physically, but would probably take a long time to heal emotionally. Donald had sworn to help make sure this psychological event occurred rapidly but naturally. All the doctors involved, all her friends and family, knowing how close Donald had become to the Blessings, seemed confident that if anyone could break through the shell that Amy Blessing had erected about herself, it would be Donald Marquette. In the meantime, though, Amy was quite capable of ordinary day-to-day business decisions involved with running the Blessing estate, insurance, et al. She just performed them perfunctorily, with no spirit or joy involved. Four months after William Blessing's murder, things were a bit in stasis concerning his books. There was a new one due for publication next month, but the one he'd been working on was only half finished. And his stories and articles and notes—no one knew much about them. Amy kept them locked away, even from Donald, who was still hard at work on the anthologies under Blessing's name.

That was part of what tonight's dinner was about.

"Yes. The gang is quite hungry. They've been swilling wine and munching chips and enjoying your piano for the past half hour. They'd like to know if you'd play for them later . . . but right now, I suppose, we should eat before the pasta gets cold."

"Of course." She pulled the top of the piano closed. "I don't want to keep people waiting."

As she got up, he offered her his arm.

She took it and sighed. "How symbolic, Donald. You know I depend on you for your support. I don't know how I would have gotten along without it."

"I feel honored to do whatever I can," he said. "You are a very important part of my life. In fact, my work now . . . and you." He paused, as though choking slightly with emotion. "Central. Absolutely . . . central."

She reached over to touch him. "Yes," she said in a small voice. "It's been so hard. So very hard."

He feigned a difficult recovery. "Hard. Yes."

He patted her hand.

This was the trick of course . . .

To show her grief and emotion, to draw *her* out. Thus, a bond was achieved. Thus they harmonized. And, gradually, he could take that composition into musical lands of his choosing.

This was a part of the strength he'd discovered in himself—the ability to withdraw into a cold, judgmental, and analytic shell deep within himself and play his emotions like a puppet master. Yes, in truth, he still had deep feelings for this woman. But now that the goal seemed more obtainable, he recognized the lustful aspect, the possession aspect.

He had goals now. Love and desire were all just a part of the mix.

Goals.

Yes.

He heard a distant snigger inside himself.

Donald Marquette once thought that if he hurt anyone, he'd never be able to live with himself. He wasn't particularly religious; he just always thought he had a sense that morally, he would be paralyzed. Now, though, that he'd actually *killed* someone . . . Well, to tell the truth, it wasn't that bad. There were occasional pangs of guilt, but they were growing less and less. And as the actual *rewards* of Blessing's passing began to kick in, Marquette became more and more grateful to Mick and especially to stony old Pallas, who had crushed Blessing's skull. A talented, learned man, certainly . . . but as he reviewed Blessing's personality more and more, Marquette realized well and truly that his original idol worship had blinded him to the man's outrageous faults.

He really had been a total *bastard*.

"I guess this conversation isn't very good for the appetite," he said. "Maybe we should just try and enjoy the evening."

He took her down to the Gothiques and all that red wine below.

The dinner was a great success.

The food was delicious, the wine was sturdy and on the right side of ten-percent alcohol.

The Count and the Marquis were loquacious and in fine fettle, prattling on about this and that in their cultural world. Baxter Brittle was charming and witty, making sure to make Amy feel a part of everything, even though she actually contributed very little in the way of words.

Marquette was very attentive, too, without being obtrusive about it. He smiled at her often and made sure that her wineglass was always full. By the time the cannoli (absolutely delicious!) were finished, Baxter had even been able to tweak a smile or two out of her.

At the behest of all she agreed to play the piano for them, after coffee.

During coffee (with cognac for Baxter, and yes, a wee drop for himself and a slightly greater tipple in Amy's cup) Donald Marquette began to bring up the subject which was truly the reason for the whole occasion.

He began casually, and had made sure that he'd dropped references to William Blessing from time to time the entire evening.

"You know, I think that we should just be grateful," he said, lifting his hands expansively. "Grateful to our departed friend for this house, for what he has left behind. None of us know how long we have upon this Earth. To be able to leave something behind, something of worth. Now that is truly something to be thankful for."

"Here, here," said Baxter, raising a glass as though in toast. "I for one shall cherish my special editions of William Blessing's work."

"Me too!" said the Count.

"And I!" chimed in the Marquis.

Amy shook her head, clearly withdrawing. "I don't know if I can ever read anything he wrote again. There was so much pain and anguish in his work, so many dark things in a man who was such a good man, a man—I thought—of light."

"Hmm. Well, you are the literary executor, my dear," said Baxter Brittle. "You inherited yourself quite a task, along with all the financial boons of an ongoing literary enterprise."

"Well, I for one have sworn to myself," said Marquette, nobly, "to dedicate a part of my life to preserving the legacy that he left. I'm even thinking of a biography." That was one of the cues for the prepared speeches.

Silence ensued.

He turned, annoyed, to Baxter Brittle, who was in the middle of pouring the dregs from a wine bottle.

"Baxter," he said, a slight wake-up edge to his voice. "What do you think? A William Blessing biography!"

As he was sitting across from him, he managed to give the foppish fellow a swift jab to the shin.

Baxter started. He barely managed to keep from spilling his wine.

Amy, still detached, didn't seem to notice any change.

"Biography? Oh, yes! Biography! What a splendid idea!" He took a few sips, letting a moment pass. He furrowed his brow thoughtfully. "But you know, it's not as though William Blessing's legacy has to be wrapped up with a biography . . . It occurs to me that his influence upon literature, upon history in fact . . . well, has a good deal more . . . potential!"

Right on cue, the Marquis asked, "What do you mean by that, Baxter?"

"Why, simply that there are short stories to be collected . . . letters to be published. Heavens, there might even be a couple of early novels hiding somewhere that Blessing never published. Plus outlines and notes . . . the unfinished novel . . . heaven knows what else." He turned a sympathetic smile toward Amy. "I can understand why all association makes you so sad . . . but . . . No. Never mind. I shouldn't even bring it up."

Brilliant! thought Donald. *Nicely played.*

Amy's interest, though still clouded with melancholy, had clearly been pricked.

She leaned toward Baxter. "No. Go ahead, Baxter. Please. You're full of clever ideas."

"Well . . . it just occurs to me that Donald here . . . Donald Marquette knows more than just about anyone else about your husband's work. Who better to lay the responsibility of co-literary executor . . . or perhaps, if you want to simply get out from under the responsibility, the *total* literary executor."

Amy blinked.

Donald watched her closely. She wasn't saying no, but she wasn't saying yes, either. Her expressions were quite difficult to read these days.

He decided to try Baxter's tactic.

"I don't know . . ." he said, hesitantly. "That would be so much . . . responsibility."

"Of course it's up to Amy," said Baxter. "But it seems to me you're already doing a great deal of work with what Blessing left behind."

Amy nodded. "That's true." She looked over at Donald. Reached over and touched him with a hand. "Would you do it, Donald? I realize that you have your own things to write . . . but it seems to be a wonderful idea to me. It would take the responsibility from my shoulders, and help to continue William's place in literature." She squeezed his arm. "I know you can do it. What's more, I trust you."

"You know, I'd like to . . ." said Donald. "But how can I? I mean, Bill's will and all . . ."

"Oh, I know some law," said Baxter. "Amy would just have to sign a few papers."

Amy nodded. "I'd be happy to. And I know that, considering these circumstances, William would want this as well."

"I think it's a great idea!" said the Count.

"Yes," continued the Marquis. "And you're a good writer! Maybe you can even finish that novel . . ."

Donald shrugged eloquently. "I'm overwhelmed." He turned

and looked soulfully into Amy's dark, mourning eyes. "But of course, I'll do the very best I can."

"Good," said Baxter, rubbing his hands. "Well, that's settled then. Now, Amy, you promised a few pieces on the piano. I've been looking forward to that the whole dinner."

Amy nodded and slowly arose from her seat.

As he ascended the stairs behind her, watching her cute butt wiggle upward, Donald Marquette knew exactly what song he'd request to celebrate, if he could.

We're in the Money!

seventeen

The boundaries which divide Life from Death, are at best shadowy and vague. Who shall say where the one ends, and where the other begins?

—Edgar A. Poe, *The Premature Burial*

WHEN HE AWOKE AND MADE TO RISE, WILLIAM BLESSING HIT HIS head on the lid of the coffin.

The coffin was lined with cushioned velvet, so he didn't hurt himself. In fact, what he felt didn't seem to quite correlate with what he remembered of pain. Nonetheless, it was disturbing and disorienting.

The closed coffin was dark beyond dark, and while it was roomy for a coffin, a few movements of his hands and feet determined that it was, in fact, a coffin. It smelled of damp earth and mildew and rot.

Naturally, his immediate conclusion was that he'd been buried alive. This did not bring up reflections or meditations upon Edgar A. Poe's *Premature Burial*.

It brought out extreme claustrophobia, total consuming terror.

The scream built up from instinct and came out loud and overwhelming.

However, the force of it startled him enough that his reason was engaged, and he paused.

The gun, the shots . . .

Donald Marquette with the bust of Pallas, bringing it down upon him, hard . . .

His reason said, a still, small voice in the darkness, *You're dead.*

Then he remembered the library. Then he remembered the librarian, the bloody dove and—

"Are you going to snooze down there all night?" asked a distinct voice. It did not seem to be coming through his ear, but directly to his mind. Nonetheless, it seemed to have timbre and tone—and a vaguely Brooklyn accent.

He remembered the crow.

"What . . . What is this place?" he asked.

"A fine and private place, Doctor," said the voice. "But none, I think, do here embrace."

"I've gone mad," he said.

"Oh, you're mad, all right. That's why you're here."

"Where?"

The voice sounded exasperated. "Six feet under! The narrow house! A sepulcher, a tope, a stupa. A cist, a tomb. Doctor, you're in a coffin in your grave! Some fun, huh?"

Oddly, although he was aware of panic deep inside of him, there was something that prevented it from taking control. His powerful cognitive abilities, yes—but also another emotion.

Anger.

Hot anger, cold anger, all the varieties of anger there were. The anger stretched from his mind and stitched together the sinews and bones and flesh of this resurrected body. It lit the fires of his being and it pumped the stuff of revenge through his veins that once held blood.

He knew now that he had been resurrected. The truth came with a surety that was as overwhelming as it was calming.

"I have returned from the dead," he said, matter-of-factly.

"Dead on, fellow! Welcome back!"

However, he was still in a coffin, below the earth a good distance. And it seemed like a very bad place to start. He did not seem to be suffocating, and he did not seem particularly hungry—but this was no place to remain for any length of time.

"Who are you?" he asked.

"Come on, don't ask stupid questions. Get your butt outta there. You've got work to do," said the voice.

"How?"

"Come on! You're the horror writer. How do revived corpses climb out of graves? Hmm? Transporter beams? No, let's try another one. How about *digging*? Duh!"

"I'm back from the dead through some supernatural agency," he said.

"Well, it sure ain't the employment agency."

"Can't I get out of here through some supernatural manner?" Blessing objected.

"Look, man. You're supernatural already, okay? You think a normal human being could dig his way out of a coffin? Just take my word and give it a try."

Even as he contemplated the voice's words, he could feel he was different. He felt as on the verge of alien senses, occult powers. The fibers and molecules that constituted his corporeal form now seemed charged with some offbeat energy.

Blessing pulled his hands up. He wiggled his fingers in the darkness before him, imagined them—

Saw them.

Even though it was pitch-dark, he saw his fingers. They seemed to glow with some supernal light. He was intensely aware of every wrinkle in the knuckles, every hair follicle, every fingernail. He noticed that they had grown very long; now they almost looked like talons rather than nails.

He lifted them up to the cool of the cushioned silk that lined the coffin.

Pushed.

The lid seemed to give way a bit. Dirt spattered through the opening casket. He could feel the pressure of the ground above, but somehow it did not seem oppressive. It felt . . . altered.

"There you go!" said the voice. "You've got the idea. Keep on! Keep on!"

Straining only slightly, he pushed the casket lid up farther and yet farther. The dirt began to tumble in upon his face and body. It tasted of humus and rocks and worms. It smelled of memories, despair, and regret.

The dirt fell upon William Blessing, but it was no dirt he'd ever experienced before. Rather than dense, it seemed merely opalescent, fluid, like some dark water. He pushed up and it gave way slowly, as though recognizing his mastery of the tomb, his triumph over the graveyard. He began to push himself up and through it, slowly but steadily pushing up and up on a gravelly stairway toward the surface.

"There you go!" cackled the voice. "You've got the knack. Comes naturally, doesn't it?"

He dug upward, upward, and then, reaching up again, he could feel his hand push up through the sod, whip past wet grass into the cold night air. The effect charged him with raw power, and the rest of his ascent was speedy. He emerged into the invigorating midnight air, breathed in the dank mist, and hauled himself from the hole where those he loved had imprisoned him.

Dirt spraying from his hair and face, he flopped onto the ground, gasping and heaving, the night swelling about him like a symphony of silence.

"I said you could do it!" piped the voice. This time not in his head, but in the near darkness. "Bravo."

He spat out dirt and coughed. "Just like an E.C. horror comic," he said bitterly, feeling bile not just in his mouth but throughout his being. He twisted his head toward the voice. "Does that make you the Cryptkeeper?"

"No, no. No such obvious antecedents for me. In fact, perhaps if I weren't very much real, I might make my home in some graphic novel. French, preferably. *Oui! Bon soir, monsieur.* Welcome back to this delightful planet. Are we ready to rumble?"

Blessing pushed himself up, unsteadily got to his feet. Around him he could see tombstones rising up, white beneath a smear of moon in a cloud-flecked night. His joints creaked like chains around an agonized soul. The place stank of history and moiled with ennui.

"Where are you?"

"Try your headstone, sirrah!"

He willed his eyes to focus, and the supernal light clicked on again, as though he were wearing infrared goggles. Although the graveyard it revealed was like no other cemetery he'd ever imagined, let alone seen.

Still, he *recognized* it.

Stunned, he stumbled and fell onto the gloaming loam,

knocking his head against a rock. He looked up. There, chiseled upon marble were dates . . . and his name.

"Most Beloved . . . Rest Well, Much Loved . . . Never, Never Forgotten."

His fingernails scrabbled up and clicked along the words.

"Amy," he whispered. "Amy."

"You'd think she'd have thrown in some Latin, huh?" said the voice. "Or Greek. One of the classic languages. Classy stuff. You know both, don't you?"

"Yes," said Blessing, distractedly.

"*Kyrie Eleison*, pal. And on the fourth month, he arose from the grave and yea, he did kick some ass!"

Blessing, irked, looked up.

The gravestone was in the form of a large Celtic cross. This must have been Amy's idea, as he never cared much for crosses of any kind. He'd always joked that all he'd wanted in his crypt was a notebook computer and a modem line.

At the top of the cross, peering down with intense dark eyes, was a large crow, radiant with blackness.

"A crow," he said, thoughtfully. "A crow . . . One of the most ancient of mankind's symbols."

"So I know what you're thinking. Heckle or Jekyll?" The crow cocked its head. "Neither. This is no cartoon, Blessing. This is Reality Noir. You're here for a reason. I'm here to help you. Period."

Blessing turned around and looked at his environs. He recognized the cemetery. It was the celebrated graveyard where none other than Edgar Allan Poe was buried! Of course! Since he'd bought himself a plot here (as a part of his Poe collection, more than with the actual intention to inhabit it) of course he'd be buried here.

"Help me," he said, slowly. "Help me."

"Yes. Help you set things . . . right," said the crow, suddenly stark and serious. "There is only chaos in the universe. But chaos randomly also creates order. And order can be retrieved from entropy, that road back to chaos . . . by that ultimate creation of order . . . Will. Consciousness. Self-awareness." The crow's voice cracked into a harsh, defiant whisper. "And though, in the end, chaos shall swallow all . . . will can control what it swallows. For will, when it is truly strong, can stand apart from chaos . . . from death and nothingness . . ." The beak snapped. "For a time. For a short time only."

Time.

A short time.

Blessing looked out upon the place of his interment.

It looked like the portrait of a graveyard that Vincent van Gogh might paint, in monochrome with breaths of azure and surreal spirit wafting. Phantom land, allusions upon illusions. Three dimensional slipping into the fourth . . . rotting and desiccating and losing its bony grip upon life, symbolism, and architecture.

Rust to dust.

Sashes to ashes.

Man lives but a short time . . .

. . . nasty, brutish, and short . . .

. . . rounded not even by a dream.

"If I cannot have the dream," said Blessing, "I shall have the nightmare."

He began to walk slowly through the groundfog, the quickened corpse upon a mission . . .

And soon he heard the wings of his avian familiar flapping behind him.

eighteen

... the unseen figure, which still grasped me by the wrist, had caused to be thrown open the graves of all mankind; and from each issued the faint phosphoric radiance of decay; so that I could see into the innermost recesses, and there view the shrouded bodies in their sad and solemn slumbers with the worm. But, alas! the real sleepers were fewer, by many millions, than those who slumbered not at all; and there was a feeble struggling; and there was a general sad unrest; and from out the depths of the countless pits there came a melancholy rustling from the garments of the buried.

—Edgar A. Poe, *The Premature Burial*

THE CITY WAS ALIVE.

For the first time, Blessing saw Baltimore as a living, breathing beast. Sweating mist now, breathing from its sewers, snoring through its telephone wires.

Smelling of smokestacks.

Tasting of destiny.

As he hobbled away from the dreamscape cemetery, the skewed streets seemed to warp and twist away from van Gogh into Picasso. Pieces and bits separated, tenuously reconnecting, like a multicolored lava lamp of triangles and squares and rectangles as well as of blobs and spheres.

"I don't know," he gasped. "I don't know where—"

Behind him, wings on air.

"Focus, Blessing. Remember. Imagine."

He stopped and leaned against a brick wall. He closed his eyes.

Baltimore.

My city.

When he opened his eyes again, he saws streets and buildings and neon lights again. Streetlamps burned halogen. Stoplights clicked.

But nothing seemed quite straight. All was slightly off, surrounded with varicolored nimbuses. There was a music in the air that had no sound, a vibration that was silent. He could sense these things, see these things with senses he'd never experienced before.

At an open avenue, he halted and looked down a hill. Spread out before him lay a view of lower downtown Baltimore. The harbor sparkled and glimmered, the buildings stood in exaggerated relief against one another. The sky seemed a vast cauldron of galaxies chased by violent shocks of clouds. Streaming above the hyper-real asphalt and concrete, the transdimensional brick, were grotesque shreds of faces, mangled remains of bodies with eyes in buttocks or mouths in chests, swimming in the air aimlessly. Occasionally a large mass of jumbled claws and fangs would, like some shark pouncing unsuspected upon a school of fish, fall upon a mass of ectoplasm and gobble it up, then sail on malevolently, searching, cruising, continuing the food chain in this fractured spirit world.

"There you go. You're starting to get it," said the crow.

Blessing shivered.

He looked away, staggering into an alley.

The crow lighted beside him, looked up. "Hey. Come on. There's work to be done."

"I . . . I just have to compose myself."

"Of course. You're decomposing!"

"God! God!" he said, looking at his hands in the light, half expecting shreds of rotten flesh hanging on skeletal phalanxes. His hand seemed perfectly formed, though. Again, he saw every detail of the hand down to the whorls of his fingerprints. He lifted the palm to his nose. He could smell no corruption.

He looked down at the crow.

"Look, don't ask me! Your will just reassembled your self. But believe me—you can't keep it together forever," said the black thing, scuttling along the ground, flicking its tail about and lifting its wings a bit, as though reshuffling its feathers.

"How long do I have?" Blessing asked.

"A few days. Longer? Who knows?" said the crow. "But you must keep your resolve. Lose your passion, lose your anger and resolve, and you shall become what you were."

"Heavens! I need a drink!"

"A little preservative never hurt!" said the crow. "I believe if you turn the corner just up there, you could well find what you're looking for."

Blessing pushed himself off the brick wall and tilted himself in the direction the crow indicated.

The crow lighted upon his shoulder. "Hope you don't mind if I take a little ride from time to time."

"No."

"Better ask any questions you might have now. I don't think they let crows into bars. Just Old Crows."

"What?"

"Whiskey."

Blessing did not respond. Maybe he'd left his sense of humor back in the grave. Or it had been segregated into the part of him that was now the crow.

As he rounded the corner, he saw the bar that the crow had promised. It was a neighborhood bar with no name displayed; just a huge neon sign showing a martini glass.

"I don't know . . . I don't know if I can do . . ." he said, stopping, ". . . what I must."

"What? Take a drink? I believe you've done that once or twice before," said the crow.

"You . . . know . . . what . . . I . . . mean."

"Hey. They've got an off license here. Grab yourself a bottle or two. Buddy, whatever it takes. Right?" Blessing reached the entrance to the bar. "I get off here. See ya!"

The crow leaped off his shoulder, and flew away into the night.

William Blessing opened the door and went into the bar.

It was one of those seedy downtown bars kept alive by regulars during the week and hard weekend drinkers; the sort of bar that would have had free lunch jars in the thirties and forties. A couple of men below a cloud of cigarette smoke were talking intensely in one of the booths. Two solitary drinkers sat far apart from each other on the long, cracked, wood bar. The bartender sat on a stool by the cash register, smoking a cigarette and reading the *Sun*. No one registered his arrival as he walked through the door.

Blessing felt apprehensive.

This was the sort of bar he had generally avoided. The cheap booze and depressing atmosphere reminded him too much of the specter of alcoholism that hovered over drinkers. As a student of Edgar A. Poe, he well knew the long-term hazards of drink. *The curse of the writing class,* as he used to joke to his students.

Also, Blessing felt self-conscious. He was dead, after all. How would the living deal with him?

However, his appetite for strong drink had been resurrected along with the rest of him. He *needed* that drink, and here he was.

He sat down at the bar. The bartender winged the paper closed and came over to him, eyeing him oddly.

"Hey bud! Just come from a fancy ball or something?"

He looked down at himself. Of course! He was still wearing his graveclothes—his best tuxedo. It was his wish that he be buried in it. "Makes me look so good!" he'd put in his will and testament.

"Uhm. Yes, as a matter of fact. A dry dinner party. I desperately need something stronger than iced tea."

"You came to the right place. What'll you have?"

"Double Old Crow," he said. "Water on the side."

"Sure."

As the bartender went to grab one of the spouted bottles perched in front of the bar-shelf mirror, Blessing reached down for his wallet.

His hand found only empty pockets.

Of course! No one was buried with money, at least not any more. He had nothing to pay for his drink with.

The bartender returned with the double shot glass and the water.

"That'll be three-fifty," he said.

"I seem to have left my wallet . . . uhm . . . in my car. Do you mind if I go and—"

"Sure. I'll guard your drink."

Embarrassed and frustrated, Blessing nodded and walked out of the bar, wondering what he could do to get money. He'd just have to give this whole drink business up.

Perched on a parking meter outside was the crow. In his beak was a hundred-dollar bill.

Blessing, surprised but gratified, reached over and took it. "Thanks."

"Thought you might be needing a little shambling-around money. You wouldn't want to *leave tomb* without it," said the crow. "Never showed you that on *Creature Feature*, did they? Resurrection can be such a bitch!"

"Maybe I will get that bottle," said Blessing.

He walked back in and handed the bartender the hundred-dollar bill.

"Jeez," said the bartender. He was a pudgy, fiftyish man with a little squib of a mustache and a receding hairline. "You ain't got anything smaller?"

"Look. I'll buy a whole bottle, okay?" said Blessing.

He noticed that the two men looked up from their beers at this interchange. They both looked deader than he was.

The bartender shrugged. "We're talkin' an extra . . . ah . . . twenty bucks."

"That'll be fine."

"Seems like I oughta be able to make some change now," said the bartender, smiling a bit with the added business. He walked over to the cash register as Blessing settled behind his drink. He took the drink half down in one swallow.

Waited.

For a moment, he simply couldn't taste it. But then, as though just waking up, his taste buds came up to speed. His throat stung, and the familiar warmth spread through him. Only oddly tinged with other things he could not place . . .

Nonetheless, there was still that hint of oblivion and relaxation, and he welcomed it. He took in some water, which was cold and much needed as well. By the time the bartender returned with his change and the wrapped bottle, he'd finished the rest of his drink.

"Another please," said Blessing. "And more water as well."

"Must have been a hard night," said the bartender.

"You don't know."

The bartender poured another double Old Crow, and then placed a fresh glass of water beside it.

Blessing sipped at both, taking his time, reflecting on what the crow had said.

Mission.

He had a mission, and he well knew what it was. He had only a short time in which to accomplish that mission. The fires of the drink mixed with the fires inside him, the relentless drive that must have driven him up out of the grave.

Justice!

Revenge!

However, even as the fires raged, the tranquilizing effect of the alcohol eased the broken glass-on-nerves that seemed to line his spirit.

He closed his eyes.

Ah, to rest!

To let go!

To have that peace of mind where there is no mind.

He could feel the very stuff of the bar throbbing in sympathy. As he breathed in the last of the whiskey, the stale fumes around him joined into the chorus.

Relax, they seemed to say. *All will be nothingness soon anyway. All comes to dust and oblivion, eventually. Join the lucky already there.*

Peace, Blessing. Comfort and joy and the sweet, sweet darkness. Light is the lie. Darkness is the truth.

He sighed and put down the whiskey glass. Oh, to taste fully of that sweet drink again.

The River Lethe and its calm currents of . . .

He opened his eyes.

There was something in the whiskey glass.

It was a nose.

Automatically, he reached up to his face.

Where his own nose had been once, was a hole.

He looked at his hands. The nails were cracked, the skin slowly drying and graying even as he watched.

No!

No, this was too soon!

He poured his nose into his left hand, then smashed it back onto the hole where it had been, holding it there. Then, with his other hand, he grabbed the change and his brown-bagged whiskey and hurried out from the bar into the night.

The slap of the cold air, the panic, and the fear seemed to arrest whatever was happening to him. However, he could still feel the skin of his face begin to draw back from his teeth and eyes.

"No!" he gasped. "No."

He halted in an alley. He put the bottle of whiskey down and felt up to his cheek. Skin was beginning to split. The hand came away green and slimy, slick with pus and . . .

What?

Embalming fluid?

Even as he stared at the mess in his hand, noxious in the distant amber glow of the streetlamp, he felt something hard and insistent poke into his back.

"Okay, asshole. Hand over your cash and you'll make it to morning."

The voice was brisk and demanding.

There was no question about what was in its owner's hand.

Again he saw the gun in the hand of Long Coat.

Saw it fire.

Felt it fire, two bullets slamming into him.

"No," he said.

He turned around.

He recognized the man as one of the drinkers at the bar. Must have figured nice dress, big cash—easy pickings. Then followed him out, hoping to catch him in some ill-lighted place.

"Jesus!" cried the man.

He fired the gun.

Blessing felt it merely as a small smack into his abdomen. There was no pain as such. Just a light tap, exploding the rage deep down inside of him.

"Scum!" he cried.

Blessing knocked aside the gun, then pulled the whiskey bottle up and slammed it against the man's head. The bottle broke and splattered the man with whiskey, blinding him. He tried to bring the gun back, to fire again.

Blessing found himself with amazing speed, power, and dexterity, driving the broken neck of the bottle into the torso of the mugger . . .

. . . straight through to the other side, all the way up to his forearm.

Blood gurgled from the man's mouth. He spasmed, head back, light in his eyes dimming—all, to Blessing's perception, a kind of slow-motion freeze.

Blood pumped onto his arm.

Blessing, in a trance, let the mugger hang limp for several long moments (the weight did not seem great) . . . and then simply lowered his arm. With a squelching sound, the man slipped off, flopping onto the ground in a messy heap.

The smell of blood and whiskey was intense. Blessing lifted the red-streaked bottle and sniffed. He felt invigorated. The night seemed to explode with a resonant electrical charge, humming, harmonizing with his anger, his indignity and sorrow . . .

His rage.

He looked down upon the dead man and felt himself Justice personified. This vile hunk of detritus would no longer trouble the living. As he stared at the cooling carcass, he saw the cankered soul leak out, tiny and shriveled, to join the spirit-fog of the night.

He had performed a service. This validation imbued Blessing with renewed purpose. He could feel power coursing back into him . . .

Resolve.

A dark-winged form hopped onto the body. It dug its beak into the steaming entrails, pulled out a tangly bit and swallowed it.

"Mmm. Guts flavored with whiskey. What a treat," said the crow.

"I must . . . be about my work," said Blessing.

"My, my," said the crow, peering up at Blessing's ruined face. "Lost a bit of inner fire, did we? Looks like *you're* off the sauce for the duration. That is, if you want to put things right. That is, if you think that, all in all, you'd rather not see your killers enjoy a prosperous old age molesting kiddies on the rides at Blessingland!"

Somehow, the rage got stronger.

"That is, if you don't want your betrayer doing the double-backed Big Nasty with your wife thousands of times . . ."

Blessing moaned and howled.

He threw the bottleneck against the wall. It shattered into minute pieces.

"There you go. That's the spirit," said the crow. "I'm here to help, William. Only to help."

"My face," said Blessing. "My nose—"

"Yes, yes. A little reconstructive surgery is in order. I do hope you saved your fallen proboscis."

Blessing looked down. Yes, it was still in his left hand.

"Good. So then, looks like your face is getting a little—shriveled, too. Well! Good thing we happen to have some nice fresh protoplasm here to aid in your reconstitution."

"How . . . ? I don't—"

"Leave that to me. We've got to fix you up for tomorrow morning, don't we? You don't want to have Amy see you without your nose."

"Amy? What?" Blessing said. He could feel his being wrench at the very thought. "Why?"

"You must find the name and address of at least one of your assailants, true? Also, I believe both you and the librarian would appreciate the Poe collection being restored to its proper room. A little bird has told me that our dear friend Donald Marquette has introduced several members of his new club—members involved with your death—to Amy." The bird paused, cocked its head thoughtfully. "Besides," it said in cold tones. "You need to remember what you've lost, Blessing. Or more will fall apart in this mission than your nose."

"Yes," said Blessing, no longer allowing reflection or hesitation into his mind. "Yes."

William Blessing knelt down by the steaming body of the man he had just killed and, with his long sharp nails, did as the crow instructed.

nineteen

On this night, *Mrs. Poe*, lingering on the bed of disease and surrounded by her children, asks your assistance; and *asks it perhaps for the last time.*

—*Richmond Enquirer*, November 29, 1811

"GOOD. YOU ARE ALL HERE, THEN," SAID ELIZA POE. "ALL MY CHIL-dren. *All my loved ones. I need to speak to you now." The death-pale woman's voice was low and very sad.*

It took little Edgar Poe's mind off that big black crow somewhere outside.

Edgar was confused, but he kept quiet and listened. He always listened when Mama spoke. She always had good things to say.

The room seemed somehow darker, even though there were lanterns and candles about. Colder, even though there was a well-stoked fire in the hearth. It smelled of camphor and tallow and the black tea with cream that the grownups were incessantly drinking. There was a stack of small cakes and jam near the teapot, but Edgar didn't really want any, even though blackberry jam was his very favorite and he hadn't had much for breakfast. Somehow, he just wasn't that hungry.

Above the sea of wool-patch quilt, Eliza Poe's head seemed sunk deep in the white linen of the feather pillow. Her dark hair had been combed out so it formed a kind of unearthly black halo about her head. All of her was pale, a deep white shade of pale, the pale of worms that Edgar had found under rocks—except her cheeks and her lips, which were colored a cherry red. She had dark black eyebrows and the biggest eyes that Edgar had ever seen—big, dark eyes that had always seemed so full of life and curiosity . . . but now, they held nothing but sadness.

Still, when they turned to Edgar, a little spark kindled in them. Edgar felt momentarily happy, for he saw the caring and attachment his Mama felt for him. There were times when he sensed that the world was a cold, nasty place, filled with cold, nasty people and not a great deal of fun or joy. However, he always felt, even in these bleak moments, that he was a fortunate soul, for in this world there was always, for him, the deep warmth and caring that Mama held for him.

"Oh, Edgar," she said in her little voice. "Your Sunday tie is crooked."

"Yes, Mama," he said, and attempted to straighten the thing. He made a botch of it, and one of the old ladies had to help him.

"There. That's better," said Eliza Poe. "Come closer, Edgar."

Edgar stepped beside William, who quietly relinquished both his place and his mother's hand. Eliza Poe stroked her son's dark hair, and then let her fingers drift fondly down his face, touching his high cheekbones, his sensitive lips and noble nose, his strong chin.

Her hand was cold and clammy and Edgar felt a shiver run through him. He felt alarmed and felt a need to cry, but he knew he had to be brave for his Mama and he clamped back the tears.

"Dear Edgar, there can be no one who doubts that you are my child," said Eliza. "For you have my eyes."

"Yes, Mama."

"Have you been good for our dear friends?"

"Yes, Mama."

"No, he hasn't," said William, suddenly. "He keeps looking for a crow. All he can talk about is crow . . . crow . . . crow."

His mother turned her eyes back to him. "Edgar, you must not dwell on dark things. Do you love Jesus, Edgar?"

"Yes, Mama."

"Jesus is the Son of Light, and there is no Darkness in him. Look to Jesus, Edgar. And always pray to God."

"Yes, Mama."

Eliza Poe took several long, difficult breaths, and closed her eyes, as though fortifying herself. Then she opened her eyes and began to speak:

"Children. I'm afraid there will be difficult times ahead for you," she said in a weak voice.

It was not the best of times.

It was not the worst of times.

It was the end of 1811.

Soon England would make another final and weak attempt to regain her lost colonies, but already America had identity and power. Its cities were growing, its sense of itself as a nation was getting stronger. Having only just formed its more perfect union, the States were having difficulty thinking of themselves as a country, but the idea was sinking in and most tradesmen were prospering. With its fine ports, the Atlantic seaboard was beginning to grow in wealth, and people flocked for work to the brave, new, and beautiful cities. Needing entertainment, this new society looked to theater and music, and one of its most popular young actresses was Eliza Arnold, who had been born into an acting family and took to the waters like a swan. She had married young to another actor named David Poe. Unfortunately, though filled with plenty of bravado and ambition, Poe was not a very good actor. His reviews were generally dismal, and he took to drinking. Alcohol at the turn of the nineteenth century was a generally acceptable libation—so much so that office workers often had snorts of whiskey at eleven A.M. breaks called "elevenses." However, drinking before breakfast was not thought to be a good idea, and David Poe did not seem to be able to control his bouts with the bottle. When failure as an actor loomed, he simply packed up and left the family.

Eliza had soldiered on.

Now, though, at the age of twenty-four, Eliza Poe was on her deathbed.

She'd been ill for months. Some said she'd never been quite the same since the birth of little Rosalie, that the fever that had taken her might have let go had she not been weakened. Without the income from her career these past months, the family had become destitute. Only the kindness, hospitality, and sheer Christian goodwill from friends such as Fanny and John Allan had kept them from starving.

However, young Edgar really understood little of this. He felt sad that Mama did not feel well and seldom rose from bed; but she never stopped touching him and holding him and professing her love for him, and this in a way was an improvement on the times when her life was a bustle from stage to stage, from social affair to rehearsals, when he seldom saw her. And it had done him good to see the sheer pleasure that his presence gave her; it made the solemn little boy's feeling of self-worth bloom.

"Difficult?" asked William, "That is the word Papa used. Things are always difficult in the 'noble profession' of acting."

"We cannot count on your papa for even proclamations anymore," said Eliza Poe. "We must all fall upon the kindness of others . . . And I must fall upon the mercy of God."

She blinked and seemed to faint a moment, but then rallied, whispering to herself. "No, Eliza, no. You must speak to the children. Speak to the children."

One of the women gave her some nasty-smelling medicine from a big silver spoon, then tilted some hot, milky tea down her throat. Her awareness flickered back on, and once more she was able to address her children.

"I am going away," she said. "Jesus is calling me."

Edgar said, "We will come, too!"

"No, child. Only I can go."

Edgar was suddenly very upset with Jesus. Jesus, who had before been such a friendly and sweet fellow . . . Not letting him stay with Mama. It seemed very wrong . . . Very wrong indeed, and Edgar intended to let Jesus know this in no uncertain terms when he said his prayers tonight.

"You and William and Rosalie must grow up and do good works and become fine people. You must love God and love Jesus and love your fellow man."

As Eliza spoke, Edgar felt suddenly cold and alone. This was not the Mama he knew who would comfort him; she was becoming like the lecturing ministers at churches they had attended, cold and distant and aloof, filled with words and precious little kindness or comfort.

Eliza spoke to them for a while, reciting Bible verses and instructing them on matters of morality and goodness. Edgar could not help noticing that the others in the room, the grownups in their stiff, starched outfits and their high collars, all smelling of rough soap and self-righteousness, would nod occasionally and add stern but approving amens to Eliza's instructions to her children.

Eliza then kissed Rosalie and whispered in the nurse's ear. She then beckoned William to come closer and kiss her cheek. William did so. She whispered something into his ear and he nodded. William's face had gone white and confused tears brimmed on his eyelids. Edgar wondered if he had caught Mama's fever; he surely hoped not.

"Edgar. Please. Come here."

Edgar neared and looked into his mother's eyes.

. . . black feathers . . .

. . . flapping . . .

. . . flapping . . .

. . . like wings of some dark angel.

Edgar backed away. His heart hammered in his chest. He felt he must get outside. There was no air here . . . Nothing to breathe but black feathers and . . .

The little boy took a step and rammed directly into the leg of a man. He felt thick, hard hands descend upon him. He looked up and found himself staring into the granite face of John Allan. "Boy!" said Allan, in the same masterly way that he spoke to his slaves. "Do your duty. Go to your mother!"

Terror added heartbeats to his confusion, but the words turned him back, and he found himself close to his mother again.

"Edgar," said Eliza. "I want you to remember me."

. . . remember . . .

. . . remember . . .

The word echoed in his mind.

"You are so young . . . I fear you will forget the mother who loves you so very much. To help you remember your mama, Edgar, I am giving you a miniature portrait of myself . . ."

. . . remember . . .

"Some letters I wrote which I feel hold some of my soul and perhaps even some literary quality, for you love reading and poetry and stories so . . ."

. . . remember. . .

"Lastly, Edgar, I am giving you a watercolor sketch of the Boston harbor. Do you remember Boston, Edgar? It's where you were born . . ."

. . . remember . . .

"It is where your mother found her best and most sympathetic friends, several of whom are here today."

Eliza's hands were cold to Edgar's touch. She smelled odd as well, and Edgar had to fight for the composure that he sensed his mama needed from him.

Mama said more things, but they made a great deal less sense. There was a great deal about Jesus and God and charity and strength and love and honor, but there were also words that made no sense together, spoken in a feverish whisper.

Finally, Eliza Poe was quiet.

A woman felt her wrist and then put a mirror to her face and nose.

"God bless her and God be thanked," she said in a stolid tone. "Her passing was peaceful."

There was some quiet weeping from Fanny Allan, but John Allan's face was like a statue. "I suppose we shall be stuck with the middle brat, then," he muttered.

Edgar couldn't understand what the fuss was about.

Passing? What did that mean? Mama hadn't gone anywhere! She hadn't gone to heaven to see Jesus. There she was . . . Looking as beautiful as ever. Sleeping . . . Couldn't they see? She was just sleeping!

"Edgar, William," said Fanny Allan. "Your mother has passed on. Kiss her now to speed her with your love."

Obediently, William went to the bed, leaned over, and kissed his mother's lips. He seemed to be in some sort of trance.

Then it was Edgar's turn. He had to be lifted onto the bed. He looked down upon his mother's pale face and he said, "Mama. Wake up."

"Blast you, child," barked John Allan. "She's dead. Can't you see? Now kiss her and let's be done with this. I've a business meeting to go to."

Edgar cringed at John Allan's voice. He touched his mother's face. Somehow, she seemed warmer than before. He kissed her lips and they too were warm. "Very well, Mama," he whispered, "I will not give away your trick."

Then he heard a sudden rapping.

He turned around and looked toward the window. There on the sill, on the other side of the windowpane, stood the crow. Its wings were spread, and the dark span cut off what little sunlight bled through the overcast sky. The feathers flapped against the glaze—a skittering of claws and peck of beak and then the creature flapped away, disappearing once more into the cloudy, barren unknown.

"Look, Mama!" said Edgar Poe. "I told them! I told them . . . A great black bird!"

But his mother said nothing.

Nor did she speak again or hold him or kiss him or smile and laugh and sing her lovely songs.

Never.

Never.

Nevermore.

"Nevermore," moaned Donald Marquette.

He woke up breathing hard. He felt disoriented.

The dream.

He'd had that damned dream again.

"Poe," he said, reaching for the glass of water by his beside. "I'm sick of Poe."

A guilty conscience?

Maybe. He rejected the thought. There were things to be done, hard things to accomplish if he meant to achieve his goals. Guilt was something he simply could not afford.

The cup was cold. He sipped at the chill liquid . . .

. . . and spat it out.

Damn!

It tasted like blood.

twenty

Take this kiss upon the brow!
And, in parting from you now,
Thus much let me avow—
You are not wrong, who deem
That my days have been a dream;
Yet if hope has flown away
In a night, or in a day,
In a vision, or in none,
Is it therefore the less *gone?*
All that we see or seem
Is but a dream within a dream.

—Edgar A. Poe, "A Dream Within a Dream"

AMY BLESSING WAS DROOPING OVER A FRESH MUG OF COFFEE IN her kitchen, when the doorbell rang.

Amy had never liked coffee terribly much, before William was killed. She'd far preferred tea. When she and Bill had gone for their trip to England last year, they had returned with mountains of different teas she'd bought at Fortnum and Mason's in London. Darjeeling, Earl Grey, Lapsang Suchong, English Breakfast, Irish Breakfast, oh, and so many more, kept fresh in splendid tins. She also had tea from various provinces of India and China, splendid, first-rate, very expensive tea.

Now, though, she mostly drank coffee.

When she drank fresh-ground coffee, now, she felt warm

and invigorated . . . and close to Bill. She could sip on the aromatic stuff sweetened with milk and just a breath of sugar, close her eyes, and she'd be with him again. The memory of his musky aftershave seemed closer, the touch of his voice, the taste of his skin in rumpled bedclothes, his protective *presence*.

She knew that she'd withdrawn, but she knew no other way of dealing with her loss. At the end of a brilliant, fun career in college, she'd thought she had her whole life mapped out. Professor William Blessing had been a stunning surprise. The college girl would have been horrified at the notion of marrying a man over twenty years older. Perhaps the writer part would have been romantic to that person, but the academic part? Oh, no! Stuffy, theoretical, painfully dull—this was not what she'd envisioned for herself. No, a life vaulting across oceans and continents, passionately pounding concert pianos, chased by exciting foreign men with burning eyes and a terrible need to bury their sensuous lips in her long, flowing hair. Yes, that was what she'd seen. Then, settling down, a life-mate, family; a musician, yes. Someone to duet with constantly.

William Blessing, of course, had been a bit of a veering off course, but every bit of it had seemed *right*, indeed almost *fateful*.

Fate, though, it would seem, had deadlier things in store.

If only Bill hadn't had to keep his Poe collection in his home and make it common knowledge. If only he hadn't insisted on keeping his professorship and living downtown, exposed. With his money, they could have had a nice big house in a guarded community, away from the threats that plagued people who did not distance themselves from the human viruses that plague society . . .

If only . . .

The bell rang again.

She went to the control wall.

After that horrible night, when he couldn't convince her to move out of the house, Donald had insisted that the security of the townhome be beefed up. This was costly, but his argument was that there was plenty of money still in the bank, and only so much life remaining in the house.

Part of the new security system (along with barred windows

and an impenetrable first floor and basement) was a video system that monitored all of the house's entrances and windows and much of its interior. In a kitchen nook was one of the control areas. Amy went to this, carrying her cup of coffee with her like a talisman.

She switched on the monitor.

The screen showed a man in a hat, dark glasses, and a long coat, his collar pulled up around his neck and up past his chin. Spring in Baltimore had been breezy and a little chilly, but not *that* cold.

Still, it was morning, and the clothes and hat looked top quality and the man hardly looked threatening. No reason to call the police.

She turned on the audio. "Yes," she said, voice monotone. She could still play music, but she could not get up enough energy to make her voice musical again.

"Mrs. Amy Blessing?" said the voice. It seemed harsh and muffled, but somehow strangely familiar.

"Yes."

"I wonder if I might . . . might speak to you?"

"Go ahead."

"In person."

A shiver of dread went through her.

That night, when Bill answered the door . . .

It was ten forty-five in the morning. Donald had come into the office bright and early, but then had gotten a phone call and had to go out for some sort of business meeting.

She was alone now, and had no intention of going to the door and talking to anyone in person. She wanted the safety of two thick doors and many locks between herself and the world.

"I'm afraid that—"

"I understand your position," said the man. "With your recent . . . tragedy, you are very cautious. However, I can assure you, I mean no harm. And I must speak to you. I have come . . . from a very long distance . . . to speak to you."

The man's voice, previously staccato, suddenly seemed filled with emotion.

"Who are you?"

"I am . . . I am Delmore Blessing."

"You're related to Bill? I've never heard of any Delmore . . . He never mentioned . . ."

"I am . . . a distant older cousin . . . Our contact was . . . rather infrequent, I fear. However, when we did correspond we shared ourselves and our secrets. There was much trust between your husband and me." He paused. "I have to speak to you of . . . of things."

She was flustered. She hesitated. "How do I know you're really my husband's cousin? How do I know anything of the sort? I've never seen a letter of yours or answered a phone call."

"You may ask me what you will about William Blessing and I can do my best to answer. But please let me say that my time is very short. May I start out by telling you . . . that your husband . . . He loved you very much. He wrote to me that on your recent wedding anniversary he gave you a poem he had written for you, and that at the end of every month he would give you a clue to the puzzle the poem presented. For the poem would lead you to a secret place and there would be a prize of prizes there. A heart of hearts."

She could feel her heart beat harder.

The memory of that poem opened something inside of her.

She welled up, full of pain.

Full of endless joy . . .

She found that there were tears in her eyes.

She had not cried since the day of William Blessing's funeral. And though the tears burned her cheeks, she welcomed them. For at least it meant that she could feel again.

"You . . . You know about that poem? No one could have known. How could—"

"I taught him to write poetry, you see," said the man who called himself Delmore Blessing. "And I gave him some early lessons in prose as well. I . . . I gave him his first book of the stories and poems of Edgar A. Poe. So you see . . . we were very . . . very close . . . a long time ago."

No one else could have known about that poem.

Her next question should have been, she supposed, why this mysterious relative of William's had not called first. She'd never even heard of him, now he suddenly appears!

However, he looked so uncomfortable out there. And he had been close to William. He *must* have been.

And wouldn't that make her closer to her dead husband . . . just being near this man?

"All right," she said. "I believe you. I'll be right there."

She turned off the monitor and went down to the front door to allow the strange but marvelous man to enter.

twenty-one

A dark unfathom'd tide
Of interminable pride—
A mystery, and a dream,
Should my early life seem;

—Edgar A. Poe, "Imitation"

"THIS IS MOST DISTURBING," SAID DONALD MARQUETTE.

"I gotta say, Mister," said the cop. "Never seen anything or heard of anything quite like it. But then, this is a damned crazy world. You never fuckin' know nothin'. Truth is stranger than fiction. That's what I say."

"Who else knows about this?" asked Marquette, an odd and eerie sensation of dragging chains across his backbone.

"Just the caretakers."

"And where were they?"

The policeman's name was Daniels. He had a donutlike rind of fat around his belt and sweat stains on his blue shirt. There was a bit of snot hanging out of his nose. *Baltimore's Finest*, thought Marquette. "That's the strange thing, Mr. Marquette. This graveyard's got security up the yin yang. I mean, it being the resting place of Edgar Allan Poe and all. But the security—the patrol boys I talked to from last night—they didn't see nuttin'."

Marquette looked down at the ground.

It looked as though a hole had been dug in the grave and then filled back in, badly. There were clumps of dirt in the grass, leading away toward the cemetery's gate. The bright, new, expensive Celtic cross at the head of the grave was untouched, unharmed. Funny. In a case of vandalism, you'd think that would be the first to go.

"Have you examined the coffin?"

"No. Got to dig it up. That's why we called you. We wanted to know if you knew anyone who'd want to dig Mister Blessing up. Him bein' a horror writer and all . . . Gotta have a lot of strange fans. I heard tell of one time, that Stephen King guy was signin' autographs. Guy comes up, slashes his own hand and asks King to sign his book—in blood."

"That was Clive Barker," said Marquette.

"No shit! I knew he was a fan, but man . . ."

"No, no. It was Clive Barker's autograph session."

They'd called this morning to tell him about Blessing's grave being desecrated. He was just damned happy they hadn't gotten ahold of Amy, the lumbering jackasses. He'd gone down straightaway to investigate, telling Amy he had a business meeting.

Grisly business.

"Oh, yeah. Shit, I don't read that kinda stuff anyway. Me, I stick to straight mysteries. I like reality. Know what I mean?"

"Well, I suppose we're going to have to exhume the coffin to make sure that nothing's been down to it or Doctor Blessing's remains," said Marquette.

"Well, that ain't in the area of police duty, Mister."

"I'll check with the cemetery officials to make arrangements. Should there be charges, the Blessing Trust will handle them. I just want to thank you, officer, for letting us know so soon about this nasty business."

"Yeah. Sure. Just doing my job."

"And doing it very well indeed."

The policeman wobbled back to his squad car and headed off, doubtless to the nearest donut shop for lunch.

Donald Marquette went and dealt with the cemetery officials. Since there was no outward evidence of anything missing, there would indeed be a fee for exhumation. Marquette did not argue. The soonest this could happen was tomorrow morning. Not to Marquette's liking, but then he didn't particularly care to grab a spade and start digging himself.

When he had finished these dealings, he found a telephone booth and called Baxter Brittle.

Baxter was not in the Tome Publishing office, which was not surprising.

Marquette tried his personal number, and got a messaging service. Again not surprising. This was very early for Baxter.

However, there was another way, short of actually going over and rousting him out of bed. After that terrible, ultimately wonderful night that everything had changed, Marquette had made Baxter see that communications had to be immediate between them, should anything arise. They had special phone lines installed, and had bought cellular phones. As Baxter hated his, he'd asked that Marquette avail himself of all other means of communication before going for the cellular. In turn, Brittle had promised to keep the channel open. At all times. No flicking the switch to off. No submerging the device beneath his pillows. No simply ignoring it (something that would be very hard indeed, as Marquette had made sure he bought him the model with the most annoying ringer).

Marquette reached into the pocket of his jacket and pulled out his phone. Clicked it open. Stabbed the pound key, which was programmed to immediately dial Baxter's number.

It rang for a long time, but finally Baxter's voice, heavily distorted, came over the line.

"Yes, dear boy."

"Baxter," said Marquette. "Are you straight?"

"I am immensely hungover. In a moment, with a sip and a pill, I shall be straight enough."

"No. Don't. Wait. Talk to me first."

"Very well. Something important, I presume."

"If it wasn't, I wouldn't be bothering you. I keep my promises, Baxter."

"Glad to hear that. Sorry to hear of problems. What seems to be the matter?"

"Mick and Theodore. They're back in town, right?"

"I did mention that last week. Indeed they are. Fit and tanned from their Caribbean adventure."

"I still wish they hadn't chosen to come back to Baltimore."

Whenever they spoke via the phone lines, they were careful

not to be too explicit, keeping to generalities as much as possible. Paranoia seemed a useful state when dealing with such delicate matters as covering up murder and robbery.

"Be that as it may, they have their uses." Baxter Brittle's voice was full of pain and emerging annoyance. "Please do get on with your subject matter, dear boy."

"A certain grave has been desecrated. I just wanted to make sure that certain friends didn't have certain odd vices."

There was a silence.

Then a short bark of a laugh.

"Maybe the occupant arose on the third day and ascended into heaven. I always thought he had a bit of a Christ complex."

Marquette's voice was harsh. "This is no time for smart remarks of extremely poor taste, Baxter. Check up on this. Now. Do you understand?"

"Certainly, dear boy. However, I don't think we exactly have to panic about this."

"There's no panic involved. Just precaution."

"Fine. Fine. Now can I go and partake of my eye-opener?"

"Just get back to me, and sooner rather than later."

"Must I use this hateful device?"

"No. I'll be back at the office."

"Best news I've heard all day, dear boy. *Ciao!*"

Marquette clicked off.

He found himself drifting back to the graveyard, and the disturbed grave. He stood by the cross thoughtfully, staring down at the troubled dirt and grass.

Marquette shook his head and laughed.

All this was giving him a *great* idea for a short story.

Feeling much better, he walked jauntily back to his car, hands stuck in the comfortable silk-lined pockets of his sporty Italian jacket.

twenty-two

It was many and many a year ago,
In a kingdom by the sea,
That a maiden there lived whom you may know
By the name of ANNABEL LEE;—
And this maiden she lived with no other thought
Than to love and be loved by me.

—Edgar A. Poe, "Annabel Lee"

DR. WILLIAM BLESSING, RISEN FROM THE GRAVE, STOOD AT THE door of the house where he had once lived and waited for the living to answer.

The crow was gone, nowhere to be seen. Just as well. After a miserable night on a park bench, it had come to him holding several more hundred-dollar bills in its beak. He'd shuffled into a downtown department store, bought new clothes and some makeup.

Staring into the men's room mirror, looking at his flaky, cracked, dead-man's facial skin, he'd splashed on pancake foundation and then, on some strange whim, color-penciled in clownlike smile lines, clown sparkles about his eyes.

On reflection, he decided that perhaps this was not the proper disguise.

He simply used the pancake to cover some of the more egregious of facial scars and fissures. The work with the fresh flesh of last night had filled in the cracks off his reattached nose. Still, even with the pancake, he looked older than when he had died.

193

Thus, from the foundation of dead William Blessing, grew the (supposedly) living Delmore Blessing, distant (but letter-close) cousin.

Standing outside now, in these clothes, waiting for the door to open, whatever served him for a heart now seemed to pump harder in him, his excitement at seeing Amy again was so great.

The sound of her voice over the speaker had nearly paralyzed him. He was grateful he'd been able to speak and tell his story, let alone do it with sincerity. Fortunately, his appearance and voice had altered sufficiently to mask his essential identity.

Steady, fellow, he told himself.

This reunion is purely for informational purposes.

But, oh!

Her voice had sounded so sweet and sad. He'd had a mad urge to just let out the truth.

Amy! I'm back! Risen from the dead to set things straight!

However, he knew he could never tell her who he really was. He had left her once . . . but he had not intended to. How could he tell her who he was when he very well knew he'd have to leave her again . . .

Soon.

So very soon.

The door opened.

He could see her cautiously peering out, a chain still latched between the door and the frame.

Oh, she was so beautiful. He thought his heart would break, so immense was the feeling that swept through him.

He stood back as far as he could, his hands, empty, at his sides. He tilted his head.

"Hello, there."

"Hello," she said tentatively.

"I thank you so much for trusting me," he said. "Again I am so sorry I didn't tell you I was going to come to Baltimore. In fact, I did not know myself until yesterday. I thought that it would be an opportune time to present myself to you, explain who I am and also tell you how you might help me . . . And how I might help you."

"I just wish that William . . . Bill . . . had told me that he had a cousin . . . who he corresponded with . . . and told such personal secrets."

"I am very embarrassed. But you see, it is necessary to tell you these things . . . in order to see that I mean you no harm." He smiled and he could feel his makeup and his dry, tense skin crack with the facial movement.

"Harm? No, of course not. It's just that—"

"Oh, yes, I understand perfectly."

"Please come in."

"Thank you."

She unlatched the door and stood back.

As he entered, it took every fiber of his being not to embrace her. Not to hold her close, to have her life in his arms again. To have again, so close, what he had lost.

He walked in and stood in the foyer. Almost automatically he had wanted to go up to the bar to make coffee, but he stopped himself, waiting obediently for instructions.

"Would you like some tea or coffee?" asked Amy.

"Yes, thank you."

"This way."

As he adjusted to being in the presence of his beloved again, Blessing had a realization.

She wasn't the same.

There was some spark missing in her. She seemed to shine less brightly now. That biblical bushel was hiding her candle.

And no wonder.

He could feel the rage build inside him. There would be no danger of parts falling off him here. In her presence, and with his anger aflame, his will would be strong.

Amy led him to the dining room table.

"I have a pot of coffee on. A Kenyan blend I like. Would you care for some of that?"

"Coffee? Not tea?" he asked.

She looked at him oddly. "Yes."

"Oh, I'm sorry. William mentioned your passion for exotic teas. It's strange to find you drinking his preference."

"I feel . . . closer to him with coffee," she said. "Besides, it helps keep me awake. I've been sleeping so much lately."

"Sleeping, I understand, is good for healing," he said. "But coffee would be fine, thank you."

She left. As he waited for her return, sitting in his own dining room, he found tears coming into his eyes. He had never really liked this dining room. He'd always felt it was too . . . too . . . American looking. He far preferred European-style dining rooms. Now, though, there was no place else he'd rather be.

Blessing choked back his tears.

When she returned with a tray, she set it down and turned to him.

"Why don't you take off your glasses?"

"Oh . . . ah . . . these," he said, touching his dark tinted glasses. "My eyes are . . . ah . . . very sensitive to light."

"Oh. Like Vincent Price in *Tomb of Ligeia*," said Amy matter-of-factly.

"Oh. Uhm . . . Yes. One of Roger Corman's classic Poe movies," said Blessing.

Amy began to pour the coffee. "Bill thought it one of the better ones."

"Yes. Scripted by Robert Towne, not Richard Matheson, the writer most closely associated with Corman's Poe cycle. I must confess that Charles Beaumont's version of *The Haunted Palace* has always been a favorite of mine." Blessing found himself chuckling. "Of course, that was really from an H. P. Lovecraft story, which could be why."

"You are a Poe fan, aren't you?" said Amy.

"As I said, I introduced William—"

"I think the one we enjoyed the most together was Corman's version of *The Raven* . . . though of course it didn't have much to do with Poe, either," said Amy. "I just loved Peter Lorre as the Raven."

"Yes, of course. Though I must admit that talking birds are getting old with me lately," said Blessing.

He added milk to his china cup of coffee.

"You take it with milk. Just like Bill."

"It seems to run in the family."

"Well, I can see the family resemblance."

"Yes. That was remarked upon the few times we actually were together."

Blessing took a self-conscious sip. He could feel the warmth, but distinguished no flavor. His rage grew.

"You said you needed to speak to me."

"Yes. I live in Vancouver, British Columbia. When word reached me of William's death, he had already been interred . . . I am so sorry I was not at his funeral."

"I'm not sure I was all there, either," she said.

"Perhaps I might have comforted you. William's violent and sudden end left much unsaid. I do not know what was happening between you at the time . . . only know that whenever he wrote me in the last few years, William could not stop talking of you . . . and his feeling for you. He loved you very, very much."

"You don't need to remind me of that. I know that," she said. "I never, ever doubted that . . ." She sighed. "I loved him. I still do."

"Love lasts beyond the grave."

"Yes," she said. "I know that now."

There was a moment of silence.

"William always hoped to share everything with you," said Blessing finally. "But he said there was much of his life that he had not told you about. Nothing terribly exciting . . . Just minutiae, you understand. I'm here, I suppose, to help fill that gap. I'm here to let you know things, small things perhaps, but relevant things, I think, about your departed husband." He sighed. "Of course, if this is too painful to you . . ."

He looked up, despite his misgivings.

Amy Blessing was staring at him.

There was a light in her eye. A light that had not been there before.

"Yes. Yes . . . I *would* like that," she said. "Please go on . . ."

Blessing took a sip of his coffee. He told his wife things about himself that he had not told her before, that he had been too busy to tell her. Somehow, their life together had been left incomplete in ways that were not necessary. Even though he'd been very much in love with her, he was not a practiced hand at intimacy, and now, he wanted to leave her with more of him.

He told of some of his failures, how his first stories had never found publishers. How he'd had a bad year in college, before he really was thoroughly sure of his literary mission in life. He told her of bad relationships, of silly, stupid things he'd done. He'd told her all the wonderful things during their too-short marriage. While he was alive he hadn't brought out all the warts; he felt, now, that this was unfair to her. Amy should remember him the way he truly had been.

Finally, an hour later, realizing that he had more to say but feeling a great weariness of the soul, he could not muster any more out.

"I'm sorry. That is all I can manage to remember now," he said. "I'm sure that William told me more . . . but perhaps I can tell you at a later time."

He looked at her again, expecting her to look disappointed. Disappointed at the woefully flawed man she'd married. Maybe, perhaps, a little relieved that she'd been saved from a lifetime with him.

Instead, she seemed happy, even through a slight sheen of tears.

"Thank you. This really . . . really means so much to me," she said. "Somehow I feel I know Bill . . . better now."

He nodded. "That is good."

"But you must stay! You can rest if you like . . . There are plenty of guest rooms."

"No. I have a room in a hotel here in Baltimore."

"Please! Check out and stay here with me!"

"I'm afraid that would be impossible. Please . . . don't ask me why."

"Very well. As you wish."

"I must go now. I will . . . call you. And tell you when I can return."

"I shall look forward to that."

"There is one more matter," he said. "I wish, during my stay here, to contact certain people. Personal business, you understand. Literary business. These are members of a group involved with an effort called, I believe, Tome Press?"

"Oh, yes! Tome Press. Of course. My associate Donald Marquette works closely with them. He can help you there, I'm sure."

"Actually, I cannot tell you why just now. You must trust me. I must be very secretive, which is why I am so happy we could speak like this, Amy. Please humor me. I would far prefer to get this information from you, and leave anyone else out of the matter."

She looked slightly baffled, but nodded. "All right. I suppose if that's the price I have to pay to get more of these lovely facts about William out of you, then so be it."

"You have information on how I can get in touch with these people?"

"Yes. I have a few cards they left me. As a matter of fact, I obtained them just recently, at a dinner party."

"I'm sure, if you could just let me borrow them . . ."

"Certainly. I've no real use for them. Do you need them now?"

"Yes. I fear I must be going."

"Very well."

She went into her office and returned with several cards, all of them fancily embroidered and embossed with occult symbols.

He took them and got up to leave. It was a wrenching business, but he could feel himself cracking inside. He needed to leave before the fissures were too deep.

"I thank you so much . . ."

"It's I who wants to thank you," she said, and before he could do or say anything, he found that she was hugging him. Her warm and giving flesh against his felt like electric bliss. The smell of her—baby powder and woman-scent—jolted him like nothing spiritual or physical he had ever felt before. She was soft and tender, the curl of her hair brushing against his cheek, the *life* in her a febrile dynamo of possibility and wonder and boundless illumination in a dark and nihilistic universe.

For a moment he thought he would literally melt into a pool of tears.

He managed to hold himself together.

"I'm so glad you came," she said. "Please promise me you'll come back."

"I promise," he said.

Gently he removed himself and left, Amy's farewell lingering in his mind like the grace notes of a great symphony.

He found himself walking aimlessly down the road, the cards she had given him gripped in his hand. He felt dazed. Was it the sunlight? He didn't know. He felt as though he were a denizen of the night, unearthed into the day—and yet, the sunlight did not burn or corrode him, as it did Christopher Lee in Hammer's classic

Dracula films. He felt somehow just the opposite: as though the sunlight imbued him with greater power and understanding. True, he was a creature of the night now. But that did not mean he hated the day.

Eventually, he found himself on the campus of Johns Hopkins University.

He sat down on a bench under the shade of a tree.

Absently, he watched as students passed by. He caught sight of a few young men and women he recognized. People he taught. God, but they were young and fresh and vigorous. He regretted now how harsh he'd been with some, how little he tried to know them. Perhaps, if he had tried to understand them, they would have better understood him. He could have buried himself in the life of the university, that sacred trust. Written under a pseudonym. Avoided this nonsense of death and resurrection.

Had a normal family.

A young man, carrying a Dean Koontz paperback and a 16-ounce bottle of soda, settled down against a tree. He eagerly started paging through the book, finding his place, intently becoming absorbed.

Slowly, as Blessing watched this young man, something dawned on him: He looked like Amy a bit, with his curly hair, the dark eyebrows, the chin.

He looked a bit like William Blessing.

This student could have been their son.

Gripping the business cards in his hand, Blessing had to leave the bench, to stalk through nastier, grimmer areas of town, remembering the last intentions that he and Amy had, before the atrocities had been visited upon them.

They shall pay! he thought.

Through vengeance shall all be redeemed.

twenty-three

I could no longer doubt the doom prepared for me by monkish ingenuity in torture. My cognizance of the pit had become known to the inquisitorial agents—*the pit* whose horrors had been destined for so bold a recusant as myself—*the pit*, typical of hell, and regarded by rumor as the Ultima Thule of all their punishments.

—Edgar A. Poe, *The Pit and the Pendulum*

THE CROSS WAS A NEW CLUB.

It was one of those clubs born from somewhere else, settled in for a time to the throbs of dance music, glitter, poppers, fumed on alcohol and the endless night hours, and probably destined to either move on to some other address—or simply die a spastic, unnatural death.

It was down an alley in the heart of downtown Baltimore, amongst office buildings, stores, and restaurants long since shut up for the evening. No neighborhood here! Tucked away in a canyon of concrete, terrible and raucous noise could be made way into the wee hours. With no peace to be disturbed, there could be no misdemeanors committed.

Of that sort, at any rate.

On the other side of the entrance was a fire exit. Supposedly only emergency was cause for it to open, but tonight, as on many other nights when the club became too hot or the groaning bathrooms were too full with carnal activity, one of the nightclubbers

201

stepped into the dimly lit area formed by stone steps and brick basement access door.

This was Evelyn Nichol, Marquis de la Cinque to his brethren.

Lordy, lordy, he thought as he put his sweaty face into the cooler air. *Hot in there for a work night!*

Ev pulled a pack of Virginia Slims from the sleek black purse at the side of his red plastic jacket and lit it with a Zippo marked with a death's head. He added some pollution to the Baltimore air of the alley, already foggy and surreal at the edges.

His head was swimming! Man, much too much swirl of lights. Too much jackhammer music, aggressive and mean, NIN, Prodigy, Ministry, et al, a pummeling megamix of anger and despair. Too many drugs, too many drinks, too much dancing.

Now he relaxed, rocking on his stiletto heels, letting cool air rise up his mini-skirt to lower the temperature of his tight, tight panties. He smoothed out his nylons carefully, admiring again his perfectly formed calves, his excellently turned ankles.

The funny thing was, although he preferred guys personally, the Marquis looked much better when he was in drag. Especially when he applied makeup. He had the precise *something* that put the *trans* in transvestite.

Yes, he'd admit merrily, *Rocky Horror made a* big *impression on me!*

Used to be, back before the Gothiques, Evelyn Nichol made most of his money as a prostitute. Getting guys off was pretty easy, and it was always fun pretending you were a woman. Unfortunately, it was all ultimately pretty gross and rancid and yucky, with all that disease threat, so when he started making decent dress money with Tome Press and company, the tricks were the first to go. He liked the hip-shaking part and the wig-shaking and the flirty part, but all that groping and grunting with deep voices, all that savage love business, just went the way of all flesh.

All right! he thought, thrusting his hands up toward the sky as though to tap some kind of power latent therein. *A whole new world awaits me! Too long has my nose been on the ground! Now my eyes are on the stars!*

The Marquis was finding a different kind of power. He was

discovering that he had abilities in administration. Imagine! At Tome Press, with its burgeoning businesses and way-relaxed office codes, he could be a top manager, helping guide the company through the exciting prospects that its association with the Blessing estate would bring. What a rush it had been that fateful night when a rich man went to death, and the Gothiques shot to greatness! And he could *still* go out and party any damned way he pleased.

No.

Correction.

Partying was *mandatory!*

Partying was part and parcel of the whole Tome Press philosophy. Already, part of the drug business that Mick Prince was bringing in meant going out to parties with select business associates. It was all this wonderful, Byzantine stuff and it was exciting, powerful, and, best of all, lucrative.

God, he was not only getting the best drugs now . . .

He was getting the best dresses!

What a fucking wonderful fantasy life, thought the Marquis, letting the rich and stimulating tobacco smoke fill his lungs, then gush through his nostrils. And all it cost was a squashed big-egoed head.

Yes, and the darker stuff. That was choice. He had no doubt that the dark stuff was part of the reason for the increased revenue, increased success. *But you know what?* he thought to himself.

The dark stuff was a gas, just by itself.

The Marquis grinned to himself and flicked the cigarette away.

Time to head back for a little boogying. Then, see if I can pick up a pretty little something to take home for later . . .

"Mr. DeMille," he whispered, patting his wig. "I'm ready for my close-up!"

He reached for the door to push back through into the noisy, delightful din, but then was stopped.

A hand reached down from above, hooked into the back of his dress, the back of his bra, and pulled.

The Marquis felt as though some crane hook had gotten hold of him. There was hardly time to even gasp as he was hoisted up onto the street level and then heaved over the side of metal rungs.

"Hey. What—"

Another hand grabbed him.

An arm readjusted around his neck and somehow managed to tie some kind of gag around his mouth. He was then dragged, kicking and groaning, down the alley and across a deserted street.

The Marquis lost both heels in the process.

Adrenaline pumped through him. Was this some kind of drug thing? *Oh no*, he thought, *were all the accounts caught up? What the hell was going on?* He knew that Mick Prince was back in town. Was this some kind of *joke?*

Something smelled bad. It smelled of blood, bad meat, something gone off—

The next thing he knew, he was being carried past a construction post marked DANGER. He saw a Caterpillar roadgrader, hulking like a giant insect in the night. The smell of asphalt and dirt and sewer pipes drifted in the air.

Suddenly, the Marquis found himself staring down into a dark hole. Below, deep, deep down, he saw vague forms of spikes poking up from the bottom of building foundations. His abductor pushed him out—

"No!" he cried, voice muffled.

And then he dangled, feet kicking, above the chasm.

"Yes, I'm afraid so, Ev. Pardon me—Marquis."

Fear filling up his head, the dank air from below sailing up his dress, the Marquis managed to get a grip on himself. He tried to speak but could get nothing decipherable past the gag.

What he was trying to say was that he had money in his purse. His attacker didn't seem to care much about that one way or the other.

"'In the confusion,'" said the Dark Man, "'attending my fall, I did not immediately apprehend a somewhat startling circumstance, which yet, in a few seconds afterward, and while I still lay prostrate, arrested my attention. It was this—my chin rested up on the floor of the prison, but my lips and the upper portion of my head, although seemingly at less elevation than the chin, touched nothing. At the same time my forehead seemed bathed in a clammy vapor, and the peculiar smell of decayed fungus arose to my nostrils. I put forward my arm and shuddered to find that I had fallen at the very brink of a circular pit, whose extent, of course, I had no means of ascertaining at the moment. Groping about the masonry just below the margin, I succeeded in dislodging a small fragment and let it fall into the abyss. For many seconds I hearkened to its reverberations as it dashed against the sides of the chasm in its descent; at length there was a sullen plunge into water, succeeded by loud echoes.'"

"Mmmph!" said the Marquis.

"Do you know why this is happening, Marquis?" asked the Dark Man.

"No," said the Marquis, muffled.

"Do you know who I am?"

"No," said the Marquis, again muffled.

"Well, perhaps I won't tell you. What difference does it make whether you know or not? You are but a bit of dimness, I think, in the greater darkness."

The Dark Man was quiet for a moment, as though considering.

The Marquis felt a wash of vertigo, despite the fact that he wasn't looking down.

He could *sense* the fall below him.

Finally, the Dark Man spoke.

"That quote. Do you know where that's from, Marquis? Tell you what. Answer me correctly and perhaps you won't go tumbling tonight, hmmmm?"

The Marquis nodded violently.

The Dark Man parked his feet against the edge.

Man, this was one powerful dude to be capable of this, the Marquis thought.

"Scream and down you go instantly," said the Dark Man, who immediately lifted the gag.

"First, tell me . . . Marquis. Where is your good companion Baxter Brittle this fair evening?"

"At home. At his bar."

"Yes. That is what I thought. Just ascertaining. Now then. Your answer. Where is the quote I gave you from?"

The Marquis shuddered.

A bit of asphalt broke off and clattered down the artificial cliff.

"Clue. Gimmee . . . clue."

"You are a demanding fellow. Shall we say . . . from a famous horror story?"

The Marquis blinked.

He'd never read all that many horror stories, a fact he'd always been afraid the rest of the Gothiques would discover. It looked like that worry would soon be over.

"Uhm . . . *The Shining?*"

"Wrong," said the Dark Man.

He slipped the gag back on.

And pushed the leaning man over the chasm.

The Marquis, falling, screamed.

It felt as though he fell forever. Abruptly, though, he impacted and it felt as though a fist from below had punched up from the darkness, directly into his gut.

The darkness filled with red, and the dressing-room curtain slammed shut.

When he awoke, the Marquis felt a vague but overwhelming pain, but mostly a feeling of nothingness below the level of his chest.

He felt a liquid lapping at his face. He smelled clay and brackish, dead water. He tasted blood in his mouth.

He tried to move, but could not. It was as though a giant high heel were stepping down on him from above, pinning him onto the ground.

Suddenly, just a few feet from his face, a match lit.

The Dark Man stood there, his face in half-shadow, regarding the fallen Marquis.

He intoned: "'While I gazed, this fissure rapidly widened— there came a fierce breath of the whirlwind—the entire orb of the satellite burst at once upon my sight—my brain reeled as I saw the mighty walls rushing asunder—there was a long tumultuous shouting sound like the voice of a thousand waters—and the deep and dank tarn at my feet closed sullenly and silently over the fragments of the House of Usher.'"

The Marquis opened his mouth. He felt blood leaking out. "Who . . . are—"

"You don't get it yet? Those books you stole . . . Part of the loot . . . ?" said the Dark Man.

"The Poe books," the Marquis gasped.

"Don't worry. I got them back today. I have . . . ways."

The match went out.

Amidst the faint buzzing in his ears, the Marquis heard a squeaking sound. A slithering sound.

Another match was lit. This time, it was much closer. "You don't recognize me yet? But of course not, how could you. You've probably never met a man who's come back from death for vengeance, have you?"

There was some kind of squeaking nearby, at the edge of the fitful light thrown by the match. The stunned pain in the Marquis's head gave way to realization. He rejected the thought as soon as it came up, but the name escaped his mouth all the same.

"Blessing?"

"That's right, Marquis. That's right. It would seem there are, in fact, forces of justice in this universe . . . If you want them enough."

The Marquis twisted his head away and tried to move again. He looked around and saw the reason for his immobility.

He had been impaled on a thick concrete reinforcement wire at the bottom of the construction site into which he'd been pushed.

"Help . . . me. Call . . . 9 . . . 1 . . . 1 . . ." he gasped. "Help!"

"You know, Marquis. The end of *Pit and the Pendulum*. Do you remember what happens there?"

The Marquis groaned.

"Of course you don't. You don't know anything about Poe. You don't care about Poe. Those first editions meant nothing to you except money. Well, the character in the story, Marquis, is a prisoner of the Spanish Inquisition. Torquemada and all that. In his dungeon, he's tortured with the pendulum . . . a sharp thing that goes back and forth, back and forth, as it descends. But there's also the pit. He almost falls into the pit, you see. However, he does not . . . But I've always wondered what would have happened if he had. Would he have been swept away by an underground river? Or would he have simply lain there, dying, gnawed upon by big fat rats with razor teeth?"

The match went out.

Louder, he could hear the squeakings, the slithers. The scratch of little feet.

"Hungry rats," said the Dark Man. "Good night, Marquis. Sweet dreams."

Something nipped at the Marquis's ear.

The muffled screams were like music. Darker than darkwave, harder than hardcore.

In the alleyway, Blessing leaned against brick and listened, composing himself, regaining energy. Two down: the Count and the Marquis. Four to go.

A black form flapped down from the sky, settled down on his shoulder.

"Crow . . ." he said. "Crow . . . I can . . . do things . . . There are . . . forces about . . . I reach out . . . and control . . ."

One more final phlegmy screech, and then the pit was quiet, a bit of mist seeping out, like escaping spirits.

"Sure. Like I say . . . Will. That's what's keeping you together," said the crow. "Pure willpower. Your love survives. And your rage—" The crow tilted his beak, regarding the edge of the pit. "Hmm. Wonder if any pickings are left. I could use a small nibble—"

"Do I have enough . . . will . . . for one more . . . tonight?" said Blessing.

"What? I certainly hope so . . . Your nerve is up. I'd say go for it."

"I don't know . . . I don't . . ." Blessing looked at his hands. "I'm a murderer now."

"More like a special messenger doing the job of the Universe, that's all," said the crow. "Just doing your job, one most people never get a chance at. So don't get all self-doubting, guy, or that nose is going to come off again. And maybe those ears. You want to see Amy again, don't you?"

Blessing said nothing for long moments.

"There are things I can do . . ." he said, finally. "No human should have the power to do. Am I damning myself by my own anger?"

"Think of what they took from you—more than Amy, more than your life—your full and rightful place in history. And they would ruin it with garbage," said the crow. "You have much to settle, yes, William Blessing. But you are also a servant to the furies who, without you, might find justice in methods less satisfactory to you."

"I . . . I . . ." said Blessing.

"Kill the bastards," said the crow. "And leave their souls to the mercy of the darkness they serve." The crow flapped away into the night.

William Blessing nodded and walked into the harbor fog again, looking for a bar.

twenty-four

The thousand injuries of Fortunato I had borne as I best could, but when he ventured upon insult I vowed revenge. You, who so well know the nature of my soul, will not suppose, however, that I gave utterance to a threat. *At length* I would be avenged; this was a point definitively settled—but the very definitiveness with which it was resolved precluded the idea of risk. I must not only punish but punish with impunity. A wrong is unredressed when retribution overtakes its redresser. It is equally unredressed when the avenger fails to make himself felt as such to him who has done the wrong.

—Edgar A. Poe, *The Cask of Amontillado*

"EITHER THIS WALLPAPER GOES, OR I DO!" SAID BAXTER BRITTLE, looking up from his booth at the back of his bar.

The remains of bad carryout Chinese food—kung-pao shrimp, moo goo gai pan, and greasy egg rolls—lay on the table before him. He lifted a bottle of Newcastle Brown Ale and dripped the last few drops of the frothing stuff into an old-fashioned dimple mug. Everything smelled of sesame oil and he was burping up hops and malt and in general felt a little on the wrong side of queasy. Before him was a fabulous horror novel from a brilliant young writer who wanted him to issue a special edition several months before his regular publisher put out the trade version. Baxter fully intended to soon be big enough to publish original novels by known writers, not just short story collections and limited editions—crumbs from the tables of New York mainstream houses. *Shit*, Baxter thought, *all it takes is money, and that commodity was becoming much more common around the Tome offices.*

Ah, yes, life was good.

But he still didn't like the wallpaper much back there. Kind of yellowing *fleur de lis*. He made a mental note to have it taken down, maybe leave the natural wood (properly treated, of course) to accentuate the array of knickknacks and paraphernalia and framed pictures.

Business was slow at the bar. The bartender of the night, cleaning some glasses, laughed. "Do you know all the Oscar Wilde quips, Mr. Brittle?"

"Yes, and I have a few of my own. But only half-wits rely solely on fully original material. We full-wits know enough to plagiarize as much as possible."

"That is," said the mustached young man, "the sincerest form of flattery."

"I believe even the esteemed Edgar Allan Poe did a bit of that even while he pointed his finger at others," said Brittle, thoughtfully. He looked down at the mess before him. He suddenly realized that he needed something stronger than British ale, and he needed to drink it somewhere other than here. "Say Joe, dear fellow," he said, getting up. "Would you be so kind as to clean the rest of this up for me? There's a good deal left you might wish to save for your lunch tomorrow. Don't say the owner of the Cork'd Sailor bar is not a generous man."

The bartender bowed deeply with an ironic flourishing bow. "Oh, thank you for the scraps, oh, master."

Baxter Brittle arose, straightened his long coat, and collected the soy-sauce stained manuscript before him.

"Oh, and Joe. I may be expecting late company. There might be a man in a dark coat arriving. His name is Mick. Please allow him entrance to the cellar. I may be distracted by this stunning bit of fiction . . . and *other* things, and not have the wherewithal to let him in."

"You bet, Mr. Brittle." Joe went over to the far end of the bar, where a group of students seemed interested in ordering another round of beers.

Baxter Brittle headed for the door to his private lair. *Ah, the comforts of one's little piece of exotica*, he thought as he smelled the familiar scents of sandalwood and hash oil, candles and rosewater, as he descended. The place was getting to look more and more like a Maxfield Parrish painting, noted Baxter as he turned on the lights. All Roman columns and satin curtains and filigrees, a-splash with bright Oriental rugs and Grecian urns filled with peacock feathers. Where there had once been merely ugly plush orange and brown thrift-store sofas there were now divine divans and fine fainting couches and silken pillows by the score.

Alas, where this very special basement had once been party central for a more sociable Gothiques and associates, now, with business purring along so well, the very reason for all this added finery was causing it to be used less. Baxter Brittle was simply too busy dealing with his growing Tome Press empire. Often as not he wasn't at the bar, but rather down the street in the new offices Tome had rented to accommodate the new personnel. More and more, now, Baxter simply used this delightful place as a retreat, a place to relax and submerge himself in his peculiar dalliances.

He put the latest Planet Dog dub collection on the new surround sound system. Pulsing heartbeat rhythms took over the room.

Baxter's head bobbed to the bass line. "And now for a cocktail!"

He licked his lips and went to the altar.

The altar had prospered and multiplied also with the fortunes of Tome. No longer did it sport merely a few cheap Magickal symbols, a pentacle here, a Goat's head there. Now it was a veritable pantheon of gods and saints and demons, from Hitler and Shiva to Lucifer and Jeffrey Dahmer. Large votive candles flickered. The sweet-and-sour smell of communion wine lingered about fallen goblets. Baxter lit a few more candles, then put a couple of joss sticks in a fat Buddha's lap and lit those as well.

"These ought to burn your balls, brother," he told the somber Buddha.

He selected his own favorite sort of incense—a lovely Cuban

cigar, an El Presedente no less—from a humidor. He lit it from one of the scented candles.

Then he pulled open the cabinet below the altar.

Lined up neatly were hand-marked bottles of absinthe.

He selected one, then went to the sink of the new built-in kitchen/bar. He poured the stuff into a goblet, sniffed it . . . ah! . . . and saluted the gleaming altar, and in fact the entirety of his domain.

"I fear that I have only one way of dealing with temptation," he announced. "Yielding to it!"

The digital drumming from the sound system gave an approving flourish. The high-test alcohol didn't take long to hit his system, giving him that amazing, illegal glow, both sedative and psychedelic, that was the delightful province of absinthe. Oh, he'd have to give it up eventually, tone down to wine and beer. Absinthe not only made the heart grow fonder, but it could kill you over protracted use. The burden of success would no doubt save him, Baxter thought. Who had the time to get stoned all day when there was so much profitable work to be done? However, not right now, not quite now. Now he would enjoy the richness the liquor gave the colors in his life, the deadness it gave whatever conscience he had left in his psyche.

He took the manuscript and goblet and plopped down in a favorite comfy chair in front of his private little hearth, the delightful candlelit altar. He was feeling much better now, evened out. He looked at the candlewicks doing their eternal dance and felt the hypnotic comfort of the smells and the wormwood and the calm of knowing that rewards of work and ambition were being showered upon him.

Ah, yes, money was nice but it was the things—the comforts and the futures you could buy with money—that were the best.

There were some things, though, that money simply couldn't buy, that Baxter Brittle had now.

Next to him was another recent addition: a sturdy, custommade bookcase, polished oak, leaded glass enclosed. He gazed inside, saw his Gurdjieff books, first editions all. His Aleister Crowley books, his ancient volumes of forgotten lore. But central, yes, most important of all, were the books and magazines and documents that occupied the upper shelf, all to themselves.

Having some knowledge of the field, he'd been very quick about making sure he got the very best of the spoils of that fateful evening at the Blessing household. Not even dear Donald Marquette did as well as he, even though doubtless Donald appropriated a larger number of volumes. Even in his cups, as he most certainly had been that evening, Baxter had been able to pick and choose most artfully.

Now, he gazed upon his prizes.

It had been in his own self-interest to help Mick and Theodore and even the Marquis sell their portions of the spoils. He'd only taken a small fee for facilitating the deals with a handful of west coast underground dealers, book fair pirates (invariably fat and malodorous) who paid cash and never asked questions. He himself could have made a pretty penny on what he'd taken, but like rare artwork, Blessing's rarest treasures were well-known in the scholarly and collecting circles, and very heavily insured, no doubt. In that respect, the books might as well be radioactive, far too dangerous to be moved, but housed in his special bookcase, they provided Baxter with a constant source of . . . well, he wasn't sure just what exactly, for once words failed him, but he knew he definitely liked it.

He loved to admire his plunder by candlelight. Muse upon the meaning, meditate upon Poe. Bask in the heat of history and genius.

He took another long sip of his absinthe and considered, with mirth, the irony of it all.

Poe! Oh, how poor and destitute the man had been. And yet he'd *invented* forms of literature that had made *fortunes* for those who simply followed the formulas he'd created, the way he'd used words.

What was it that he'd read once about Poe's principal contribution to literature? Oh, yes—and it wasn't something Baxter had actually considered, yet it was most certainly, upon reflection, quite true.

The critic had pointed out that Edgar Poe was the first writer of fiction who had introduced the use of the full gamut of the devices of poetry into prose. Rhythm, meter, sibilance, assonance, tropes—you name it—Poe had dumped the whole bag of tricks into his stories. This was why, even when you read the tales today, there was a certain modernity of style, despite the nineteenth-century trappings. This, after all, was because Poe created a style that continued on to this day.

Vaguely, as he stared at the volumes before him, Baxter Brittle wondered if he should re-read Poe.

Maybe, once he was able to parcel out more responsibilities of the Press and its growing concerns . . . Maybe, he'd start writing again. Yes, business had consumed him so much . . . There was a whole industry being created here, under the brilliance of dear Donald Marquette's editorial guidance, and Mick Prince's unique ideas on marketing.

Why not claim a piece of the literary pie himself?

Lesser writers than he were certainly scattered on the bestseller lists, idolized by readers around the world . . .

Idolized . . .

Baxter Brittle wondered what that kind of fame would be like. Delicious, certainly. Quite, quite delicious . . .

Suddenly, a breeze shuffled along the tops of the candles, snuffing them out.

The room was suddenly full of wispy shadows.

Baxter looked around.

He felt a draught. A chill.

A presence.

"Who's there—?"

He tried to rise to his feet, but he'd gulped more absinthe than he'd intended and found himself too drunk to leave his chair, at least not without extra concentration.

He fell back, blearily peering into the darkness that had swept the rest of the room.

A figure stepped from the shadows.

"Hello, Baxter. Enjoying your new acquisitions, are you?"

Baxter squinted. "Mick? Mick, is that you?"

He'd called the fellow earlier to arrange for a meeting. Yes, surely this must be Mick, playing some sort of ghoulish prank.

Naughty fellow.

"Come over and have a drink, Mick," said Baxter. "I know you don't particularly enjoy absinthe, but I'm sure I can find something more to your taste."

The figure stepped forward. It was wearing a dark coat, but

nothing as showy or attention-demanding as Mick Prince's. Ahead of the figure wafted an odd smell. Once, on one of their drunken larks, the gang had visited an abattoir on a field trip. Tanned hides, rotting carcasses, bones, and animal glue. A camera had caught some of the more interesting images available of after-death, bizarre juxtapositions of light, dark, and the inclinations of death. But the starkest memory that Baxter still retained was the smell, a strange otherworldly yet very immediate valentine from the dead to the living. A thing of instinct and promise, as though this odor were intoning: "We are the flesh beyond flesh now. The reverberations of blood. The resonance of what was. Take your time or not. You will join us soon."

Somehow, above the smell of the incense, and the taste of the absinthe, Baxter detected a breath of that now.

"No, Baxter. Not Mick. And nothing to drink, thank you."

The figure stopped. Folded its arms together. "Someone you requested to meet once. Perhaps I should have been more attentive at the time and responded. Perhaps things would have been different then. Then again . . . perhaps not."

The blur in Baxter's mind prevented thought from moving very quickly. "How did you get down here?" he said, realizing that the visitor was a stranger.

"There are ways I have now . . . abilities . . . things I can do now . . . *Now.* Such a qualitative sort of word, don't you think? My now, is not very long. In fact, in a very real sense, my now is a projection of the past, a lingering shadow."

Baxter was confused, but the whiff of decay he'd caught triggered alarm, an automatic fear. The fear cleared his head enough to allow him to rise to his feet, still gripping his absinthe.

"Who are you?"

Even as he spoke, he put his goblet down and stepped back a bit.

"Someone I don't think you ever expected to see again, Baxter Brittle. I am here for two reasons."

Baxter inched back toward a chest. He pulled one of the drawers open, slowly and unobtrusively put a hand back into it. He'd always been paranoid about intruders into his sanctum sanctorum, and he had taken precautions. Now, it would seem, those precautions had been wise. He sensed immediate danger, strong danger. However, fortunately, he was still too drunk to panic.

Just get hold of it, he thought, bleariness lifting only slightly. *Grab it, and things will be fine. Just grab it and everything will be absolutely fabulous.*

The guy was talking. Talk took time, which was good in this situation. Baxter knew that even if he had to report this particular adventure, a corpse would not be a particular problem. After all, this would be a situation of *self-defense*, right?

"I don't know what you're talking about. Then again, I don't know who you are, do I?" asked Baxter.

The figure stepped forward.

Its face was lit by a convergence of candlelight and halogen.

Pale and ashen was that face. Slightly cracked and shriveled, but still handsome. There were dark glasses around the eyes, but the man took them off.

The eyes were dark but familiar.

The realization of the intruder's identity stunned Baxter so deeply that for a moment his hand paused in its search. His mind rebelled against accepting the image being relayed to it.

"Blessing?" he said.

"That's right, Baxter."

Baxter Brittle found himself giggling. "But this only happens in particularly odious and banal stories!" he said. "I simply won't accept it."

"I had the same thought, myself, Baxter. But then, perhaps, we are both simply odious and banal characters, hmm? Trapped in some shlocky, tossed-off pennydreadful, acting in a dreary tale by a writer more desperate even than we are!"

Baxter couldn't help himself from chuckling. "No, I'm just hallucinating." He shook his head.

"A bit of undigested gruel? No, I'm no Jacob Marley, Baxter Brittle, come to summon ghostly redemption. And I know Ebenezer Scrooge. And you, sir, are no Ebenezer Scrooge." The Dark Man shook his head sadly. "No redemption involved here, Baxter. Merely . . . retribution!"

Donald Marquette's call.

. . . the grave . . .

. . . disturbed . . .

And now, here was a man dressed in dark clothes who looked very much like William Blessing.

Baxter Brittle had always been an atheist. His dabblings in dark things were always, he thought, an exercise in psychological self-manipulation. An amusement, a method of hypnotic control over self and others. The powers were all, he'd felt, on the inside, and through ceremony and ritual could be unlocked. All the peripheral stuff was whimsical rococo window dressing. Interior decoration.

If nothing else, then the black arts had always been a good excuse to drink and use drugs.

Now, though, here was evidence that he'd been wrong.

His mind bent.

But it did not break.

"Oh, dear me," he said. "Come back from the dead for revenge. But why on me, dear boy?"

His hand rummaged farther back in the dresser drawer.

"You helped steal my wife from me, my wife . . . my entire life," stated the man, baldly. "You seek to steal my good name. And you also have something that belongs to me—that I'd like back."

"And what, Mr. Corpse, would that be, pray tell?"

"What you stole from my library."

"What? You're going to take it back to the grave with you?" Baxter chuckled. "Not much light to read by, dear boy."

"You may do me a favor, Baxter."

"A favor? Why, of course."

"Tell me where I can find the man named Mick Prince."

"Certainly." Baxter gave him the address where Mick was staying. "You'll find Theodore Melvins there as well. They're the ones you're after, Blessing. Not me. Mick shot you. Theodore raped your wife. Me . . . I just wanted to be your friend! It was all a ruse. I just wanted to know you!"

"But it was *your* plan."

"My plan. Alas, gone wrong. But I assure you, my intentions were good. Oh, yes, my intentions were very good indeed."

The dark man named Blessing stood still.

Baxter's fingers touched his gun. His hand closed around it, finger finding the trigger.

But he paused, waiting to see what this . . . this . . . *whatever* was going to do.

"Intentions are pavement, Baxter Brittle," said William Blessing. "You're already on the road. It is my duty to give you a small push."

Damn, thought Baxter Brittle.

He pulled out the gun and fired.

There were scant feet between the two of them. Aiming was not difficult. A quick succession of three shots pounded into the Dark Man. Baxter saw bits of flesh and clothing rip out of the man. However, William Blessing did not fall.

Rather, he simply stepped forward, grabbed the gun, and twisted it from his attacker's hands.

"Sorry, Baxter. You've just made things more difficult for yourself."

Baxter gasped and turned away.

The Dark Man's free hand swung, casting Baxter Brittle into darkness.

He awoke in gloom.

There was a faint pain in his head, but mostly he felt the continued effects of the absinthe. He was still drunk.

For a moment, Baxter Brittle was fogged and perplexed.

Where was he? His back was against some kind of rough wall, and he was sitting. There was a slight glow coming from the darkness above. There was a scraping and clacking, muted, beyond the darkness before him.

Then, it all came back to him.

The Poe books. The gun . . .

William Blessing, risen from the grave, standing before him.

"No," he said.

As he made to get up, there was a clanking and clinking. His hands and feet were restrained. God, what were these?

"Chains?" he gasped, with disbelief. "Where am I?"

He heard scraping. A slap of something wet.

The glow of candlelight in a crevice of the darkness above him.

"'At the most remote end of the crypt,'" intoned the voice, "'there appeared another less spacious. Its walls had been lined with human remains, piled to the vault overhead, in the fashion of the great catacombs of Paris. Three sides of this interior crypt were still ornamented in this manner. From the fourth, the bones had been thrown down, and lay promiscuously upon the earth, forming at one point a mound of some size. Within the wall thus exposed by the displacing of the bones, we perceived a still interior recess, in depth about four feet, in width three, in height six or seven. It seemed to have been constructed for no especial use within itself, but formed merely the interval between two of the colossal supports of the roof of the catacombs, and was backed by one of their circumscribing walls of solid granite.'"

"Stop it!" cried Baxter. He found himself laughing maniacally despite himself. "Where . . . where is this place . . . ?"

There was a scraping, as of a trowel working with cement.

"Very, very handy, this," said Blessing. "You're in your unfinished subbasement—"

"Subbasement?" Baxter blinked in the gloom. Yes, he could smell the damp and the fungus and the cool cellar smells—and something more . . .

Old rot. Dead flesh. Ancient corpses of rats, perhaps?

"Yes. The work was pretty much done for me. I just availed myself of it."

Scrape, scrape.

Clink, clink.

"Did you recognize the source of my recitation, Brittle?"

Baxter laughed drunkenly. *Cask of Amontillado.*"

"A perfectly constructed story, don't you think? I could not help but seize the opportunity presented here to act it out."

Brittle kept panic at bay, giggling.

He was still alive, and if alive, there was certainly hope.

Moreover, there was something that Blessing—or whoever this madman was—could not have known!

Carefully, so as not to jingle his chains too much and let his captor know what he was about, Baxter Brittle crept his hand into the inner jacket of his coat pocket.

Yes.

There it was.

Snug and safe in there was a hard bit of electronics. Baxter Brittle chuckled to himself. Oh, Donald, my boy! Marquette, my lad, he thought. Thank you!

His cellular phone.

He could call for help on his cellular phone.

He laughed. "Walled up alive!" said Brittle. "How original." He let his hands fall back. "My question is now, Blessing . . . or whoever you are . . . where's the Amontillado, then?"

A flicker of light. Baxter could see that there was just enough room to slip one more brick in the wall.

Eyes, lit by candlelight, stared through, directly at the captive.

"No Amontillado, I'm afraid, Brittle. No, something much more to your liking. I took the liberty of installing several bottles of what appears to be your favorite drink."

Baxter laughed. "Absinthe! You left me absinthe . . . Oh, the quality of mercy!" He looked around. "Unfortunately, I can't see a thing!"

"By your side, there is a candle with some matches."

"You are most kind."

"'For the love of God, Montressor!'" quoted Blessing.

"'Yes,' I said. 'For the love of God!'

"'But to these words I hearkened in vain for a reply. I grew impatient. I called aloud.

"'Fortunato!'

"'No answer. I called again—

"'Fortunato!'

"'No answer still. I thrust a torch through the remaining aperture and let it fall within. There came forth in return only jingling of the bells. My heart grew sick; on account of the dampness of the catacombs. I hastened to make an end of my labor. I forced the last stone into its position; I plastered it up. Against the new masonry I re-erected the old rampart of bones. For the half of a century no mortal has disturbed them. *In pace requiescat!*'"

"Bravo!" said Baxter Brittle. "Excellent. Far hammier than Vincent Price's reading. A true accomplishment."

His chains jingled as he clapped.

"Farewell, Brittle," said Blessing.

The last brick began to slip into place. Then, abruptly, it

stopped. Was pulled back out. The eyes peered in again. "Oh, one more thing. You might have some company."

"Ciao!" said Baxter.

The brick was pushed into place, cutting out what little light there was in this dank tomb.

Baxter fumbled about immediately for those matches and the candle. Reaching out, he found the candle. He gripped it. He could feel the wick. His hand patted out, looking for the promised matches. At first he felt nothing, but then, as his hand moved outward in a wider arc, his fingers touched a box that clattered when he touched it.

He grabbed and pulled it against him, doing as best he could, considering the iron bracelets he wore.

With the darkness descending, for the first time, he felt as though the alcohol was wearing off. He could feel stark, glaring fear threatening at the base of his spine.

Baxter really, really needed a drink.

Especially knowing that drink was absinthe.

Yes, he would light the candle. He would find the promised bottles of his brand of Amontillado. And, then, unlike poor Fortunato, he would be able to get out of this prison. All he had to do, after all, was pull out the cellular phone and call Marquette. Should Marquette not be available . . . hmmm. What? Members of the gang? Yes, perhaps, but if worse came to worst, surely he could just call 911.

Hello. This is Baxter Brittle. Help. I've been walled up alive!

Carefully, Baxter pulled out a match. He held the match-head against the side of the box, struck it on the flint. The flare was magnificent, a beacon of hope, and the smell of sulfur was delicious. Carefully, eagerly, he guided the flame over to the top of the candle. Touched down.

The wick came to life almost immediately. It cast a bold bright light across the expanse of the compartment.

Baxter held the candle up for better illumination, and he immediately saw the bottles that had been promised.

They were held between the arms of a corpse, obviously long dead. The flesh was decayed, and bones showed through, but there were enough features left, primarily the hair, to make it familiar to Baxter.

That, and the ceremonial knife still stuck in the chest.

The punk girl! Oh, jeez, when Mick had said he would take care of the body, he thought he'd meant drag it out and dump it in the bay or something—not entomb it beneath his own bar!

The eyes were rotted out, leaving dark obscene orbs staring out above a twist of cartilage that had been a nose. Those orbs stared forward, directly at Baxter, as though saying, "Here you are, Baxter. Come and get your drink."

A paroxysm of panic hit Baxter. He lost hold of the candle.

It fell to the ground and the light flashed out, filling the tomb again with darkness.

Silence shrouded him then, except for the sound of his beating heart.

Like Poe's *Tell-Tale Heart:*

. . . a low, dull, quick sound—such a sound as a watch makes when enveloped in cotton.

It grew louder—louder—louder!

And the harsh sound of his own terrified breathing.

"Hey, Party Guy," he thought he heard a voice from the very throat of night. "Let's get Gothic!"

Then he heard the sound of a bottle breaking against the wall, the slither of a knife sliding from between ribs . . .

I left you some company, Blessing had said.

And the stirring of old bones and dry flesh, rasping toward him, were like the flapping of the wings of some bird of prey.

twenty-five

And then came, as if to my final and irrevocable overthrow, the spirit of PERVERSENESS. Of this spirit philosophy takes no account. Yet I am not more sure that my soul lives, than I am that perverseness is one of the primitive impulses of the human heart—one of the indivisible primary faculties, or sentiments, which give direction to the character of Man. Who has not, a hundred times, found himself committing a vile or a silly action, for no other reason than because he knows he should *not?*

—Edgar A. Poe, *The Black Cat*

DONALD MARQUETTE'S CELLULAR PHONE RANG.

Marquette was standing at the window, staring down at the street pensively, sipping strong coffee and milk, feeling as odd as he'd ever felt in his life, when the insistent annoying beep, beep, beep whined from the technological wonder in his pocket like the motor of an artificial heart.

It was morning at the Blessing house. Outside, it was a moody day, warm and muggy, with dark rain clouds threatening. The air smelled like storm.

Donald had arrived early to start work. He hadn't been able to sleep well last night. What drowsing he'd experienced had been charged by nightmares he could not exactly remember. So he'd come in early and started business up. He didn't think he'd be able to write any fiction today, something he did at home. No, there were practical matters to be taken care of today, especially since he was now in control of the Blessing literary estate, the Blessing name . . . everything. Amy fortunately no longer came into the office. It held disturbing memories for her. There was a secretary, but she was out today.

Donald Marquette flipped open the cellular phone.

"Hello?"

On the other end, silence.

Some kind of grating, an echo . . .

"Hello!" he said again, exasperated. His nerves were such that he wanted to just cut off all communications.

That, of course, in the present situation, would be extremely unwise.

"Oh. Sorry! Donald! It's Roscoe! Roscoe Mithers!"

Donald's heart skipped a beat. "Oh, yes. Mr. Mithers. Good morning."

"Just call me Roscoe, Donald. I hope you don't mind that I called on this number. I got voice messaging on the other services and you did say this was your private line . . . I thought that would be appropriate."

"Yes, yes. That's fine. Glad to hear from you so soon."

"I got your proposal, of course. And I've got some ideas myself. But I want to tell you from the very outset . . . I'm very, very interested. Like Ricardo the Vampire says, it's something I can sink my teeth into! Now, I'm having a meeting this afternoon with higher people. I'm going to present these ideas, and a few of my own. I think that there's a very good chance we're going to be able to start up a very lucrative program here, and with our corporate tentacles in every media, every merchandising area, every licensing possibility—I think we can come up with an excellent arrangement. Of course, we'd have to work out the details with your agent, but I think we'll be able to handle that."

Of course he could have taken the Blessing properties elsewhere. There were also contracts to be fulfilled. The anthologies, the novels . . . but there were other possibilities, and in Roscoe Mithers, Donald Marquette saw other opportunities.

"Have you had a chance to look at the other material, Roscoe?"

"Yes, I have, Donald. What can I say? It's excellent. You

know, I can't pretend this isn't giving me a real opportunity for my own career. Naturally, I'd very much like to publish your solo efforts as well as the proposed collaborations with the Blessing material—"

Yes!

"—and since it will be under my auspices, I'll put just as much elbow grease and promotion into those solo efforts."

Yes! Yes!

"But I can't do anything until I get the okay from above, as well as input from sales and marketing."

"I understand, Roscoe. When will I hear from you?"

"Either late this afternoon or tomorrow morning. In any event, on the other side of the meeting."

"Thank you, Roscoe. I'll look forward to your call."

"Right. Thanks, Donald. Go with the Golem!"

The connection ended.

Marquette was always fairly irked by the way that Mithers always related everything to the *Dark Sunset* universe. Personally, the only reason he dealt with that putrid material was for the money and the career advancement. But Roscoe Mithers was exactly the sort of guy who could do for Marquette what he wished done: wed his name inseparably with that of William Blessing.

From this launching pad (also highly lucrative!) could his own work take off into the stratosphere.

Donald Marquette.

A good name to see regularly on bestseller lists!

The call lifted his spirits. He sat down in the leather chair, feeling a rush. He swallowed the rest of his coffee, letting the caffeine push him into a kind of elevated trance.

All kinds of possibilities, he thought.

The future was boundless.

The cellular phone rang again.

He picked it out of his pocket faster this time, wondering if it was the New York editor again.

It wasn't.

"Marquette?" said a terse, gruff voice.

"Yes?"

"Trouble."

"Mick?"

"Yeah. Man, somethin' goin' on. The Count and the Marquis, man. Fuckin' wasted. And I can't find Baxter. He's just . . . gone. No sign of him, and he didn't pack or take his passport."

Marquette gawked at the receiver. "Wasted? I don't understand."

"Dead. Big-time dead. Like . . . like in one of my stories."

He'd never heard Mick Prince sound like this before.

Unnerved.

Scared.

"Something's going on, man. I can feel the vibes," Mick stated. "Theodore wants to leave town again, and I'm thinking that's a damned good idea."

"Dead?" said Marquette. "How—"

Mick told him.

"Police won't come to you," he said upon finishing. "I heard about it because they tried to find Baxter and we were at the Tome office. Got out damned fast, and we gotta keep goin' before they think to pin these fuckin' bodies on us. Hey man, Baxter ever tell you about . . . about any enemies that Theodore and I never knew about? Some other Goth crew or something?"

What about your *enemies?* thought Marquette. *You're the over-the-edge mad-dog psycho who pushed us into this.*

"No. But then, you were involved before I was."

"Shit, man. Don't lay this on me."

"Look. This shouldn't be dealt with through the phone lines."

"Shit. Jeez. You're right." Marquette could hear the paranoia in his voice. "You want to come here?"

"Yes. But I've got to deal with some things first. Can you guys stay put for a while?"

"Yeah. Sure. But don't be too long."

"Look, Mick. All I can say is, hang tough. There's too much at stake."

"Yeah. Like a fuckin' *witch,* burnin'."

The connection was severed.

What had he meant by that?

Marquette felt dizzy. He leaned against a desk. Distantly, he heard the doorbell buzz. He sat down. Someone else could take care of that. Someone else . . . He had to assimilate all this . . .

He'd thought that the violence would end after that dreadful night. He could live with the excellent consequences, yes, but he was not by nature someone who preferred violence or enjoyed it. He'd always felt that violence was the instinctual response of the uncreative mind and had vowed to leave that part of things, if any, up to Baxter and his cronies. That night . . . he really hadn't been himself.

Baxter, missing.

The Count and the Marquis . . . dead?

And the disturbed grave . . . That must have been a clue. There was someone stalking them. Someone perhaps who knew that Blessing's death was more complex than surface presentations. Someone from left field. Someone out of the blue.

He could call the police, he supposed. But there was too much he'd have to tell them. Too much that implicated him in the burglary, the rape, the death . . .

No. He'd have to deal with all this himself.

On the verge . . . On the verge of the ambitions of any writer. Success, wealth . . . fame!

Maybe even literary immortality.

When he was in high school, the yearbook staff had asked him about his goals in life. The answer that appeared below the smiling youth in the Dubuque High yearbook was: "I want to be a world-famous writer!"

Donald Marquette slapped the desk.

"No," he spat.

It was so close he could taste it.

Nothing would stop him.

Nothing!

Suddenly, the intercom buzzed. "Donald?" came Amy's voice. "Donald, are you up there? There's been the strangest delivery."

"I'm sorry, Amy," he said into the speaker. "I can't look at it now. I have to go out for a while."

twenty-six

Then, methought, the air grew denser, perfumed from an unseen
  censer
Swung by Seraphim whose foot-falls tinkled on the tufted floor.
"Wretch," I cried, "thy God hath lent thee—by these angels he
  hath sent thee
Respite—respite and nepenthe from thy memories of Lenore;
Quaff, oh quaff this kind nepenthe and forget this lost Lenore!"
Quoth the Raven, "Nevermore."

—Edgar A. Poe, *The Raven*

HE CHECKED HIS NOSE, HIS EARS, HIS APPENDAGES.

All seemed firmly in place.

The wealth of blood and flesh last night had been a boon.
The morning had dawned on a healthier than ever undead man.
He fancied that now, sitting here in the park within sight of his
townhome, he could smell the spring flowers that grew in rows
here, feel the warm pressure of the sun against his cracked, gray
skin.

As though I were really alive, thought William Blessing. *As
though I were truly human, and not this vengeful husk of faux-life,
shaking a bloody fist at eternal night.*

There came a flapping.

The crow settled on the bench beside him.

"What a champ!" said the crow. "You've got him rattled all
right. Murderer Marquette is heading toward the graveyard.

Maybe with a stop at the hardware store for a spade, first, eh? Plenty of time to go and talk to Amy."

"Talk to her one last time," whispered Blessing. He bowed his head into his hands. "Suddenly I'm so tired of this. The pain never ends, and this won't stop it."

"Whoa there, chum," said the crow. "Do I hear the sound of your nose falling off into the drink? You've gone too far to turn back now! You have to pick up the backbeat, amigo! You haven't even settled with your murderers yet, to say nothing of the brute who raped your wife . . ." The crow's voice filled with venom. ". . . or the assassin who wants to do the same to your art!"

"Marquette," said Blessing. Cold, raw fury filled him again.

"You didn't notice him pawing her as much as he could? The laughter between the two . . . The chemistry he tried to evoke? On some level, Master Blessing, you must have smelled the rank lust oozing from the monster when he was around your wife. Hmm? Just one more reason to heave old Pallas, eh? The student deposing the teacher."

Blessing nodded. "Yes."

"So go and do what you must. Why?" said the crow. Its eyes flashed and its beak snapped. "*Because you* must!"

William Blessing rose from the park bench and headed for the townhouse.

The crow flapped off in the opposite direction, to follow the progress of their enemies.

The boxes were scattered about the living room, all open now.

Amy Blessing held the carving knife over them.

She stared down, still stunned at what they held.

The books . . .

The magazines . . .

The letters and the artifacts . . .

The Poe collection . . .

It wasn't all here. Something instinctual told her that. But the bulk of it was, the corner-stone items.

They'd been placed in boxes, taped, and then put through a local messenger service.

When she called Donald down, she'd thought he'd be as astonished and happy as she was. Instead, she thought he was going to fall over with shock. He'd turned the whitest shade of pale she'd ever seen on a face. He'd helped her with another package then disappeared into the dining room. She thought she'd heard the clinking of glasses. Drinking so early in the morning? No, surely not. That wasn't like Donald at all. Although, in truth, he had been drinking more lately. Well, then again, so had they all—she included. All that wine!

Then Donald had said he was going down to the messenger service to see who sent the books. Then, perhaps, to the police. That had sounded quite reasonable to Amy.

She leaned over a box. The comforting fragrance of ancient vellum and old print touched her, made her feel astonished and filled with awe.

The buzzer sounded again. She was happy to hear the voice of William's cousin come over the speaker system. She let him in immediately.

"The most astonishing thing has happened!" she told him. "Look."

The man looked much the same. For some reason, though, he seemed stronger now, missing that hint of frailness.

He knelt down by the books. Touched them.

"Yes," he said. "Good. Very good. They are home now."

Amy had the oddest feeling. "You don't seem surprised to see them."

He stood, holding a copy of *Tales of the Grotesque and Arabesque*, smoothing his hand over it in a cherishing fashion. "I told you there were things I had to do in Baltimore, Amy."

"You . . . *You* sent these books?"

"I recovered them. Yes, Amy. I trust you will take care of them now. Place them back in the collection where they belong."

"Of . . . of course . . . But how . . . ?"

"I cannot tell you that. Just be assured, I am working to preserve that which your husband strove so hard for. And I have more yet to do—"

"Well, I must say that I'm happy to see these books back. William loved them so . . . and I have feelings for them myself.

But more than that, William had hoped to save them for posterity. For a foundation . . ."

"That is what you must remember, Amy. Yes, he spoke of that to me, when he wrote."

"Look. Let me make you some coffee or something . . . You must stay . . . You must tell me about this. And you must talk to Donald. He needs to meet you."

"No coffee. I must go," said the man. "However, Amy, there is one more thing I must tell you. Something that your husband meant for you to know . . . Something that he meant for you to have."

The man in the dark coat quietly told her.

twenty-seven

"Keeping now steadily in mind the points to which I have drawn your attention—that peculiar voice, that unusual agility, and that startling absence of motive in a murder so singularly atrocious as this—let us glance at the butchery itself . . ."

—Edgar A. Poe, *The Murders in the Rue Morgue*

MICK PRINCE SWUNG A LAMP INTO A MIRROR. THE GLASS SMASHED, sending down dozens of shards to rain down onto the opulent antiques of the subterranean lair. The strong scent of ropy incense in the air. A flash of candle, a stir of tassels.

Mick Prince's chest heaved. "Damn him, the fuckin' bastard. He'd better have my money here someplace."

Theodore Melvins tossed back a swallow of wine from a bottle he'd found in a corner. "Maybe he just took off with all the money."

"I'll find him," said Mick.

"Maybe . . . maybe he's dead like those other geeks."

"I'll find him," roared Mick Prince. "And then I'll fuckin' kill him again."

It has to be here! thought Mick Prince, ripping off upholstery from a couch. He pulled out the knife from his boot and started attacking pillows. Stuffing flew, but nothing more was revealed.

Once, when drunk (a common enough condition for Brittle), Baxter had mentioned the he kept "reserves" for emergencies, scattered hither and thither. Especially now since his financial condition had improved, those reserves should have swelled. The previous day when they had talked, and it had been suggested that maybe Mick Prince and Theodore Melvins might best leave town again, Baxter had promised Mick money that he'd owed him. Mick was supposed to drop by the previous night to discuss strategy and pick up that money. It had also been his full intention at that point to reveal his major plan to Baxter, and thereby obtain *more* funds to begin executing that plan. Mick was particularly annoyed to find Baxter gone, possibly having absconded with the seed money for a huge fortune, when he, Mick, was just on the cusp of a brilliant endeavor. The little crimes and drug money that he'd brought into the business had been good for him and certainly for Tome Press. Now, though, with stone deadly muscle like Theodore, Mick Prince realized that he had to think *macro*.

"You see, B.B.," he was going to say, familiar hand draped over his comrade's shoulder, the mug of ale in his fist strengthening the bond. "It's very simple. Now that Tome, in conjunction of course with our good friend Donald Marquette and the estate of William Blessing, is starting to produce products and our fortunes are particularly tied to these books' placements on the bestseller lists, I figure, what's the best way to make sure we get a healthy market share. Hmmm?"

And Baxter would have shaken his head woozily, breathed some absinthe into Mick's face and said, "I don't know, Mick."

"Why, eliminate the competition, of course! Clear the way for our success. It's quite simple, really. With my talents for burglary, and Theodore's mercenary soldier talents, and our conjoined talent for murder . . . why, all we have to do is to pay . . . uhm . . . visits to other writers of horror literature whose books perform as well or better, and then remove them from the planet! Of course, we'll make sure to get signed first editions before we kill them and I'm sure pillaging their homes will be extremely remunerative. But the main thrust of our mission would be to follow the traditional American capitalist dictate: Bury the competition!"

And Baxter Brittle would have said, "Oh, excellent idea, dear chum. Please, *please* obtain souvenirs for me. Just don't have anything *personally* inscribed!"

Mick Prince had come up with the idea while he and Theodore had been in Antigua, laying low and living high. It seemed the perfect area for improvement of the literary business. Mick wondered why organized crime hadn't thought of it first. In fact, when it worked, maybe this would be the beginning of a new force in media. Yeah. Drugs, racketeering, prostitution, gambling, and bestsellers! Sheesh, it was *brilliant!*

And then he'd be able to sell his own novels to big publishers. Yeah, that was what Donald Marquette had promised. He could be a part of that new line that was being proposed: *William Blessing Presents: Sliced Eyeballs* by Mick Prince.

Oh, man, what a *rush* that would be!

"Find anything?" he called across the room.

"Shit, no," said Theodore. "Just a bunch of bottles and old crappy videos!"

"Keep on looking. There's gotta be somethin' down here!"

Mick went over to the altar. Crazy Baxt venerated this place. Maybe he felt that a plastic Satan was going to protect his stash!

"Sorry, bro," said Mick Prince to the picture of the pentagrammed goat hanging on a curtain. "Need some dough."

He cast his arm out across the altar. Idols and icons crashed to the floor. He pulled off the red altar cloth. Below this was a cabinet. Mick began to rifle the drawers.

Yes, yes. Now that the Enemy was gone, the world was his oyster, Mick thought.

Ever since that night at the Blessing house, when he discovered the true reason he was in Baltimore, he felt like a free man. Mick Prince had always been aware of some Other—some terrible enemy—ever since his days in reform school. He'd never known his parents—probably just some whore and her john had always been his theory. But still, he hadn't ever done well at the orphanages, and foster parents just weren't his bag. It was only when he got busted for dealing at the age of fourteen and got stuck in a reformatory in the San Francisco Bay area that he realized that he loved to read. And what he loved to read were wild and creepy and crazy stories, nonfiction and fiction. Man, he was just as happy with the Marquis de Sade as Clive Barker, with books about the Holocaust or the Khmer Rouge as Stephen King, and he devoured them all.

It was a good hobby, yeah.

Most outlaws (and that was what Mick Prince considered himself—an outlaw) just diddled their time away, gambling and womanizing or whatever. What a waste. Man, reading was the thing. You could do it outside the pen, or inside the pen, it didn't make any difference. Books were books and you could read 'em fuckin' anywhere.

Mick pulled a drawer so hard, it pulled all the way out and off its track, spilling candles all over the floor. Mick picked one up, lit it, and pushed the flame back into the shadowy recesses to check if there was anything hidden back there.

Nothing.

Shit!

A black rage flung itself over him. He started kicking and smashing away at the altar, splintering the balsa and plywood. Abruptly, the spell was over as soon as it had begun. Now that the Enemy was dead, Mick had better things to do than scrounge around for spare change.

He had goals!

He had *dreams!*

The Enemy had seemed to haunt his dreams as long as he could remember. A dim form, hidden in the shadows, that always made things go wrong in Mick's life.

Of all the horror stories and tales of mystery Mick had read, the ones he'd had the most trouble with were those of Edgar A. Poe. Once he'd read a biography of Poe. Man, what a bastard the guy had been! No wonder he'd had so many enemies. The figure that Mick had identified with the most was the literary executor, Rufus Griswold. Good ol' Rufus had told the truth about Edgar, all right. The A. in the middle wasn't really for "Allan." It was for *asshole*.

Too bad he'd already sold his share of the Poe collection, though. He sure could use the funds right now!

"Hey, Mick!" said Theodore from across the room. "We got company!"

"Baxter?"

Mick's shout was half-anger, half-relief.

Man, if that was Baxter Brittle, that would solve a shitload of problems. They could get the money they needed and *vamoose*, amigo! Adios Baltimoron *muchachos!*

"No, pard. Ain't Brittle."

Mick spun around. His long coat twirled and his brow furrowed deeply.

A man stood in the shadows besides the entrance to the subterranean lair. He was dressed in black and his face was in darkness.

Something else moved farther back in the dimness.

"Who are you?" Mick demanded, sauntering forward a step, chest stuck out, using his deepest and most intimidating tone. "How the *fuck* did you get down here?"

"I walked down the steps," said the figure. "As to the first question—Mick . . . That is your name, yes? Mick Prince?"

"Yeah," said Mick, trying to figure out what the hell to do in this situation.

A forefinger pointed toward his big, gruff, scar-faced partner. Theodore had gotten more tattoos and piercings on their recent "vacation." Earrings dangled from him now like baubles on some muscle-slab Christmas tree.

"And you . . . you're Theodore."

"What of it?" said Theodore.

"Yes. I recognize you both. I'd hate to be dealing with the wrong people. That just wouldn't do. No, not at all."

"Look buddy, you want to tell us what this is about?" demanded Mick. "We got work to do!"

"Looks as though you're doing some of my work for me," said the man.

He stepped forward.

The man was in dark glasses, despite the low light. His hands were beneath a dark coat.

"I'm the dead man whose wife you raped, Theodore," he said. "Let me apologize in advance for the lack of imagination here."

An arm lifted from the coat, holding a Heckler and Koch. The scabby finger tightened on the trigger, banging a slug straight into Theodore's crotch.

Theodore screamed.

He doubled over and fell to the floor, writhing.

"Shit!" said Mick.

He pulled his knife up.

The gun swung over to cover him.

"I wouldn't do that, Mick. I'd just stay where you are for now and let me deal with Mr. Theodore here. I can't quite decide if I should let him go on with his life without male apparatus . . . or send him to Hell without male apparatus. Any thoughts, Mr. Rapist?"

All that came from Theodore were agonized moans.

"As you wish, sir."

The gun swung again.

This time the bullet tore apart the man's head. Blood and gray matter splattered across the floor like a wash of particularly vile vomit.

"Now that's my kind of body piercing, Theodore," said the Dark Man.

Theodore's body shuddered, spasmed, kicked—then was still.

Mick Prince flinched. He stepped a pace back, trying to figure out what to do.

Dead man? The guy had said he was the dead man?

What the fuck was he talking about? Mick Prince didn't know yet, but that the dude had killed Theodore was pretty clear, he could see that, no problem. His experiences with street and prison violence, as well as other delightful modes of self-expression, put him in good stead. Wasn't there some quote about keeping your head when others were losing theirs?

So Mick just raised his hands up to show he held no weapon. He knew he needed to buy time. Then he might be able to do something appropriate. With time, he might be able to wax Mr. Mysterioso here.

"Shit, man! I ain't got a beef with you, whoever you are!"

"You don't? Then why did you shoot me?"

Then Mick Prince got it.

Didn't make a lick of sense, but he got it.

This son-of-a-bitch *thought* he was William Blessing!

That *must* be the case. Because no fuckin' way could this motherfucker actually *be* Blessing! He himself shot Blessing—and then watched as Marquette, bless 'im, bashed his skull in with that bust!

"Buddy, when I shoot people . . . they're dead. Real dead."

"No argument there, Mick . . . I'm dead, all right. Real dead."

"You? You're William Blessing?"

"Correct. Who else would know his murderers in an unsolved case—except for the murdered man himself."

"Oh, man." Mick's mind kind of *twisted* at the very notion—but he kept his calm, his cool, and his belief that deep down, there had to be some kind of explanation here. In the meantime, the number-one priority was to keep on breathing. "So . . . you just . . . pushed up out of the grave, got yourself a gun, and went after the people who you thought had killed—"

Then he got the buzz.

It was in the air . . .

The electric charge he got late at night, when his extra senses caught wind of that scent . . .

That *smell* of the Other. . .

The Enemy . . .

Mick froze, unable to move, even though he wanted to. Here he was, staring at a guy who'd just shot his buddy—who claimed he was a corpse come back to life.

And suddenly, every bit of him told him that this was the *thing* that he'd been dreading all his life, the force that haunted his dreams, his anathema, his nemesis.

Still, he hung tough.

He'd been tough all his life, and he intended to stay tough.

"So then," he managed to growl. "Back from the dead, you say. Well, that gun's alive enough for me."

"It works. That's the important factor."

Something clicked in Mick's head.

"Shit. You're the guy that killed the Count . . . And the Marquis, too . . ."

"I have a mission, yes."

"And Baxter . . . What about him?"

"I'm afraid that Baxter went the way of all flesh as well."

"Okay, damn you. I been expecting this all my life. I could feel you creepin' around my brain since I was a kid, gunnin' for me. Why—I don't know. Maybe you made me what I am. I just got one question for you."

The Dark Man didn't respond.

"Just tell me, shadow man, who was my real mother? Why

did she give me away? I figure you must know." Mick's eyes betrayed his own surprise at saying these unbidden words.

"That's two questions. And I'm afraid you're mistaking me for a therapist. I'm your undertaker."

"Then what are you waiting for? Do it and quit wasting my time."

"You're pretty tough, aren't you, Mick?"

"Yes," said Mick. "Tough as you want."

"You scared now?"

"Shit, no!" Mick spat the words.

"I like your bravery, Mick," commented the Dark Man. "I like your attitude. So, tell you what. I'm going to give you a chance. You look like a street-fighting man."

Mick felt a glow of pride despite himself. "Damned straight."

"You beat my boy here, I'll let you out of here alive!"

"Your boy?"

"'As the sailor looked in,'" the Dark Man quoted, "'the gigantic animal had seized Madame L'Espanaye by the hair, (which was loose, as she had been combing it,) and was flourishing the razor about her face, in imitation of the motions of a barber. The daughter lay prostrate and motionless; she had swooned. The screams and struggles of the old lady (during which the hair was torn from her head) had the effect of changing the pacific purposes of the orangutan into those of wrath. With one determined sweep of its muscular arm, it nearly severed her head from her body.'

"So," said the Dark Man, "First test, then. What's that quote from?"

"Sure. I read that. *Murders in the Rue Morgue.*"

"Excellent. You'll be familiar with my boy, then."

The Dark Man stepped aside.

Shuffling up from the gloom came the movement that Mick had noticed before. A hulking presence, a congruence of form and darkness . . .

And masses of hair.

It was an ape. A primate . . . an orangutan.

Bulgy and ugly and awkward but unusually big and powerful looking.

"What do you say, Mick? Beat my boy here, you get to go."

"Then bring him on, I got better places to be," said Mick.

The Dark Man stepped aside.

Gangly and menacing, the orangutan moved forward, long arms outstretched, smelling of offal and wildness. Mick was glad of the lump he felt in his boot—his butterfly knife—a street-fighting tool if there ever was one.

The orangutan grimaced and peeled its lips back, turning to the Dark Man as if to receive instructions.

Mick quickly retrieved his knife, bringing the blade out in one fluid motion.

But with a lightning-fast swipe of its massive arm, the giant ape knocked the blade from Mick's hand, breaking his wrist in the process.

Grabbing his wrist, Mick bit back a howl of pain.

The ape took a slow step forward. Showing its sharp yellow teeth as it brought up a massive hand. It in was a jagged straight razor.

Then, in his mind, Mick heard the ape speak. A strangled low rumble, the inchoate voice of the Other, splintering his last coherent thoughts.

Mick, old friend, the ape said, *I'm going to fuck you up*.

When it was finished, the orangutan stepped back from what had once been a man, tossed its sharp instrument aside, and stepped back into the shadows again.

The shadows shifted.

The figure that re-emerged was no longer a primate, but a raptor.

A crow.

"Plenty of material over there to work with, if you need a little cosmetic surgery," piped the creature.

"I'll consider it," said William Blessing.

"I'd take it if I were you. You're looking a little rough."

"That's the way I'm feeling."

"There's one more for us to deal with, and then we're through and you can rest."

Blessing nodded.

Yes. Rest. He had only one more bit of justice to mete out. He'd told Amy what he had to tell her.

From time to time during their living relationship, he'd written poems for her. Some he'd given to her. Others, though, he'd kept back and collected into a volume, because they seemed to be of a thematic piece. She'd never even known about that volume, let alone read any of the poems, before he'd been killed.

He had them hidden behind the *Complete Works of William Shakespeare* and volumes by Keats and Shelley.

This was the information that he'd given to Amy, in his role as his own mysterious cousin.

"Ah, c'mon," said the crow. It fluttered down to the mass of corpse, sipped a little blood, pecked a little flesh. "No telling if you're going to see Amy again. Want to look your best. Dip in! It will put some color in your cheeks!"

The crow returned to its sacramental repast.

Just on the edge of the pool of blood, William Blessing knelt.

His kneeling, though, had nothing to do with prayer.

twenty-eight

"Prophet!" said I, "thing of evil!—prophet still, if bird or devil!—
Whether Tempter sent, or whether tempest tossed thee
    here ashore,
Desolate yet all undaunted, on this desert land enchanted—
On this home by Horror haunted—tell me truly, I implore—
Is there—*is* there balm in Gilead?—tell me—tell me, I implore!"
Quoth the Raven, "Nevermore."

    —Edgar A. Poe, *The Raven*

THE GRAVE WAS EMPTY.

Donald Marquette stared down at the casket that the workers had pulled up out of the ground. What he saw appalled him.

The coffin had filled with dirt, which of course had been dumped out. Its lid had been busted through, splintered in half, torn apart.

"Damnedest thing I ever did see," said one of the diggers, scratching his head. "Looks as though the corpse bashed itself through from the inside!"

The sun had just set, and a breeze fluttered leaves of a nearby tree. The place smelled strongly of overturned earth and diesel fumes from the coughing truck on a nearby road.

"Impossible, of course," continued the worker, a coarse-looking man who smelled of beer-laced sweat and cigarettes.

"I should hope so!" said another of the men, stepping back.

"Impossible. Obviously," said Donald Marquette. "What is

245

important is that the grave has been defiled and the body *stolen.*"
He turned to the night-shift cemetery keeper, a grizzled old coot
munching on a bacon, lettuce, and tomato sandwich. "How do I
report this to the proper authorities? Not that idiot beat cop I
dealt with yesterday."

The old guy wiped off some mayonnaise from a bushy mustache. "Don't know. This ain't ever happened before, as far as I
know." He took off his cloth cap and scratched a tuft of hair on a
generally balding dome. Dandruff and dead skin flaked down.
"My guess is, the night police have their hands full with live people. You're going to have to file a report tomorrow, I suppose."
He shrugged. "And talk to the day people as well."

It had taken Marquette all day to get this project started.
Only because of his persistence, and his willingness to pay extra
money, had the grave been dug up this quickly. And despite his
anger at the policeman last night, now he wasn't so sure that
having a bunch of cops nosing around was really such a good
thing. It would surely mean more questions about the events sur-
rounding Blessing's death.

As the cool of the evening seemed to caress his bones like
slimy tentacles, it was everything he could do to hold himself
together. And a new thought began drumming at the back of his
head like a scrap of music repeating itself incessantly:

What if Blessing had pushed through the lid of that coffin?

*What if he was back, returned from the grave, to avenge his wife,
to restore his scattered Poe collection, to drag those who killed him
back with him?*

Absolute nonsense, of course.

Utter foolishness.

Something was going on, yes. With the Count and the Marquis dead, Baxter missing, and now *this* staring at him, the pat-
tern could not be denied.

But surely this was the work of some living group, perhaps
some rival group of death-obsessed Goths, or just Baxter himself,
or any one of a hundred possibilities. When you ran with a mor-
bid bunch like the Gothiques, was it any wonder that a body
would get dug up now and then? Big joke! Ha ha! Sheesh, maybe
it was even the nut-case *Dark Sunset* editor, or even Blessing's
publisher. He could see the headlines now:

HORROR AUTHOR'S DECOMPOSING BODY DISCOVERED IN *NEW YORK TIMES BOOK REVIEW* OFFICE.

Great publicity!

Yes. What was that philosophical and scientific principle?

Right. Occam's Razor.

The simplest solution to a puzzle was usually the *correct* solution!

And surely a body with two bullets in its vital organs and a smashed-open head, declared way dead and filled with embalming fluid, was not a likely candidate to liberate itself from a strong oak box six feet under heavy rock and dirt!

"I can't deal with it tonight?" he asked the groundskeeper.

"'Fraid not," said the man. He spat out a wad of chewing tobacco on the ground. "Funny business. Horror writer, wasn't he?"

"That's right," said Marquette.

The limbs of the trees were knocking together now. The breeze had stepped up to just-approaching-wind status. Dark clouds were rolling across the stars and the moon, more storm weather. Nothing unusual in a place where the weather is moody and fitful; but all the same, not a comfortable experience in a graveyard.

"Mister Poe been here a century and a half. He never tried to get out of his grave," said the cemetery man.

"As far as you know," quipped one of the diggers.

"Usually, people come out of graves cos they're pissed off," said another of the men, resting on his spade, smiling with the joke. "Wonder what Mister Poe would want to come out of his grave for?"

"Royalties, most like!" sniffed the keeper. "Poor fellow died a pauper. Not like Mister Blessing here. No sirree, Bob. I seen the funeral party, I seen the casket. Mister Blessing was a rich man. He didn't need no royalties to take with him into the afterlife."

A flash of anger fell upon Marquette.

"All right. That's enough of that!" he said. "This is a crime scene. Blessing's grave has been despoiled, violated, and the body taken. It's a sick desecration, and I'm going to find out who's responsible." His voice was snappish and deep. Marquette had discovered he'd gained in authority and stature these past months. Killing someone had certainly matured him. "It looks like rain. I want you to put plastic and a tarp here. There might be evidence for the police."

"Right," said the keeper, understanding and agreeing. "I'll keep an eye out for wandering corpses, too!"

"Just direct him back here where he belongs!" replied the joker.

Marquette swirled around and stalked off.

Whatever was going on, he didn't like it. He'd already told Mick and Theodore to clear out. There was danger afoot, he could feel it in the air.

A shudder ripped through him as he headed back for his car.

A fat raindrop splatted onto his head.

No, it was time to get to safer territory. Time for that vacation he'd been promising himself. He could deal with business through phone and fax from some other location just as well as from here. At least until all this blew over.

Problem was, he also had to convince Amy to leave. What was a danger to him could well be a danger to her. And there were many, many reasons he wanted to keep Amy Blessing alive and healthy.

Because he *loved* her?

Was that what it was? he thought as he hurried through the gates of the cemetery and ran for his car. Cold rain slashed from the sky.

As he opened the door of his new BMW, and slipped into the fresh new-car smell, Donald Marquette smiled grimly to himself.

Yeah.

Love was always *such a useful word.*

A loud clap of thunder rumbled outside.

Amy Blessing awoke.

She was sitting at the table of the Poe collection room, the book mashed against her chest. She felt the salty wet of tears on her cheeks. The laser-printed pieces of paper, which William had bound carefully into the book himself, were still slick. Her hair was loose and tangled. She smelled of herself, mixed with the scent of the candles she had lit around her on the reading table, by a copy of the Sunday *New York Times* which she'd been looking at here last week, to be close to William and that which he held dear, despite the troubling memories the room held.

She'd fallen asleep.

She'd brought the book she'd found, the book of poems that William had meant to give her, down here to read in this special place, the place that William had filled with the poetry of the author who had meant so much to him.

The candles she'd lit, smelling of lavender, were nearly to their end. She'd only been asleep for a short while. Why?

And then she remembered.

She looked down at the page the book was open to. The poem there, a short one, spoke of the time they had spent in a rustic cabin by a beautiful lake. She had cut his hair one morning after a delicious breakfast of blueberry muffins. The cabin still smelled of the fresh-baked stuff, and she felt alert and awake and aware with the taste of the bracing Earl Grey tea she sipped. Looking out at the blue of the lake, the green of the evergreens, and the bright red of berries on a bush by the veranda, he had told her that he had just experienced the true meaning of eternity. Eternity, he said, wasn't measured from birth to death, wasn't linear at all. You had eternal life, if your life was full of life's true deepness. Each moment of Now was an eternity. But the key, he said, was truly being in love, and regarding the beloved in the beauty of that moment.

Forever.

Forever was lateral, for those in love.

And William said then that he was truly and eternally in love with her. Forever and ever. Then and now.

That sentiment had been gorgeously reflected in this poem, and she'd been overwhelmed with emotion. She cried and cried, leaning into the singular book as though to be nearer to it. Cried into her folded arms.

And there, she'd fallen asleep.

She closed the book and rubbed her eyes. She felt odd.

"No more of these tonight," she whispered to herself. She would take it with her and place it on the spare pillow on the king-sized bed upstairs.

William's pillow.

There, she could read another poem tomorrow, if she felt up to it.

The night seemed very thick outside and bleary. Then she realized that it was raining, and it was the thunder that had awoken her.

A haze of lightning brightened the window. Flickered. Faded away.

A moment.

Thunder again.

She had a pot of tea and a teacup before her. Gone cold, of course. She picked up the cup.

She still felt odd. Very odd, indeed. Something seemed very off. She'd been dreaming the strangest dreams, none of which she could remember. They seemed cut off by some gauzy, opaque curtain. Half-recalled forms seemed to move beyond that veil, none tangible . . .

She still felt very *close* to William. It was as though his death were the dream, and she was just waking up.

The pain of the rape, the trauma of that evening—whole chunks of it she simply couldn't remember. Like some alcoholic blackout.

Repression, the psychiatrist who'd treated her had said. Perfectly normal and healthy. The way the mind deals with things too horrible to accept. She'd never heard the shots that had killed William, or seen which of those dreadful men picked up that bust of Pallas and brought it down on her husband's head.

She'd woken up in a hospital, already tapped into drugs. She still took anti-depressants. All her friends and family had been so kind, but still, with all their support, she seemed to move in a kind of half-lit, shadow-floor of an alien ocean, from the time she had learned that William was dead. She sometimes wished she hadn't decided to stay in the townhouse, but then she couldn't imagine leaving it either.

Another burst of lightning, this time brighter. It threw a wash of light over the end of the room. A part that had once been in darkness.

Something was wrong there.

Something was *very* wrong with that end of the room!

The melancholy and sadness, the *lost* feeling was swept

away in a spurt of adrenaline. Amy arose, went to the side of the room, and turned on the overhead electric light. They were track lights, positioned to subtly illuminate key elements of the collection. The farthest away had been angled to throw a spot directly upon the bust of Pallas with the stuffed raven perched upon its head. The bust, though, had been taken away by the police to fingerprint and use as evidence. The raven had been taken away as well, to where Amy wasn't sure and hadn't cared to ask.

Now, though, there they were.

The white marble head statue of Pallas Athena, the Greek goddess of wisdom.

The black bird.

Undamaged. Defiant.

As she stood gawking at this (had Donald put them back there? If so, *why*?) Amy heard the door bang loudly on the first floor.

She heard the pounding of feet, coming up the stairs.

"Amy! Amy, are you here?"

It was Donald's voice, loud.

Quickly she went to the door of the collection room, and opened it.

"Donald!" she called. "I'm in here."

The whole house was lit up. He'd turned on all the lights. He hurried up the stairs now, his eyes wide, looking definitely disheveled.

"Amy? Are you all right?" he asked.

"Well yes, I guess so . . . I'm very upset, though."

He grabbed her by the shoulders and breathlessly asked, "What's happened?" He looked past her, into the library. "What are you doing in *here*, Amy?"

"The bust of Pallas. The raven . . . Did you put them back here?"

"*What?*"

Donald swept past her into the room, eyes targeting the back area. Amy watched as Donald, shocked, noticed the re-erected statuary. Then he noticed the boxes that she had returned to the room. The boxes of books that she had opened and carried up here and not unpacked.

He drifted over to these, bent down, let his hand touch the spines of a few books.

When he turned back to look at her, his eyes were full of surprise, even shock.

"These books . . . These are . . ." Donald shook his head as though to realign jarred portions of his brain. "I mean, these were part of the stolen collection . . . "

"Yes. Yes, isn't it amazing? They came after you left this morning!" she said. "They've been returned to where they're supposed to be. But I have absolutely no idea where the bust and the raven came from. You didn't—"

He shook his head, still trying to put something together. "No. No, Amy." He stepped over to her, touched her arm. "But those books delivered here this morning. Do you have any idea who —"

Donald noticed the handmade book of poems on the table by the candles. He stepped over and turned the book over.

"A book of poems by William Blessing. I wasn't aware of these!"

"No. William had intended to give them to me . . . His cousin told me about them."

"Cousin?" said Donald. "I didn't know about any cousin who was in contact with you."

"Yes. His name is Delmore Blessing. They hadn't had much contact lately. He knew a great deal about Bill that I didn't know," said Amy. "Delmore's the man who retrieved these books."

"Retrieved . . ." said Donald. "But . . . how?"

"I don't know."

"How do you know . . . this man?"

"He came by . . . yesterday. He introduced himself to me. We talked. I wanted to tell you about him, but he said not to. Not right away, anyway. He said that you two would meet in due time."

Donald gripped Amy by both of her forearms. He looked deeply into her eyes with an intensity she'd never seen before.

"Amy," he said. "Listen to me carefully. You're in great danger. I may be in danger as well, by association."

"Danger. But why? How?"

"Some madman—perhaps this man who has visited you, I don't know for certain—is committing atrocities here in Baltimore. Atrocities associated with William Blessing."

"Atrocities? What do you mean?"

"There have been . . . murders! And Bill's body." He looked away, biting his lip, looking vastly indecisive. "It's—"

"My husband's *body?* What about my husband's body? Tell me!" she said, almost on the verge of hysteria. "Tell me what's happened to my husband's body!"

"It's been stolen from his grave."

"What!"

"Yes. I'm notifying the proper authorities. But tonight . . . listen carefully . . . tonight we should go someplace else. Away from here. I don't feel that you are safe in this house."

She still couldn't quite comprehend what Donald had said. "Stolen . . . stolen from his grave? But why? Who would want to *do* such a thing!"

"Amy, your husband had a very long life before he met you. There could have been secrets he kept from you. God knew what strange associations he had. Maybe he wronged someone . . . Maybe there was some sort of . . . I don't know . . . *curse*. That we can discover later. But right now, I am convinced that you must pack some things very quickly. I'll take you to a hotel, get you your own room, and I'll take one right beside you. Maybe notify the police for security. I don't know, but what I feel absolutely certain of is that *we must get out of this house!*"

"But I live here . . . And I have to guard . . ."

"I'll notify the police. We can even hire a security person or something, Amy. Everything in this house will be safe. But I feel that *we* must get *out!*"

Something deep inside of her not only rebelled against the notion of leaving the house, but made her look at Donald Marquette in a new and altered fashion.

A little voice spoke in the back of her mind:

Who's truly been keeping secrets?

"If we're worried, why can't we just call the police from here, have them check on us?"

"I'm not comfortable with that alone, Amy," he said, shaking his head insistently.

"Well then—if there are security men to be hired, Donald . . . Can't we hire them from here? Can't we just have them come over *here*?" She gestured about. "This collection, these books and memorabilia, they were so important to William. Now that they're back, I don't want to risk losing them again."

"These things are worth *nothing* compared to you. To your safety, to your *life*." Donald looked terribly stressed, as though something that had been weighing on his mind for a time was beginning to exert the full extent of its pressure.

Amy shook her head. "Why is my life threatened? I don't understand, Donald. Before I leave my house, I have to know exactly why you think that I'm in danger!"

For a moment, Donald was at a total loss for words.

"This man—this so-called cousin of William's—it sounds strange to me. He could be the one who's the danger. He could be a *madman!*"

"If he wanted to be *dangerous* to me, Donald," said Amy defiantly, "he had his opportunity on two separate occasions! Now I demand that you tell me everything you know. Why do you think I might be in danger tonight?"

Amy was beginning to feel as though she were coming out of some kind of fog. And what she was seeing was different than she'd ever imagined it would be. Before, she didn't want to know anything but the drugged stupor of melancholy that padded herself away from existence. Now, though, she felt herself emerging from sleep to discover a very strange world indeed. "Tell me. I need to know!"

Donald opened his mouth, but nothing came out. His eyes darted about, but they seemed filled with panic and indecision, not any kind of answer.

Then a voice spoke from the doorway.

"Yes, Donald. Perhaps you should tell her."

twenty-nine

"M. Valdemar, can you explain to us what are your feelings or wishes now?"

—Edgar A. Poe, *The Facts in the Case of M. Valdemar*

"Be that word our sign of parting, bird or fiend!" I shrieked,
      upstarting—
"Get thee back into the tempest and the Night's Plutonian shore!
Leave no black plume as a token of that lie thy soul hath spoken!
Leave my loneliness unbroken!—quit the bust above my door!
Take thy beak from out my heart, and take thy form from off my
      door!"
Quoth the Raven, "Nevermore."

—Edgar A. Poe, *The Raven*

HIS HEART HAD BEEN POUNDING, POUNDING, POUNDING IN HIS CHEST, and his ears seemed to be ringing, ringing, ringing with a dizzy tintinnabulation of disjointed words, fears, and jumbled emotions.

However, when the words came from the doorway, they were like a cold hand of night slapping him across the face, and pulling Donald Marquette into an attentive focus.

He swung his head over to the door.

Standing there was a man in a dark coat. He wore a hat,

pulled down over his brow. The lapels of his long coat were pulled up over the lower portion of his face. In between, dark glasses obscured most of the rest of his face.

Donald Marquette found words.

"Who are you? How did you get *in* here!"

Panic and fear seemed gone, erased in a flood of adrenaline. He seemed in control again. But he sensed nothing but threat from this figure in the doorway, and something deep, instinctual and competent, some survival instinct took over him.

Amy did not respond with the same kind of alarm.

"Delmore," she said, stepping forward. "I'm so glad you're here. You were right! I found that book of poems . . ." Amy hurried back to the desk, pulled up the book to show the stranger. "You see?"

"I'm so glad," said the Dark Man. "Did you have the opportunity to read any yet?" His voice softened discernibly.

"Yes! Oh, yes, they're *wonderful*. It's like . . . It's like they've brought William back to me. I can let him go now because I now how he truly felt. I can let him go, because I know how much he'll always be in my heart."

The Dark Man nodded. "That is how, Amy, he . . . he would . . . he would have . . . liked it . . ."

Donald Marquette heard the voice breaking . . . as though with tears . . . or something else.

"This is the mystery cousin, I take it?" Donald said, voice freighted with suspicion.

"Oh, yes. I'm sorry. Delmore, this is Donald Marquette. William's colleague. He's stayed on, to help with the estate . . . and deal with so many things."

"Yes, of course," said the man. "William wrote about him." His voice hardened. "In fact, it is Donald with whom I wish to speak. That is why I have come back tonight, Amy. I had hoped not to disturb you. Perhaps you might want to go and occupy yourself with things upstairs. Your piano? Work? It's a shame it is such a wet and dreary night outside. You might go visiting a friend. Still, I'd be willing to call you a cab."

Fierce doubt arose in Donald. "Does this concern the Blessing estate?"

"In a way, yes," said the Dark Man.

"Then why have Amy leave? She is still directly involved. I have nothing to hide from Amy in my dealings concerning the estate. She should stay if she likes."

The Dark Man shook his head. "I would prefer it if she went—"

"Amy," said Donald in a taut, hard voice. "All these things I spoke of—the reasons I wished for us to leave this house until we know we are safe—they have begun with the arrival of this man. I fear that this is the man behind it all. This is the man we should fear!"

"But . . . But *why?*" Amy turned to him, emphatic. "He's told me so much. He's somehow restored the stolen books . . ."

Donald turned to the man who called himself Delmore Blessing. "The body of William Blessing is missing from its grave. Is it *you* who took it?"

The Dark Man held out gloved hands, imploringly. "Amy. Please. You *must* go!"

Amy shook her head, her eyes becoming hard. "What? Is that true? Are you the one who took William's body? Are you the one who's been causing so much alarm from Donald? Is this true?"

"Trust me, Amy!" The man's voice was teetering toward despair. "Go! Go, I say! Now!"

"William always told me, the truth is the hardest, yet it is the best. It will always bond together the good, and destroy the evil," whispered Amy. "Are you evil, Delmore? Are you bringing evil to the memory of your cousin?"

"No, Amy! No, I swear."

The Dark Man held up his hands imploringly.

"Then what is the issue that you cannot reveal in front of me?" she demanded.

Donald heard a strength there—a strength that he had not heard in Amy Blessing's voice ever before.

"Yes," demanded Donald, already doing mental calculations on how he could get some time to himself to call the police. Dash into another room and quickly tap out 911 on the cellular in his pocket. He wished he'd called some kind of security patrol before he'd even gotten here. "What is it that you don't want to reveal to Amy about yourself?"

The Dark Man swung toward Donald Marquette. He suddenly looked like an animated statue, aloof and cold—and yet still burning with something intense.

"Very well. You leave me no choice, Amy. I wished to spare you, but I am running out of time."

Slowly, the man removed his hat.

Then he lowered his collar.

Lastly, he took off his dark glasses.

The man's features were vague, waxy, and rough. Like a modern sculptor's impressionistic version of a face rather than a face that any normal human being wore. Bits of skin were flaking off, and scablike protrusions grew on the cheeks and neck. Marquette could see that one of the ears was half gone, and the other one was bent at a strange angle.

The eyes, though slightly milky, burned with identity and personality.

A personality that Marquette recognized, and yet could not bring himself to accept.

"In the future," said William Blessing, "I want you to think of this as a dream. A dream, Amy. Do you understand? I do not want it to be included in your scheme of reality."

"I don't . . ." Her voice came out choked and aghast. "I don't understand. You look . . . You look even more like . . . your—"

"There is no cousin, Amy," said the Dark Man. "I am William Blessing. It's me, your husband. There is . . . unfinished business. I have somehow been given . . . another short chance—" He turned to Donald, and those eyes burned hard and fiery. "—to make things right again. To preserve my legacy . . . and you . . . from further atrocity."

Donald Marquette shook his head adamantly. He could feel madness nipping at his heels, but the strong thing in him, the vital thing that had taken control, that had preserved him in times of catastrophe, returned again.

"No, Amy. It's a trick. Some sort of trick. This can't be William Blessing. William Blessing is dead!" he shouted.

The Dark Man shook his head sadly. "I never claimed to be alive, Marquette."

The Dark Man took a shuffling step toward him, holding out a pointing, accusing forefinger toward him.

"I killed them all, Donald. Your cronies, the Gothiques. I destroyed them and the blight they were going to present to my house . . . and perhaps to literature. Vengeance? Perhaps. Justice? Definitely! And now it is with you I must settle."

"William . . ." said Amy, voice trembling. "Bill . . . ?"

Donald took a step back, but before he could get far, the Dark Man rushed forward.

A cold, waxy hand clamped around Donald's throat.

"No!" shrieked Amy. "No!"

The arm and hand were unbelievably strong. This close, in his grip, with the smell of the grave clinging to him, and the sense of otherwhere defiant and strong, Donald could not deny—despite the rational side of him in strong objection—that this was William Blessing.

Choking, he reached out and grabbed at the face. A chunk of skin flaked off.

Strangling, gasping, Donald grabbed at the arm that held him, trying with all his might to pull the hand away from its grip around his windpipe.

"It was this villain," said the Dark Man. "This villain, Amy, who killed me. This noxious traitor who we took into our home—who we *trusted*—who introduced the forces of chaos and corrosion into our lives!"

"Help . . . Amy!" Donald managed to squeeze out of his windpipe. "Call . . . police!"

"No!" shrieked Amy Blessing.

Donald's vision was growing red and dimmer as he struggled desperately. He caught sight of Amy's movement. Beside the doorway was an antique chair. A chair, it was claimed, in which Edgar Poe had once sat. Amy grabbed this chair and ran toward them. Her face a mask of inchoate emotion, she slammed the old wood against the back of the man who claimed to be arisen from the dead.

With a loud crack, the antique flew apart.

The death grip upon Donald's throat disengaged. He flung himself back, away from his attacker, holding onto his throat as though to yank breaths through it into his famished lungs. He staggered, falling against the table.

Gun! Why hadn't he thought to get a gun!

The Dark Man stood, not so much harmed as astonished by the attack.

"Amy!"

"People don't come back from the dead!" Amy cried. "They just *don't*."

"But it's me . . . Amy . . . It's me . . . Bill."

Amy's words were high-pitched with stress and disbelief. "If you are indeed my husband, then my husband was not killed! I did not witness his death," she said. "But if you *are* Bill . . . then it's a Bill that has gone *insane!* Bill Blessing would never, ever hurt anyone. Ever. He was a gentle, *civilized* man. Not . . . not some *monster!*"

The Dark Man staggered a bit. He moved his arms in an ungainly, spastic, uncertain manner as he moved around toward Amy Blessing. "Amy . . . you don't . . . understand."

Donald was reminded of Boris Karloff as Frankenstein's monster, groping pitifully toward light and compassion.

A strip of skin from his face fell off onto the floor.

The strong part of Donald Marquette, the survival part that *comprehended* things, suddenly understood on a deeper level than his mind ever could. It *sensed* the being's true character, the truth of its statement, the dire danger it posed, the structure of meaning this imprinted on the dark underpinnings of the universe . . . What it meant to him . . .

And how he could intervene to save himself.

The survival part, the dark instinct pushed back the sheer horror of the moment, and dove in to the attack:

"She's right!" said Donald. "You can't be Blessing! Blessing would never, never murder wantonly. Blessing would never cause pain! His work said as much! Yes, death and destruction was in his writing—but it had the moral structure of comedy, of tragedy, of the great things in man. Not the utter banality of revenge plays, the melodrama of lesser artists!"

The Dark Man turned toward the speaker.

Donald caught the bleak glimmer of doubt in his eyes.

A larger piece of skin flaked from his temple, flopping down onto the floor. Some kind of crimson goo began to leak there on that face, as though from a pestilent sore.

Yes! thought the instinct. *That's it!*

"No!" said the Dark Man. "Punishment! There must be punishment . . . prevention!"

"You're mad! Mad, whoever you are! Prevention of *what?!*" He sidestepped a lunge of the Dark Man and stepped beside Amy, holding her around her waist in a comforting way. She grabbed him, held on to him, terrified of this dark specter before them.

"You need help!" said Amy. "Let us call help for you . . . whoever you are!"

"Punishment," growled the Dark Man, more of a bent creature now, a grim shadow of Basil Rathbone playing humpbacked Richard the Third. He scrabbled forward slowly, but his gait now seemed hamstrung. More of a hobble. "Prevention!"

"I've done nothing to harm Amy! I've done nothing but good for the memory and the estate of William Blessing. His books will continue to be popular because of my work. His name will remain on the bestseller lists, his stories and novels taught in schools. He will be remembered for posterity . . . kept alive by the values of good and virtue and love which he epitomized in his best work," said Donald Marquette. "Whatever you are, you are an instrument of insanity, a black and squalid thing, bringing destruction upon the true friends and believers in the legacy that William Blessing left!"

The Dark Man held out a hand.

"Please! Don't hurt us!" said Amy. "Whoever . . . Whatever you are . . . know that William Blessing was full of love and goodwill. Not murder and vengeance!"

Two of the lower fingers of the outstretched hand fell off, lying in pieces on the floor.

"Amy . . . No. I must . . . There are forces: Destiny. Love. Memory. Justice. Will. Forces that must hold back . . . the Evil . . . the Darkness . . . I have returned to fight the darkness. I have returned . . . *for love!* For love of you. For love of my art . . . *For what my work stands for!* Value! Virtue! Art! Beauty!" He moaned toward the ceiling. "Oh, Time. Poetry! Oh, Muses. Give me the words I need to *convince!*"

"Haven't you read the articles, monster?" said Donald Marquette, just the right amount of irony in his voice to be venomous. "Gothic writers are gentle people! They are civilized.

They shape the darkness to bring forth the light. Besides, William Blessing . . . or whatever part of you *thinks* it is William Blessing, this whole business reeks—reeks of the recklessness and crassness of the exploitive literature that you so despised! Weren't you more a proponent of the subtle? Of *quiet* horror? All this . . . Blessing . . . poor fellow . . . It's straight out of a cheap horror movie!"

The Dark Man gurgled.

He shook and shuddered.

Part of his face began to cave in. The whole left side started melting off, showing dark skull beneath. Tiny white maggots began to squirm though the eyeballs.

Will! the voice of the dark instinct told Donald. *It's losing its will!*

"Amy," the thing gasped, bubbling pus through its gash of a mouth. "Am—"

The jaw fell, dripping down like an overheated candle, and splashing and clacking onto the floor.

The Dark Man's nose fell off, more corruption oozing out.

The stink of rot advanced before the thing.

Amy groaned. Her grip around Marquette loosened. She wilted away from him.

She'd fainted.

Amy collapsed in a heap onto the floor, unconscious.

"You inconsiderate bastard!" spat Marquette. "Look what you've done!"

The remaining, unruined eye swung down and stared at the woman, lying lovely on the floor. A long moan emerged from the creature, origins deeper than any mouth or throat or diaphragm.

"You know, Blessing. She never really loved you," said Donald. "She told me that . . . Yes . . . She merely had some sort of strange father fixation on you. Something psychological. You truly were deluding yourself."

The will . . . he heard the voice in his mind. *Kill the will!*

"Yes, Blessing. She told me that. And we flirted—even while you were alive. Behind your back. We flirted. And we giggled. And we kissed! Did you know that? Those, sweet, sweet lips touched mine." Marquette chuckled throatily. "And I could tell . . . Oh, I could tell . . . that she lusted for me. And that when your old, old loins couldn't squirt anymore, it would be mine that she would want . . . *Mine!*"

"No . . ."

The corpse continued its messy deterioration.

"You know, Blessing, you are some sight! Like that Wicked Witch of the West in *The Wizard of Oz!* Only I didn't use water on you . . . I used *Truth!*"

With a sigh of escaping gases, the bones of the dead man gave way, and the decomposing heap collapsed upon itself, leaving a heap of crepuscular material amidst the mass of clothing that remained upon the soiled rug.

For a moment, Donald Marquette just stared at the horrendous pile of corruption on the rug.

Gone! said his dark instinct. *Pffft!*

Then Marquette began to laugh.

The laughter started deep down inside him, as though from the dark instinct itself. It crept up from his spirit, through his soul, into the nether parts of him. Up and up and up, it moved through his body to his throat and his mouth and came out dark and maniacal.

A cosmic joke!

The famous horror writer—

—returned from the dead!

And there he was: a bucket of greasy guts spotting the Oriental rug!

"I've won!" he said. "The midwestern boy truly makes good!"

The pile of slop said nothing at all.

Giddy hilarity filled Marquette.

"And here's the biggest joke of all, Blessing! You became horror's biggest cliché! What do you think of that! A cover from a pathetic comic book! Something out of a schlocky movie!"

The pile of shattered bone and moribund gore did not reply.

His laughter was the dark instinct's relief; he felt high from it. He felt as though, finally, he had discovered himself. Felt his destiny. Alcoholics had their Higher Power; he had his Lower Power. And now it reverberated within him like a song that had just found its singer. Its power simply filled Marquette with the thrill of discovery, puissance of purpose—and a rapidly growing euphoria that was raw with passion, need, and desire. Feeling death glide by his eyes seemed to pump lust from his glands with a heady rush.

He looked away from the pile of death. (Oh, what other truths were there of life that he had denied! The vistas before him because of this were so much broader than simple creativity and wealth. What brave dimensions awaited!) Amy Blessing came into view. Her prostrate body was astonishingly carnal, her long hair flashed out with erotic abandon, her mouth half open as though sucking the member of some invisible incubus.

He reached out his hand and touched the firm yet soft roundness of her buttock, covered with dress. Then, experiencing a thrill sharper than he'd ever known before, he let his hand drift under her long, woolen skirt, past her thigh, beyond the elastic band of her panties . . . And made acquaintance with flesh as soft and sweet and electric as any he had ever known. The secret . . . the forbidden . . . the best . . .

"You see, Bill," he said. "It is whimsical fate—fate and destiny involved here. I am truly the superior writer! However, in usurping your world . . . merely obeying, I might add, the laws of nature in the process, I shall burst forth into the greatness that is due me from the springboard of your accomplishments . . . and drag your work with mine into history. I think, posterity would have just as soon forgotten you. My work, I promise, will be remembered. And I shall write it in the utmost of luxury and success."

He could feel the pulse in his temples quicken. The smell of Amy was thick in his nostrils, and he could feel need building in him, turgid and complex. Withdrawing his hand from Amy's skirt, he began to unbutton her sweater.

He laughed again.

Amy remained unconscious; he sensed that she would remain so for some time. It was impossible now to control himself, and it seemed to be the nature of his dark instinct to mock the vanquished.

So be it.

"Oh, and thank you so much for finding Amy for me as well. I don't know if years of combing through the world would have found a flower so sweet to plant in my bed!" He pulled the sweater aside, exposing a black lace bra. Not white! My, how he had tossed and turned at night, unable to sleep, imagining this moment.

A little peek! A little feel! What harm would it do? Then he would wrap her back up as nice as you please, tuck her into bed, put some wine and pills on the nightstand, and come tomorrow tell her a terrible tale about how she had overdosed and had cried out in her sleep with dreadful nightmares. Dreadful!

"My, my, Billy boy! What a lucky fellow you were. What sweet fruit to taste. What a bouncy little bundle we have here! You don't mind if I take a little preliminary sample, do you?" He giggled. "Of course not. Then I shall simply sweep you up and the nasty bits that remain of you. And the authorities will never, ever discover the mystery of what became of the stolen body of William Blessing. But they truly won't care much. Besides, it will simply augment the legend. Yes, I shall make sure that the *National Enquirer* gets a hold of the story. HORROR WRITER'S GRAVE DEFILED! And every supermarket will start stocking your paperbacks at the checkout line!"

He pulled back the black lace.

The nipple of Amy's right breast was perfect. Absolutely perfect! Pink and saucy, bright and pert.

His fingers trembled slightly as he reached for it.

His fingertips brushed across the nipple. The feeling was electric, utterly what he had dreamed it would be. He could sense the blood rushing to his loins.

"Soon, Blessing," he said. "Soon I shall be sucking on this sweet bud. Soon—"

Something closed around his ankle.

Gripped.

Gripped very hard indeed.

"What?"

He swung his head around and down, startled.

Around the bottom of his pants leg was a hand. Half flesh and half skeleton. Yet even as he looked down upon it, aghast, he could see the sinews and the flesh reassembling, growing back into a full hand.

Beyond the hand, a half-face pulled itself back together over a leering skull. Pieces of skin wiggled like a sea anemone. Veins and arteries materialized, skin reassembled, hair appeared from a protoplasmic stew.

"No!" cried Marquette.

He raised a fist and struck at the grinning skull. The spine cracked and the head swung back, off its precarious perch. He was in the midst of lifting his left foot to push the grip of the dead thing's hand off his ankle when a sudden "Caw!" squawked from another part of the room.

He looked up.

There was the bust of Pallas, returned. However, what was on top of the bust was far more alarming. The stuffed raven had returned as well, perched above the head—now it was blurring and growing and turning blacker, blacker, even as its wings spread.

The raven became a crow.

Reddish-brown eyes ignited.

The bird launched. Flapped and flapped. Slammed into Marquette, pushing him back.

As the crow wheeled around in the room, Marquette's hand came away from his face bloody. He struggled again with the leg, finally knocking the dead man's hand off. He rolled, got on all fours and started for the door.

The crow wheeled around again.

Instead of attacking, though, it fluttered down between Marquette and the door.

You're not going anywhere, pal, the crow seemed to be saying.

Marquette paused for just a moment.

Then he plunged ahead toward the door, driven by the voice of his dark instinct which demanded immediate evacuation.

The crow stood firmly in place, glaring at him.

He made to kick it out of his way, but even before his foot began to fly, he was grabbed from the rear by an arm, ropy with exposed muscle and half knitted-together skin. The arm pulled him back, back, and he smelled the grave again, though this time it was a different smell, a different grave:

His grave.

Donald Marquette was flung against the table. Papers and books stacked there flew. He made a superhuman effort to push himself away, driven by panic and every last bit of power left to him. However, the less-than-human creature kept him pinned.

"I brought something along with me from your friend Baxter Brittle's chambers," said the reassembled corpse, grating harshly into Marquette's ear.

Marquette saw a flash of metal as the thing appeared.

He'd seen it on Baxter's absurd altar. It was an elaborately detailed and curlicued knife. A knife often used for animal sacrifice—and who knew what else.

A ceremonial knife.

"No!" cried Donald Marquette. "You can't do this . . . Can't—Please . . . *Please* . . . !"

"No, no, Donald," the voice said harshly. "You don't understand. You're going to get your wish! I promise. You're going to get exactly what you wanted!"

The knife arced in a silvery trail as it swung around.

It buried itself, hilt-deep, into Donald Marquette's lower abdomen.

The pain raged molten and fierce.

Donald watched with disbelief as blood spurted across the scattering of papers on the desk.

The images began to flicker, strobing before him. He looked down and saw the unhuman hand pull the knife up, watched as his viscera spilled out upon the paper. With disbelief he saw it was the *New York Times Book Review*, opened to a certain familiar page.

"There you go, Donald," the undead voice snapped in his ear. "You always wanted to be on the *Times* bestseller list, didn't you?"

And then, the dark instinct reached up to claim him, enfolding him, like deep bay fog upon a Fells Point alley.

William Blessing held the body until he felt its spirit flee. Then he let it and the knife go. Donald Marquette, quite dead, fell against the table, then, dragging the knife along with him, flopped down onto the floor.

The crow fluttered onto the table.

"The last one," said William Blessing.

"The last one," agreed the crow.

"I can . . . I can rest," said Blessing.

"Yes," said the crow. "And I can move on . . . and do what I must do."

Blessing looked at his hand. The skin was back on. It still looked a fright, but it was certainly a hand again. He reached up and felt at his face.

Yes. Reassembled, for the most part.

And yet, with his mission accomplished, he could feel his will diminishing again. He had reserves, he knew, but he did not want to leave himself as a splattered ruin within his own home.

No, he had another home now. A home in a cemetery, where he truly belonged.

"I must return to my grave," said Marquette.

"As we all must, eventually," agreed the crow. "But nothing lasts forever. You'll see."

William Blessing turned and looked down at his wife. Amy lay a-sprawl, still unconscious.

"I cannot leave her like this, with these memories."

"No," said the crow. "You have the power to make things right, Blessing."

William Blessing nodded.

He went to his wife. He bent and pulled her sweater back on, rebuttoning it. Then, carefully and reverently, he reached down and pulled her up to him.

William Blessing carried her upstairs. He laid her down in their bed. He let her head rest gently upon the pillow. Now that his rage was slaked, he only felt love. The love burned bright inside of him, holding him whole.

Amy's beautiful hair spread out upon the embroidered pillow. She took what breath the dead man had away. She looked like some fairy princess, resting, awaiting the kiss of her prince.

He rested a hand upon her brow.

"Rest, Amy. Rest for a full day. Dream. Remember me as I was. Do not recall what I had to become."

He could feel these powers move within him, gentling down upon his wife.

Emotion moiled inside William Blessing.

"I'll let you go now, Amy," he whispered. "When you awake from your sleep, the horror will be gone, and you will heal, soon.

Soon. Then . . . Then . . . I leave you only my name, if you still want it . . . a blessing. A blessing for you to get on with your life, knowing the value and meaning and beauty you gave to mine."

William Blessing leaned down and, with decomposing lips, kissed the flushed cheek of the living.

As they moved past the office, heading back toward the grave and eternity, the crow took its perch upon Blessing's left shoulder. Then the phone rang.

For some reason he did not know, William Blessing stopped and listened.

"This is Blessing Enterprises!" said Donald Marquette's cheery voice from the answering machine. "We're not in right now, but please do leave a message after the beep."

Beep.

"Donald!" said a voice. "This is Roscoe Mithers! Yes, yes, I know it's late, but the meeting went late and then I had a private dinner with the publisher. This is the most exciting day of my life. They loved *all* your ideas! And I had a few of my own! The department heads were all there, and it just so happened that the top creative executive from the media division was in New York on business from the Coast. There is *vast, vast* interest in fully exploiting the William Blessing name and association. We're talking not just books, but movies, television, videos, merchandising, licensing . . . The action figure rights alone are going to be a breakthrough! The ideas for your collaborations with the Blessing name sent everyone into ecstasy. And they want me to be the editor on it all!

"Best of all, though, I have another idea that I ran past the publisher at dinner that he's approved immediately: a line of William Blessing *Dark Sunset* books, that you can create. Crossover, Donald. Synergy! Brilliant marketing, huh? The possibilities are endless. So please, please, I need to talk to you. Call me immediately anytime tomorrow at the office or even tonight, at my home. You have the number. Wake me up! No problem. Jesus, Donald! I had no idea how far this was going to go! You're a genius. I owe you! May your sunsets always be da—"

Blessing picked up the phone.

"Hello, hello?" said Mithers. "That you, Donald? I knew if I rambled enough you'd finally pick up. How much did you hear?"

"Enough," replied the dead man.

"Hey, this isn't Donald. Who is this?"

"The keeper of William Blessing's literary heritage. Donald Marquette had to resign his position."

"That was rather sudden," said Mithers, not trying to mask his doubts about the situation, if he was being hoaxed in some way.

"A matter of grave importance suddenly arose and he found himself unable to perform his duties."

"But we had a deal. It was being worked out," objected Mithers.

"He signed a contract? A letter of agreement?"

"Not exactly, but a deal's a deal."

"Yes, I suppose it is. Even a deal with a devil. Especially so."

There a long silence as Mithers tried to frame a response. He was getting a bad feeling about this. The odd voice on the telephone seemed half-caked in wet dirt. *Damn creepy*, thought the editor. He could almost imagine that a zombie, or some other dead thing from the *Dark Sunset* pantheon, was actually on the other end of the line.

"Mr. Mithers," the eerie voice continued, "any agreements you might have thought you had with the Blessing estate are revoked and rescinded. Do you understand?"

"Frankly, no, I don't. Just who are you? Where's Marquette? This doesn't make any sense."

"But it does, Mr. Mithers. Perfectly. Here, let me make it clear to you."

A shock wave of horror reached out through the phone lines, through the digital optical cable, striking Mithers in mid-breath. A barrage of death images assaulted his mind. His hand gripped the phone so tightly the plastic receiver cracked. All he could do was tremble as Death in all its forms boiled through his brain, freezing his blood. He began to whimper, spittle appearing at the corners of his mouth, as hot and cold blasts of fear shot through his soul.

You see why it's impossible to continue with your projects? the voice seemed to say from behind his left ear. *It would be very hazardous to your health. Now sleep.*

As if dropping from a gallow's pole, Mithers gasped and fell to floor, unconscious.

Back in Baltimore, the crow flapped onto the desk. "Impressive," it said to Blessing. "You're really getting the hang of this undead avenging stuff. Too bad you weren't killed by a lynch mob."

"Think he'll get the message?" asked Blessing, placing the phone back in its cradle.

"He won't know why exactly," replied the bird, "but just hearing your name will invoke a particularly personal brand of terror in Mr. Mithers. He'll be contemplating a career change in the very near future."

"Yes. A career change. I could use one as well," said Blessing.

He stopped at the Poe collection room to take sustenance from what remained in this dimension of Donald Marquette. One for the road.

Then William Blessing continued shuffling toward the night outside, toward his rendezvous with the grave.

epilogue

And the Raven, never flitting, still is sitting, *still* is sitting
On the pallid bust of Pallas just above my chamber door;
And his eyes have all the seeming of a demon's that is dreaming,
And the lamp-light o'er him streaming throws his shadow
    on the floor;
And my soul from out that shadow that lies floating on the floor
Shall be lifted—nevermore!

—Edgar A. Poe, *The Raven*

1849

HE FELT THE BAY FOG, ROLLING IN HEAVILY UPON HIM AS HE LAY IN the Fells Point alley.

As he woke, the tremors hit him violently. The cold, the horrific *cold!* It knifed through him mercilessly. The man shook violently as he agonizingly got to his feet and dragged himself across the cobblestones.

His teeth chattered.

The smell of sea and rot was heavy and wet upon him. He felt waves of hot and cold and violent horror toss him into paroxysms of hot and chill, hot and chill . . .

Shivering, he staggered out and saw the fog moving over old buildings and piers, the languid movement of dark water . . .

Above a horse-drawn carriage, he saw a huge, dark bird, flapping away into the mist.

Ahead of him a man in a top hat and a suit with a waistcoat walked arm in arm with a woman in a bonnet carrying a frilled umbrella. The street smelled of horses and an open-air market-place.

As he staggered out toward them, his knees gave way. Shivering and gasping, he splashed down into a muddy rainpool.

Even shortened, his legs could not support him. He fell forward, and unconsciousness swarmed around him, like angry pieces of winged night.

My name? came a voice. *What is my name?*

And another voice answered, but he could not hear.

"Sir! Are you all right?" asked the man.

"Yes," he insisted, somehow dragging himself up. "Yes, I am merely . . . wet. Taken with cold from these accursed rains. A drink! A drink is all I need. To warm myself. Could you direct me, sir?"

"Why yes. Across the way is Gunner's Hall. Today is election day, so there will be plenty of folk polling there," said the man. "You may find drink . . . And help as well, if you need it."

"Yes," he muttered as he turned and headed blearily toward the building that the man had indicated. "Away from my enemies . . ."

As he staggered toward the hall, the Fells Point fog seemed to pour into his mind again . . .

"Mr. Poe," called a voice. "Drink this, Mr. Poe. You need to drink this water."

He came awake to the fuzzy images of a man dressed in black with large sideburn whiskers, proffering a glass of water. He was immediately filled with the ache and ravage of fever and sweating. Seeing that he was awake, the doctor pressed the glass of water against his lips, dribbling some onto his parched tongue. Much of it splashed down his mouth, landing upon his bedclothes.

Poe, he thought. *My name is not Poe!*

But if it was not Poe, he thought, shaking with the alternating chill and the stabs of pain, then what was it?

Another splash of water into his mouth, and then he was allowed to lie back upon his pillow. He smelled lye and sickness in the air: He was in some sort of primitive hospital.

As he drifted off, snatches of memory came to him . . . all bathed in spasms of pain and dismal melancholy.

Virginia, dead of tuberculosis. A long, tortuous death.

The long and dreadful battle with alcohol, that angel of easement against the torture of a life filled with penury and loss . . .

Alcohol, that devil of distress, casting him into headache and heartache, soul-searing pain and fretful depression . . .

The occasional island of liberation of verse and story, review and article in a sea of ache and trouble.

This was his pitiful life.

And it was, he realized, the life of Edgar Allan Poe.

The man shot up in the bed, gasping. "But I am not Poe!" he screamed. "What am I doing here?"

"I am Dr. John J. Moran. You are at Washington Medical College in Baltimore," said the man. "You were found in a semiconscious state at Gunner's Hall. You're very ill. You've been babbling."

He tried to get out of bed. He was immediately surrounded by attendants. He had to get back home, back to Iowa . . . back to work.

"Back to work!" he cried out loud. "Back to work! I must succeed as a writer! That is my life's goal!"

The forms around him pushed him back, holding him down. "But you *are* a writer, sir. And a well-known poet as well. Now be calm, sir! You must be still. It is not good for your condition to thrash about so!"

The strong hands of his attendant soon gave way to straps which tied him to the bedposts and prevented all but the most useless of movement.

As dimness approached, he heard the doctor whisper, "The sad and hopeless ravages of demon drink has him in its jaws."

No! he thought. *Rabies! Poe died of rabies!*

And I am not Poe!

No, I am Donald Marquette!

But he could not speak these words. Dimness and oblivion reached out, grabbed him. All he could do was babble.

He seemed to be afloat in a sea of darkness and confusion. He was too baffled and delirious to be capable of regret or reflection or repentance for the blood and the pain he felt heavy upon him.

Only once more did he emerge from his confusion.

"Lord help my poor soul!" he gasped, his head moving back and forth.

Hearing the words come from his mouth he recognized them. Poe's last words. He opened himself and readied for the blessed relief and nothingness of death.

Death, instead, came upon black wings.

It carried him off, swirled him around like a sailor clinging to a piece of shipwreck, spinning around in a maelstrom. Down, down, into a deep, dark center . . .

And that center suddenly came alive.

Blinking, he found himself staring out of a window. Beyond the window were the empty forests and fields of a bleak, late fall. Dark clouds hung in the air. The smell of camphor and dusty gloom surrounded him. He felt a heaviness in his chest.

The black bird that had brought him here flapped up onto a porch, perched there. It stared at him with eyes of crimson and piercing brown.

"A bird!" he found himself saying. "I told you! See the black bird!"

The reflection in the windowpane was of a child.

He was staring out of the eyes of a child!

"Edgar!" said a woman's voice. "Come away from there. Come and sit by your poor, dead mama!"

"Blast," barked the stern voice of a man. "I can see this one's going to be trouble."

He turned around.

On a bed, surrounded by people dressed in the costumery of the early nineteenth century, was a dead woman.

Somehow Marquette knew it was Poe's mother.

His mother now as well . . .

He remembered his dream . . . His nightmare.

This year, then—the thought came uncontrollably—would be, what . . . 1811? 1812?

What was he doing here?

But even as the thought came, so did the overwhelming hint of an answer.

A woman came up beside him. "It's a crow, John. There's a big, black crow out there!"

"Well, chase the cursed thing away," said the nasty, grim man. "It's a bad omen!"

The soul of Donald Marquette stared out of the eyes of Edgar Poe to the creature that had carried him here.

Trapped!

He was trapped in the body of a man, doomed to agonies and melancholy and wretchedness beyond imagining!

Trapped in some sort of infernal time loop!

To live and die . . . and live again . . .

In this accursed being . . .

The final revenge . . .

For his sins . . .

He thought he heard the crow speak to him.

"You're a world-famous writer now, Donald," it said, a snap and bite to its eerie voice. *"Just as you always wished!"*

He leaned against the windowpane, icy and dark, and he managed, for a moment, to speak through this child, knowing that he would never be able to do so ever again, nor influence his environment or host.

Merely *suffer.*

"Pray for me," begged Donald Marquette of whatever fate had brought him this hell. "For I am a soul damned as no soul has been damned before.

"How long!" he asked the crow, knowing his time of full awareness was almost over. "How long, crow!"

The bird cocked its eyes and for a moment those eyes became human eyes. Eyes that had lost things beyond telling.

How long? cried Donald Marquette's screaming soul. *How long?*

And the bird opened its mouth to speak.

Quoth the crow:

"Evermore!"